I0761240

HOLLOW

HOLLOW

CELINA MYERS

HANOVER
SQUARE
PRESS

ISBN-13: 978-0-7783-8785-5

Hollow

Hanover Square Press
22 Adelaide St. West, 41st Floor
Toronto, Ontario M5H 4E3, Canada
HanoverSqPress.com

Printed in Lithuania.

For My Adam,
I never truly understood love until I met you.
You have stood like an unwavering lighthouse in the densest fog of my life.
You were the whisper in my deepest silence, the voice that told me to keep going when I had never felt more lost.
You are everything.
In every lifetime, I will find you.
I love you. I love you. I love you.

AUTHOR'S NOTE

Some stories sink their teeth into you and never let go. *Hollow* was one of those stories for me.

I grew up obsessed with vampires. I was the typical teen who devoured anything vampire-related—from the classics of years forgotten to modern-day vampire brothers. The idea of living forever, of having the chance to right my wrongs, to truly discover who I was before youth slipped away, lived so deeply in me.

Hollow was my passion project—the book I was most excited to write. I spent a decade shaping these characters, crafting their world, and weaving their stories before I ever put pen to paper. But what makes *Hollow* different from anything else I've written is that I didn't write it alone.

I've been a writer my entire life, but in 2020 I found another way to create—I found TikTok. I'd always been a bit of an introvert, but in that app I found my people. It awakened a confidence in me I had never known, and I started sharing my comedy, creativity, and writing with the world. Over the course of two years, I gained a collective following of over thirty-two million. These people who'd found me from behind the locked doors of COVID were now cheering for me. I'd spent my whole life doubting myself, my internal monologue full of voices I never should have listened to.

This changed everything for me. *Hollow* was shifting gears in my mind, and I knew it was time to get writing. For a year, I went live at all hours across my platforms. We typed in silence together at 3 a.m., pressing the secrets of the night into pages. I shared bits and pieces and took everyone's feedback. This book became a shared experience—a novel built in the quiet moments between me and you. And that is why *Hollow* means so much.

Mia, like so many of us, felt lost before she found her place. She didn't know where she belonged or if she ever truly would. Life can feel like that sometimes—a whirlwind of uncertainty, of searching, of feeling adrift before finally finding home. Maybe that's why Mia's story feels so real, maybe because it could be. *Hollow* is the kind of novel that makes you wonder if these vampires really do live in the shadows of our everyday lives.

Hollow is for the ones who crave stories that make their hearts race. It's for the dreamers who believe in epic love, in fate, in the kind of magic that lingers long after the final page. It's for the ones who feel a little different, a little lost, a little hungry for something they can't quite name.

This is for you.

I love you forever. Thank you.

Celina Myers

HOLLOW

1725

The air had never been colder than it was that winter. It was preceded by the hottest summer the quaint village of Black Creek had ever witnessed; even the elders had never experienced heat like they did that year. The trees around the small town wilted under the sun's weight; the wooden veins of soft maples were brittle to the touch. For the first time in the forty-two years since the founding of Black Creek, the creek that the community was named after ran dry.

Then, in July, the beloved town priest became delusional with a disease of the mind; the local healer and doctor said he would have more time, but the heat seeped in and dried up his head, just like the river. He called out late into the darkness of the nights and the wee morning hours. He cursed the God he had so faithfully worshipped and preached about for his entire life. Somehow, the only thing he had ever believed in brought him no peace in his last moments. His bedside was lined with aging women at all hours of the day and night. The numbers had started to drastically decline as his hallucinations took physical form. The ladies had never witnessed such vulgarity. He screamed hate-filled sentences at the top of his lungs, his breath escaping as if the fire from the heat of the day had built inside him. He had been at the births of all the village children, and the mothers he had tended now dabbed tepid cloths at his brow, silently reflecting on how this man who now ranted and raved had blessed their babies with the Lord's Prayer, had gently made tiny crosses on their soft, newborn foreheads.

In August, he hung naked out the window of his small cabin screaming at the sun, telling the town that they were cursed, and that they were witnessing the End of Days. At first, the people were scared of his warnings. They pulled back, shrinking against their walls as if mere closeness to his words would make them true. But by the last two weeks of his life, they were laughing at the crazy old man down the street as if his ramblings were entertainment.

He passed away on the twentieth of September.

A week later, the heat broke.

The villagers looked with despair at their meager harvest; there was not enough food to last to the end of the year, let alone through the long winter. The dry summer had destroyed most of their crops and livestock. Any prosperity and supplies that had survived the drought were dwindling quickly. They rationed their food, even going without when they could stand it. New mothers found their milk running dry. The nights were full of the sounds of murmured prayers of relief to God himself, and the ear-piercing cries of children's hunger pains.

The villagers recalled the priest's words and now found no humor in them. It truly did seem to be the End of Days.

In November, the cool weather rolled in, and with that, a stranger.

///////

Eli Bellamy, who had been born and raised in Black Creek, stood deep in thought. His errand to buy what little grain he could was all but forgotten as he looked at the plain buildings where the villagers lived and worked. At this time of day, people should have been milling about bartering goods, the street full of children dodging carts and horses and playing the same games he had played as a child. Instead, the road was bare except for a few miserable-looking folk who sat with their backs propped up against the walls of their dwellings, arms crossed and deep in their black thoughts.

Life in the village had always been hard. When Eli was only three years old, his mother died giving birth to her second child. The baby boy died as well. Stricken with grief, Eli's father, Matthieu, spent more time lamenting his wife's death than paying attention to his only living child. Within weeks, his unmarried sister-in-law Agnes stepped in and took charge of her younger sister's child. Aunt Aggie was the closest thing to a mother Eli could remember, and he spent more and more time in the rooms where she lived behind her cheese shop. He spent hours with his aunt in the kitchen, helping make the cheeses she sold in the front of the shop and listening to her gossip about the goings-on in town. Eli often spent the night with Aggie, as his father barely acknowledged his existence when he was home on the farm. Eli even looked forward to one day running the cheese shop himself.

By the time Eli was twelve, Matthieu had grown tired of his son spending more time in the shop than the fields. He put a stop to the visits with Aunt Aggie, though she continued to keep a close eye on Eli.

///////

The Suttons arrived in town in a horse-drawn cart with their daughters, sixteen-year-old Elenora and eight-year-old Jeanne. The entire family was dressed in much more expensive clothing than the people of the village wore, and they brought with them jewelry and artwork, the likes of which had never been seen in Black Creek. Some folks were wary of the family's wealth, but the Suttons moved in with the Martins in their simple old cottage and were kind and generous to their new neighbors. Soon, those who had once felt intimidated welcomed them with open arms.

Elenora's skin was pale, and a slight splatter of brown freckles graced the cheeks of her ever-smiling face. Her hair was copper, her eyes chestnut, her day dresses perfect pale yellows, and all blended as neatly as a painting.

Elenora carried her own hue that stood out against the dimness of the colors of the village. The village wasn't dim in her eyes, though—she associated the people she saw every day with specific colors. Her parents were the blue of the sky, always watching over her and protecting her. The baker was the white of the flour he turned into soft bread; her little sister, Jeanne—a soft, kind child—was pink; the beloved village priest was maroon, warm with the love he bestowed upon his congregation; and the man on the edge of town who drank too much and beat his wife was the grayness of despair and misery. Whenever Elenora strolled through the village, everyone around her shimmered with their various colors. She never understood how others couldn't see the colors that emanated from the people around her.

She found herself quite enjoying life in the village. She had grown close with Alice, the girl who lived next door, and they often spent what little free time they had in each other's company, sitting and chatting near the creek or helping each other with the housework. Alice devised an ingenious way for the girls to say good morning and good night to each other. She had two small matching brass bells, and she gave one to Elenora. Alice rang hers every morning, and Elenora would answer with her own ring. They repeated the ritual every evening before blowing out the last candle. When she looked at Alice, Elenora saw bright red; her friend was feisty and full of love and passion. Everyone she loved collected in her mind, their colors representing flowers. She felt so blessed that her mind was always full of the bouquet of the ones who meant the most to her.

///////

Eli had been struck speechless the first time he laid eyes on the new girl. She graced him with her radiant smile whenever their paths crossed, but as she was usually in the company of her friend Alice, Eli found himself unable to respond. Instead, he peeked through windows and from behind trees just to watch her walk by and take in the soft melodies that she hummed as she strolled through the streets.

He was not alone in his quiet observance. Elenora had taken as much notice of him as he had of her. It had started one evening when she was walking to the butchers to pay her family's weekly bill. Eli walked past her with some friends on their way to the public house. He hadn't seen her, but she'd noticed him immediately. His tall, muscular frame caught her eye, and when he laughed a deep, genuine laugh at something his friend said, she knew he was the one for her.

After that, she looked for him whenever she could. She sat in the window claiming she needed the light to work on her embroidery, but in actuality, she was waiting to see him walk past. At the fair that summer, she snuck glances down the tables so she could observe him chatting confidently with the other local boys. In the evenings, she drew soft portraits of him by candlelight with her dull charcoal pencils. She would ring her bell to say good night to Alice; then, pushing the scraps of paper under her pillow, Elenora would fall asleep hoping for dreams full of images of Eli's face.

Alice often teased her, asking if she had her eye on any of the village boys, but Elenora always said no. Yet, when she looked at Eli, he shimmered with the yellow of the sun.

Aunt Aggie was the one who finally got them to speak to each other. Aggie had seen her nephew blush whenever the girl was in sight and had observed Elenora turn and watch him after he passed her on the street. She couldn't help but notice that despite their obvious attraction, neither had ever spoken to the other. She waited for the perfect opportunity to get them face-to-face.

One afternoon Eli stopped by the shop to lend a hand wrapping cheese wheels. Aggie was about to close up for the night when Elenora walked past the window. Rushing into the kitchen, Aggie grabbed her nephew and babbled something about needing his help, then dragged him out of the shop. The moment they were outside, she looked around frantically; her quarry was only a short distance down the street.

"Elenora!" The words sounded sharp coming from Aggie's mouth. Eli watched in horror as the girl turned. "See here; my boy has been watching you intently since you arrived." Eli tried to shrink from his aunt, but she held his wrist tightly. "I have also seen *you* staring at *him* when he is not looking." Elenora's eyes shot to the dirt road in embarrassment as curious onlookers began to gather, but Aggie was not finished. "It seems to me that neither of you knows what you're doing, so I am taking matters into my own hands."

Aggie pushed Eli forward, a smile engulfing her entire face as she stood back in triumph. Eli stumbled a bit but righted himself a mere foot from Elenora. To his surprise, her cheeks were as red as the harvest moon, so much so that her freckles had all but disappeared into her blush.

He cleared his throat. "Hello, Elenora."

"Hello, Eli." The girl bit her lip, then smiled.

"Aha!" Aggie exclaimed, seeing the connection as their eyes met. She almost felt the pull, like two magnets drawing together.

“I need a pail of water from the well. You two can fetch it for me.” When neither moved, she gave Eli another push.

And that was it.

///////

They married two summers later. Elenora was the definition of perfection on her wedding day. She and her mother had dyed rolls of cotton a soft, buttery yellow for her wedding dress, and Jeanne wove her a crown made of flowers. Eli stood with his father at the front of the church and watched his beautiful bride walk down the aisle.

After the ceremony, they held a dinner in the field of wildflowers that lay just out of town. There were blossoms that went on as far as the eye could see, reminding one of the stories that the elders told the children. As the light faded from the sky and the tables were aglow with candlelight and lanterns, the scene looked almost magical.

That was the greatest day of the new couple’s lives. In the two years that followed, the only happiness they found was in each other. At first, all seemed to go well. Eli’s father, Matthieu, was practically a new man; Elenora’s happy presence was a balm to him, and he began to let go of the anger and pain he’d carried around for nearly twenty years. He relaxed and started showing real kindness toward Eli, and for the first time, they exchanged pleasant words more frequently than angry ones. But two months after his son’s marriage, Matthieu complained of a pain in his shoulder, then simply sat down in the field and died.

Though Eli grieved, he knew that his parents were finally reunited and that his father was at peace. Still, he couldn't help but feel that he'd finally connected with his father, only to lose him.

Not one year later, sweet Jeanne was playing on the street with her friends when a passing horse spooked and ran straight at the children. Jeanne was trampled, but she somehow made it back home before collapsing. That day she went to sleep; her breath was even, her heart still beat, but her eyes never fluttered. Elenora spent every moment at her sister's side, smoothing her golden hair, dribbling water between her rosy lips. The village healer sprinkled some herbs around the bed, then proclaimed there was nothing else to be done. The Suttons refused to give up. Leaving Elenora to nurse Jeanne, they hitched the horses to their cart and set out toward a village nine days to the west, where someone had heard that a real doctor lived. They were determined to find the man and bring him back to tend to their youngest child.

Three days later, while Elenora slept mere feet away, Jeanne quietly drew her final breath. Elenora woke to check on her sister, only to find her cold. Her poor little arms were stiff at her sides. Jeanne was buried in the small churchyard; the entire village turned out to support Elenora and Eli in their grief.

After that, Elenora could not sleep. She refused to go to bed with Eli, choosing instead to sit up late into the night with a cup of tea and stare down the road for hours, waiting for her parents to come home.

The Suttons never returned.

They knew the dangers when they set off that day; the roads leading to the town were full of stories of robbers.

Elenora had begged her mother to stay with her, but she knew a group of two would be safer than one. She had hugged her parents fiercely the morning they left, promising she would take the best care of Jeanne. The afternoon before Jeanne died, Elenora had been sitting in the small window at the front of the cabin. The biggest fear that she had ever felt drifted through her. It wasn't until Jeanne passed that she knew: something had happened to her parents. The drought must be in other places, with panicked people everywhere; had her family been taken for their supplies?

Elenora kept her hope. For six weeks after her parents left, she stood guard in the family's cabin, with her embroidery in her hands. Her eyes trained hard on the horizon, looking for them to crest the land. Nothing.

Without Eli, Elenora may have never moved on. His sunny yellow aura brought her out of the darkness and kept her in the light. And in turn, he took comfort in his wife. Eli loved the way she looked in the early-morning light, the soft rays making love to the contours of her cheekbones. Her smile held the magic to make his heart flutter the same way it did when he first saw her.

Then the peak of the hot, dry summer was upon them. The crops shriveled and their cows died of thirst, but Eli and Elenora continued to struggle forward. In October, Elenora found that she was with child, but before it even quickened, it was gone. Elenora had thought of the baby as a gift from the universe. As soon as she knew, she had crawled into Eli's arms and told him she was absolutely sure it was a girl. She would name her Rose because roses were such a beautiful physical expression of love, just like their daughter would be.

After the loss, she was distraught and spent several weeks in bed while Aunt Aggie tended to the household. Eli secretly believed it was for the best that they'd lost the child then, instead of months later to starvation, like several of the village's infants, but he did not dare say it aloud. Elenora had become a fragile shell of her former self. Though Aunt Aggie did her best to coax broth and what little cheese she had left down Elenora's throat, she refused to eat. Eli was more afraid than ever that he would lose her, too.

And then the stranger arrived.

//////

Outside the old lodge while the sun beat down on the dirt path, Eli was jolted from his thoughts as a hand reached out to clasp his slight shoulder.

"Good sir," an unfamiliar voice said. "Are you well? I have already hailed you twice." The stranger dropped his hand and stepped back. "I am passing through and meant to ask where I could purchase supplies, but from the troubled look on your face, I would guess there is little to spare."

A chilly wind swept down the road, brushing Eli's dark hair into his green eyes. "No, sir," he replied. "If you had told me half a year ago that this would be our sad state, I would not have believed you."

The stranger's smile dropped into a frown. "The same has been true everywhere I have gone. The elders of my town say that hot summers are always followed by bitterly cold winters. They predict countless deaths from the cold alone."

"We will most likely starve first," Eli muttered.

The man sighed. "Well, sir, I might as well make myself useful as I pass through. I see you have a downed wall there on that building." Eli followed the man's hand as it pointed to a broken pile of wooden slats that had been lying on the ground for the past two weeks like a metaphorical reminder of the village's failings. "I will help you to repair it if you can find a few more hands to help."

"Thank you," Eli said automatically, still staring blankly at the half-fallen timbers. "I am afraid that we do not have much to offer you in return."

"I have the food I need, though I would gladly accept a place to lay my head. I have spent too many nights beneath trees. They are lovely company, but alas, with the cooler nights, they do more harm than good." He held out his hand. "I am Gregor."

Eli and Gregor rounded up the village's stronger men to dismantle and rebuild the fallen wall. These moments would usually be full of talk and stories, but the stress of reality and the need to conserve as much energy as possible worked as a needle and thread on the villagers' lips.

Gregor worked quietly, noticing how thin the men were, how heavy their tools seemed in their hands. He paused in his work, standing up straight to stretch his back. "There is a town to the east, about a thirteen days' walk from here, one with plenty of food and assistance."

Eli wiped the droplets of sweat from his forehead with a dirty hand before resting it on his bony hip. "We heard it was more like a month's travel." He looked at the man quizzically.

"Nay, it is not that far. This is my second trek there and my last. I was staying in a forest community about six days' walk west." Gregor pointed from the direction he came. "We were dealing with the same as you folk, but worse. I begged them to come with me, but they were too afraid."

Eli could see in the man's eyes that there was a heavy story behind those words, though he did not feel it was his place to ask. Some stories were best kept untold; some could unsettle a soul.

"I have a lass where I am going," Gregor continued. "Or at least, I used to. A kind, sturdy woman I never should have stopped chasing. I just hope she is still there waiting for me." He turned to Eli. "You should come with me."

A glimmer of hope sprung in Eli's chest, but just as quickly, it was snuffed out. "We could not impose upon another town," he said. "They would not be able to feed and house all of us."

"Nay, your village is small compared to theirs. A few more people would make no difference."

Eli returned his attention to the slat he was hammering into place. He thought about how he had spent the morning trying to ration the remaining food and how he had been unable to figure out how to make it last. Supplies were that low for everyone, even if they combined all they had. He did not see how the villagers could last the winter. This new city that Gregor spoke of might be their only option for survival. If they put faith in this stranger and pooled their resources, they should make the journey and arrive with full stomachs.

//////

That evening Eli had a few quiet words with the village elders, who in turn called a meeting of all the residents.

Gregor again explained about the town to the east and how they would find plenty of food and shelter.

"I do not feel easy about this," said Michel Berger, an auburn-haired, red-faced man. His butcher barn was full of more opinions than cattle. "All we have is this man's word that such a town exists, and if it does, why should they welcome us?"

"I speak the truth," Gregor replied.

"But how did they manage to escape the drought when the rest of us have suffered for months?" Aunt Aggie wanted to know.

"They have many underground springs from which water flows continuously," the trader replied.

By the end of the meeting, most of the villagers were willing to set out to find the town, but there were still some who had reservations about taking such a risk.

"What other choice do we have?" Aunt Aggie asked. "The way I see it, we are going to die if we stay here."

"We will die if this city turns us away!" shouted Michel.

"Maybe," Aggie replied, "but at least we would have a chance. If we do nothing, we have no chance."

"We must give this more thought," Elder Caron said.

"I am leaving in the morning," Gregor said, "but I will draw you a map of the route to the city."

The villagers returned to their homes to consider the situation. That night Gregor slept on the floor before Eli's hearth, and by morning he was gone, leaving a drawn map on the kitchen table. By late afternoon, the town had reconvened; as they looked at each other, they knew that they had all reached the same conclusion, even Michel. They all felt the hunger pangs. They all saw the empty stock. Winter was a horrible time to travel, but it was either that or die.

The next day was full of preparation and, some might have said, hope. Yes, it was terrifying, but they knew they had no other choice. They turned their fear into excitement as they called back and forth with their neighbors.

All that could be packed was loaded onto whatever form of transportation was available. The wagons and carts were filled with bags of grain, jugs of water, and sides of salted meat. Looking at the combined rations, they saw that they had enough food and water for nearly three weeks if they ate their fill, six if they rationed. Blankets, boots, warm coats, and lard for chapped hands were stuffed into every inch of space. A few women tucked what little jewelry or other precious items they might be able to sell or trade into their pockets but left everything else in a safe place. Aunt Aggie even wrapped her mother's best teacup in a length of muslin and hid it under the seat of the privy.

Elenora spent the day beside the grave of her sister, pressing dried flowers into the frozen earth. Eli watched her from the window. He thought of going to her, convincing her to come inside to the warmth of his arms, but he knew she would refuse. He finished packing the cart alone.

When he awoke the next morning and turned toward his wife, he saw that she was smiling. It was such a different sight than the one he'd laid his eyes on the night before.

"Today is the day," she said, touching her delicate fingertips to his lips. "I was up early—your tea is ready. I am going out to hitch up the horses." She spun out of the bed. Eli put his hand on the warm spot of the bed that was imprinted with her shape, the loose threads snagging on his calloused fingertips.

The street outside was full of horses, mules, and carts. Children were laughing; their parents were nervous but wore tentative smiles on their faces. Everyone was ready. There was a light buzz in the air Eli had never felt in his life, a sense of adventure and hope he had only read about. Aunt Aggie was one of the first people ready, having bolted and locked the door to her shop before climbing up into the seat of her own small wagon. When the entire village had assembled, they set off east in a long line.

Aunt Aggie's cart was in front of the Bellamys' wagon, and Alice and Pierre Travers were directly behind. They all spent the day calling out to each other, laughing, and pointing out interesting features in the landscape. Near dusk, the party stopped for the evening and made camp. Those in carts or wagons stretched large quilts or tarps over the tops to create shelters. The villagers who had ridden horses or walked created makeshift tents using whatever materials they had. They cooked their food around tiny campfires and retired early, exhausted from the first day of travel. In a return to their childhood tradition, Alice rang her bell, and Elenora answered.

In the morning, they packed up as quickly as possible and ate their meals on the road. The day passed more slowly as the excitement of the journey died away.

//////

It was the third day when the strange symptoms started to show. The head of the Jones family, Tomas, was the first to fall ill. He awoke that morning moaning terribly. A fevered chill crawled like pinpricks across his body. He left the shelter of his cart to fetch water, but after a few steps, he collapsed to the ground. His wife, Ann, and a few men rushed to him. Eli watched as they rolled him over. Tomas's face was a mottled grayish purple. The people stepped back in shock, Ann clutching their newborn son to her chest.

"Water," Tomas gasped. Eli hurried to the closest container. Helping the man sit up, he tipped a dribble of water into Tomas's mouth.

"We must keep going," Elder Caron said tersely. As the villagers hurried away to finish breakfast and pack up, Eli helped Tomas climb back into the cart and covered him with as many blankets as the family had brought. The village healer brought an infusion of herbs for Tomas to drink to help reduce the fever. Knowing Elenora was more than capable of driving their own wagon, Eli hitched up the Joneses' horses and climbed up next to Ann and the baby.

The villagers moved out of camp, knowing they needed to travel a full day before they could rest again. Tomas spent the day in a deep sleep. The air might have been cold, but sweat glistened on his forehead. He occasionally moaned in his slumber, and when they took a break to rest the horses at noon, Eli saw that his fever had worsened. By the time they stopped for the night in a clearing, Tomas was too weak to leave the cart, yet he claimed he could feel the fever breaking and would be better by morning. His words gave the townsfolk some relief, as it looked as if the fever had been a simple sickness, one cured by rest.

///////

At first light, the villagers were awakened by screams. Eli rushed from his wagon to the Joneses'. Ann was huddled in the corner farthest from her husband, crying and rocking the baby back and forth.

Tomas was stiff and cold—he had passed in his sleep. A small pool of coagulated blood lay on the blanket beside his gaping mouth, his eyes open ever so slightly. Ann's panicked cries were soon joined by others as they awoke to find their family members shaking and sweating with fever themselves.

Eli and Elder Caron wrapped Tomas's body in the bloodstained blanket and set him at the edge of the clearing. By midmorning, a quarter of the villagers had been struck by the mysterious fever.

Eli and Elenora were wracked with fear, but at the same time, felt relief that neither of them had developed symptoms. They retreated to the safety of their cart while the healer went from wagon to wagon, attending to the sick. He had never seen such a thing and could only suggest keeping the patients warm and frequently giving them water mixed with his herbal potion to keep them from drying out. Those who had ill family members drew their carts to the other side of the clearing, away from those who hadn't been touched by the sickness. The camp grew quiet as the villagers huddled in their wagons beneath blankets or at isolated fires where they stared unseeing into the flames.

In the silence of the afternoon, Eli walked to the eastern side of the hill with the map to see if he could tell how close they were to the city. He studied the drawing, the cold air tugging at his chapped uncovered skin when he saw it.

Below him on the downward slope of the hill was a strange-looking mass, a snow-covered hump protruding from the ground, but something about its shape gave him pause. With a frown on his face, Eli began to pick his way down the hill. He had just about convinced himself that he was merely looking at a rock when he saw a set of thick leather boots resting in the lee of a snowdrift. He realized he was looking at a man.

"Hello? Sir?" Eli's voice trembled slightly. He moved closer to the body, and as the wind slid down the hill, he saw the flutter of a beard. With a feeling of dread, Eli grasped the man's shoulder and turned him over.

It was Gregor. His lifeless eyes gazed up at Eli. A dark line of frozen blood ran from his mouth and down his neck. Eli reeled back in horror, recalling the man's words about the forest community he'd been staying at, that they were worse off than Black Creek.

Gregor had infected them.

Eli staggered back up the hill, calling for Elder Caron. He blurted out what he had found as villagers peeked out of their wagons, and several made their way down the hill to look at the body. The healer was the first to return to camp.

"I can't help you, any of you," he said slowly. "This is like nothing I've ever seen before. Tomas perished from the fever in less than a day. If you already have the symptoms, there is no stopping it."

"What are you saying?" demanded Michel Berger. "Are all of our sick going to die?"

"I hope not," the healer responded, "but my medicine didn't help Tomas. It may not help anyone else. And if you rode in the same wagon with someone who woke up with a fever, then you most likely have this sickness, too." The healer hung his head.

Elder Caron turned to his people now, tears in his eyes. "We laughed at the priest; now look at us. We cannot travel with so many ill, so as I see it, we only have one option—we stay here until this sickness passes. If the map is correct, the city is about six days away, and there is enough food to last for at least a fortnight. Stay inside your shelters with your kin. Leave only to cook and use the privy. Watch the sun rise three times; then, on the fourth day, we will all meet to see where we stand." He looked around at the solemn people gathered there. "This is our darkest time yet, my friends. Say the words you need to say to God."

The villagers looked at each other from the small circles they had created with their family members before pulling their silent children closer. Everyone then turned around and walked back to their wagons and makeshift tents like it was a funeral march. Elenora was about to crawl into the wagon when she heard a bell ringing. Glancing around, she saw that Alice and her husband had pulled their wagon next to the Bellamys'. She smiled at her friend, then dug her own bell out from her pack and rang it in response.

The snow came heavily that night, cushioning itself around the shelters, creating an insulated pocket of warmth. The first morning was filled with soft sobs as some of those who had shown symptoms expired. Families spoke in whispers inside their wagons as they prayed together. The few who ventured outside gave each other encouraging smiles, though some avoided their neighbors altogether. Eli called to Aunt Aggie, who responded that she was feeling fine, just bored.

Eli and Elenora spent the first day of confinement reminiscing about their childhoods, telling each other stories they had not heard before. But terror lurked just under the surface of their words. They shared a plate of salted pork and a small loaf of bread for dinner, then pulled up the blankets as the sun sank behind the horizon. Elenora believed that a person never got over a death, never healed completely from someone leaving you forever. You just learned to tuck all the memories of them into every fold of your being and let them become a part of you. Since losing her family and then the baby, she had become more paranoid about losing Eli.

"If this is the end, I will not mind as long as we die together," Elenora whispered as she fell back hard into the down pillow, and Eli drifted off to sleep. But Eli awoke in the dark to feel her cool hand testing his forehead for fever every half an hour. He was not even sure if she had slept.

The next day was quieter, though heart-wrenching sobs echoed from across the clearing around noon. Eli left the wagon to water and feed the horses, and as he turned, he saw three snow-covered bodies lying in front of the tents. He could only guess that they had died in the night but their families were too weak to do more than remove them from their shelters. He did the cooking that day to spare his wife from the gruesome sight. That evening Elenora and Alice rang their bells gently, though the noise seemed to shatter the stillness.

The third morning started with slow moans that dwindled into silence before the sun disappeared into the trees. Elenora was becoming restless and agitated, and the cries unsettled her. She clasped her hands to her ears and murmured songs to herself to block out the soft sounds of grief. All day Eli thought he heard a slow muttering among the tents, but he wasn't sure if what he heard was merely the wind tricking his ears.

As the sun faded from the sky, Elenora reached for her bell and rang it quickly, flinching at the cheerful toll.

The other bell did not ring.

Elenora waited a minute, then rang again.

There was no answer.

She glanced frantically at Eli, then moved to ring her bell a third time. He reached out to silence the sound, but she pulled away.

"She did not ring back!" she said in a panicked voice.

"Alice is probably visiting their privy," Eli said quietly. "Or perhaps she is already asleep." He trained his eyes on his wife's fingers, which were squeezing the handle of the delicate bell tightly. She had experienced so much loss in the past two years; how could she bear any more?

The darkness seemed to come on much faster that evening. Maybe it was the weight of knowing that in the morning, the healer would call the people out. Everyone would be forced to see who was alive and who had not survived.

That night Eli and Elenora sat with their foreheads pressed together, hands and legs intertwined, and prayed to whatever would listen that tomorrow they would find most of the villagers spared. They spoke softly about continuing on to the city, where they would be saved from the long winter.

It was not the light that awoke Eli the next morning but a horse's whinny. The sun must have been high as glorious light filled the covered wagon. As he gently stroked Elenora's hair, she stretched and turned toward him.

"Today will be good, my love," she said, smiling. "I wished for it, so it will be." She reached up and stroked his face.

"So it should be," Eli replied, grabbing her hand and kissing it. "The sun is a good sign." He and Elenora hurriedly rose and pulled on their warmest clothes. They opened the flap of their tarp, and the light glancing off the snow momentarily blinded them. A gust of early-winter air hit their faces and stung their lungs. When their sight cleared, they saw that they were the only ones awake. No footsteps were pressed into the night's snowfall.

"That's strange." Eli frowned. "It must be midmorning already." He gazed hard into the sun; it sat in the center of the sky.

"Hello?" Elenora called hesitantly. No one stirred.

Eli took a few steps from the wagon, then turned to his wife. "Go back inside, my love, and I will find out what I can." Elenora opened her mouth as if to question him, but then she nodded and slipped back under the covering. Eli watched to make sure the tarp was back down before he turned his attention to the campsite.

The flap to the healer's tent was open, a blanket partially pulled out into the snow. Eli covered his mouth with the fabric of his shirt, then slowly squatted down and looked inside. The healer lay unmoving. His heart pounding in his chest, Eli leaned in just enough to confirm what he had suspected: the man was dead. His open eyes looked eerily up into Eli's, the irises frozen white. A smear of blood was crusted upon his jaw.

The hair rose on Eli's neck as he backed out of the shelter. Suddenly, he was afraid of what the silence that now lay heavily over the camp meant. Seeing him, a horse whinnied, and then another, but there was still no sound from any of the villagers.

Before he ventured any farther, he broke a branch off a tree. He trudged through the snow to Aunt Aggie's small cart, where she had constructed a quilt as a roof. The quilt had collapsed under the weight of snow, and there was no movement from underneath. Eli only had to lift a corner to see one of Aggie's thin legs sticking out from beneath a blanket. The skin was gray, the flesh frozen.

Eli choked back a sob for the woman who had raised him, but he knew he had to see if anyone was alive before he could grieve. He held his breath as he approached Alice's wagon, where she and her husband, Pierre, should have been snuggling their five-month-old daughter. Eli used the branch to push aside their tarp, but he had little hope. Still, the shock sent him reeling; the family inside was dead, their faces marred by blood. The baby lay at Alice's side like a discarded doll. Eli backed up, then stumbled and fell into the snow.

He sat in the snow for a few minutes, his head in his hands. Finally, roused by the wetness soaking into his trousers, Eli got to his feet and looked around the clearing at the other wagons. The horses were now eyeing him eagerly in the hopes of being fed, but he ignored them. He wanted to call out again, but he knew if he did so, it would scare Elenora, and he was not ready for her to face his grisly discoveries. Eli stepped over the snow-covered lumps he had found the second day and peered into the shelters, his hand covering his mouth. With every new body he found, his ragged gasps grew louder, and he did his best to stifle them.

At last, Eli knew the horrible truth: there was no one else left.

Other than Elenora, everyone he had known his entire life was gone. They were people he had known from childhood, friends who had attended his wedding, and those he had sat with at church on Sundays.

All gone. All ghosts.

Eli heard a muffled cry and turned. Elenora was standing beside the wagon, her fur wrapped around her face, making her skin seem brighter than the snow. Even from across the clearing, he could see the tear tracks on her cheeks. As soon as his eyes met hers, she turned and ran to Alice's wagon.

"Alice!" she cried, running to the opening in the tarp.

"Elenora, no!" Eli followed her as fast as he could, but he was too far away. He did not want her to discover what he had seen. He wished he could wrap her up into warm blankets and protect her from this horror.

Elenora's scream tore through the air so loudly it echoed through the trees. It was the kind of primal scream that only came from a moment that changed a life forever. Eli managed to reach Elenora just as she started to stretch out a hand for Alice's baby. He pulled her back and held her tight.

"No! You cannot touch them," Eli cried as he watched his wife's heart break yet again. She sobbed as he turned her toward his chest and clung to her with all his strength.

"Her color is gone," Elenora gasped. "I can't see her color anymore."

Eli picked Elenora up like a doll and pulled her into their wagon. He tried to think of words to comfort her, but there were none. She needed silence. She needed sleep. He needed to turn off the world for her.

Another horse cried out, and Eli reluctantly left Elenora with a kiss. He went from animal to animal, giving them minute amounts of feed and water. He did not know how long they had gone without sustenance, and if he gave them their normal amounts, they would eat too quickly and become ill. While the horses ate, Eli went to the carriage that held the last of the supplies and saw that there was plenty of food left. He rearranged everything until he had room for the rest of the horse feed and their own belongings. Once the horses were finished with their meal, he hitched a team to the supply wagon and drove over to his own.

There, he found Elenora lying on her side, staring blankly at the wall. He took her warm hand in his cold one. "We should get moving," he said gently. "We cannot stay here." Elenora slowly looked up at him, but her eyes were blank. When he tenderly pulled her up into a sitting position, she did not resist. Eli remained silent, letting her sit numbly, wrapped in a blanket as he transferred all their belongings into the larger wagon before leading the remaining animals to the rear and securing their leads. He had no intention of leaving any of them behind to starve. With Eli's help, Elenora managed to climb up onto the seat of the large wagon. He made sure she was wrapped warmly before he snapped the reins and moved out of camp.

Only as they pulled away from the campsite did Elenora turn and stare at the snow-covered tents. She sat like that until they crested the hill and the camp was no longer visible.

As night fell, Eli found a flat, tree-covered area to set the wagon and put up the tarp. A steep cliff dropped off on one side, but with the horses tethered at the tree line, they would be safe. After he fed and watered the animals, he rubbed them down.

Eli heard a low melody coming from the wagon. It was Elenora. "Love?" he called out. She climbed out from beneath the tarp.

"I feel better," she said softly. "What has happened has happened, and I cannot change that. I will pretend this is only a story, and once we reach the city, we will be safe. Then—and only then—I will let myself think of it. After all, I have you. That is all that matters to me." She wrapped her arms around her chest and continued humming her melody. Eli took a deep breath and continued brushing the horses.

Later that night, Elenora tucked herself into Eli's arms and closed her eyes as though she hadn't a care in the world. He kissed her hair and drifted off to sleep.

It was just before dawn that Eli awoke to the sharp sound of Elenora's gasp. "No!" she cried. "No, no, no!"

"Elenora, what's wrong?" Eli said, trying to push himself up. His head felt like it held the weight of a boulder, and with a groan, he sank back onto his pillow. Elenora scuttled into the far corner of the wagon with a look of fear in her eyes. "Oh God," Eli whispered as he reached up a leaden arm to feel the slick sweat on his hot forehead. He tried again to sit up, but he did not have the strength to move.

"No," Eli said softly into the morning air. "How is this happening now?"

"You will be fine," Elenora said quickly, sounding irrational. "You must be. I cannot go on without you."

"Yes," Eli agreed in a whisper. "I will get better." Eli could see the sanity leaving Elenora's eyes as the panic filled them.

But as the sun crept over the trees, Eli worsened. They both knew deep down what was going to happen. His breath came in short gasps, and his body felt as though it was on fire. Elenora brought him the water he begged for, but as the day wore on, it was clear he was fading quickly.

"Elenora," he murmured, "I am so sorry."

The whisper that came from Elenora's mouth was barely audible. "We were supposed to be together forever. What will I do without you?" Her question went unanswered. "Eli?" He was asleep. Elenora was barely aware of the tears that poured down her face. She laid her head on his chest and listened to the strong beat of his heart. Yet, she knew that he would likely be gone by the morning's light, gone like all the others in their sleep.

Even in the days they were confined to the wagon, Elenora had never let herself truly think about what she might do if one of them became ill. She knew that if she started thinking about it, she would never be able to stop. Elenora sat back on her heels, holding Eli's hand in hers. "We were supposed to die together," she murmured. Her husband's teeth began to chatter, and she drew the blanket up under his chin and tenderly tucked it around his body. She clasped his hand and kissed it one last time. "I love you," she whispered.

Elenora maneuvered herself out of the wagon without pausing to put on her shoes. The snow's coldness would not bother her much longer. She would not watch Eli die, could not stand seeing the line of blood that she knew would soon trickle from his mouth. She would soon fall ill as well, and she would not suffer alone next to her husband's cold body.

Eli had warned her of the cliff behind the wagon, but she put one foot in front of the other as she slowly moved toward the deep gorge. It seemed only moments later that she felt her toes wrap around the cliff's edge. She gazed down upon bare treetops and steeled her resolve. She closed her eyes and took a final deep breath, raising her arms to the sky as she prepared to fall.

"Do not do that, girl," a haggard voice called from her left side. Elenora gasped as a rough hand grabbed her arm and pulled her back from the edge of the cliff. She spun around to see a squat, elderly woman wearing a frown. "What exactly are you doing?"

Elenora took a moment to collect her composure. "Excuse me," she responded, "but what business is it of yours?"

"Well, now," the woman said. "It looks to me like you were about to jump, and I don't fancy cleaning your remains from my property."

"What are you talking about?" Elenora said angrily. The woman grabbed her arm again and then pointed into the gorge below. Elenora could just make out a stone house at the base of the cliff.

"My house is down there," she said. "If you are trying to kill yourself, I would greatly appreciate it if you would find another way." Elenora stared at her in disbelief. "What exactly is it that troubles a pretty young thing such as yourself?"

"My Eli is dying," Elenora said. "I cannot live without him."

"Oh, pish-posh," the woman said, flapping her hand. "Plenty of women live without their menfolk. You're not the first to lose a man, and you certainly won't be the last."

"You do not understand!" Elenora protested. "The disease that is killing him will soon take me, too."

"In that case," the woman responded curiously, "let me take a look." She turned and trotted toward the wagon.

"No!" Elenora cried, rushing to catch up with her. "Do not go any closer! Everyone who has gotten sick dies within a day's time." She threw out her arms to stop the woman.

"Ha, nothing can take me out!" the woman replied gruffly as she pushed Elenora aside and yanked back the tarp. Elenora looked on desperately as the woman examined Eli's feverish body.

"Your man has the plague," she announced. "It has wiped out thousands, but it will not touch me. It would not dare!" She pointed at Elenora and laughed. Elenora stared at the old woman in terror. She could not believe that in what should have been her final moments, she had been found by a lunatic.

The woman sprang out of the wagon and hurried off as Elenora gaped after her. "Come with me, girl," the woman called over her shoulder. For a moment, Elenora hesitated, but then the woman called, "I am not asking."

Blinking her eyes in confusion, Elenora followed the small figure to a hidden track in the cliff, and they slowly picked their way through the bare brush and brambles. The woman scrambled down with the skill of a mountain goat, but Elenora took her time lest she fall and break her neck. When they reached the bottom of the gorge, she saw that a small stone house was right ahead.

It looked so welcoming, like a cozy cottage out of a fairy tale. When the woman opened the door, a tantalizing scent wafted out. Elenora entered and was immediately enveloped by the warmth that a cooking fire gave off. A kettle hung over the fire; stew, by the looks of it. Elenora breathed in and felt surprisingly comforted. The rest of the cottage was sparsely decorated, with heavy wooden furniture taking up most of the room. A man sat at the table sharpening a knife.

"This is my son, Alexander." The old woman motioned toward the man as she walked to a basin.

"Hello," Elenora said apprehensively, feeling embarrassed. She could only imagine how she looked, probably half-wild with her windblown hair, her face chafed by tears and the cold, her torn stockings all that she wore on her feet. Alexander nodded in acknowledgment.

The woman slowly made her way back across the stone floor, a tin cup in her hands. "I have what will cure you and your love up there," she said, offering the cup. Elenora glanced at Alexander to see what he made of this crazy proclamation, but his face was expressionless.

"What could possibly cure this disease?" Elenora asked. "Our village healer said he has never heard of anything like this before."

"Well, your healer never met me, did he? Worth a chance, is it not? If you both will die anyway, what is the worst that could happen?"

Elenora looked at the tin cup suspiciously; it was filled with a dark liquid. Still, the old woman was right. What did she have to lose? She reached out and took the cup.

"Now, pinch your nose and swallow it down," the woman instructed her. Elenora took a breath and gulped the liquid. It was warm, and the taste reminded her of when the slaughter stone was bathed in sunlight for a whole day. It was metallic and musky. A hot feeling shot from her throat to her stomach, and she shuddered.

"This one is for your love at the top of the hill." The woman handed Elenora another cup. "My old bones can only make that climb once a day, but Alexander will take you."

The walk back to the wagon made Elenora's heart pound—not from exertion but fear. What if they were too late and Eli was already dead? But when they reached the wagon, she was relieved to see that Eli was still breathing, his chest rising and falling regularly. Alexander pulled Eli's limp body into a sitting position, and Elenora tipped the cup between his lips. He coughed a few times as his body instinctively tried to swallow the foreign liquid. Only then did Elenora notice that the liquid was a deep red hue. In the darkness of the cabin, she had not been able to discern its color, and she recoiled slightly as it dripped down Eli's chin like blood.

"What is this?" she asked Alexander in horror.

"It does not matter," the man replied, his dark eyes carrying a threat. "He needs to drink it all, or it will not work."

With shaky hands, Elenora continued to pour the thick concoction into Eli's mouth. When the cup was empty, she set it down and concentrated on her husband.

"How long until he is healed?" she asked.

"It is already working." Alexander laid Eli back down on the blankets. "You will feel like new in three days." Suddenly, there was a glint of light as he pulled something out of his belt; he moved like lightning. A sickening crack filled the air as he plunged his knife into Eli's chest.

"What are you doing?" Elenora cried, lurching backward. She threw herself off the wagon and hit the ground hard, but immediately she was back on her feet and running. The horses reared and shrieked in terror as Alexander easily grabbed her around the waist and threw her down.

"I will explain when you wake up," he said calmly. Elenora's scream abruptly ended as the knife slid through her chest like butter.

"Welcome to the Family."

CHAPTER ONE

The embroidered edges of the curtains that framed Mia's double-paned windows moved in smooth ripples just above her head, the breeze brushing against her face. Nearly every morning of her life began this way, no matter the temperature.

Mia was in love with the night and the mystery the silence carried. Every evening her mother would storm into her bedroom to slam the window closed. But regardless of how many times her mother asked her to leave the window shut, she couldn't. The moon just called to her; in her mind, if the window was open, the sky and her were connected in a way that was only feasible if the glass wasn't there to separate them. She thought herself a moon child.

When Mia was younger, she thought her mother was more concerned with the energy bills than anything else. She'd had no idea then that there was such a thing as bad people who sometimes crawled through windows and stole little girls. It would have made zero sense to her anyway, as the people who *did* make their way into her room didn't need windows or even a door, and they never meant any harm. Her mother knew this. When Mia was barely old enough to go to school, people-like things would show up as faint dustings in the air. Maybe they were just a shadow or a faint outline, but she used her childlike mind to try to rationalize what she saw. Even at that young age, she could make connections with the things she had seen on TV and learned in books.

Her mother also knew that only Mia could see these people.

Mia's mother was Elizabeth Adair, a world-renowned psychiatrist, and her passion was parapsychology. In her childhood and early teens, Mia was her mother's most famous case. She was known as Case 37 in the book her mother had written, the work of literature that was almost a handbook for paranormal enthusiasts across the globe. It was strange for Mia during the few times she had been coaxed into sitting through one of her mom's presentations in front of hundreds, or even thousands, of fans. The second she heard her number, 37, called out, she watched the faces of strangers light up.

She had been born with the ability to see and hear things other people didn't. From the day she started speaking, she talked about the people in her bedroom. Seeing those strangers was as normal to Mia as breathing. Sometimes she got a few visitors a week, sometimes every night. Some of the spirits spoke to her, but most did not. Their strange movements sometimes scared her. It was strange to see a person who appeared lost and found all in the same moment. They would pace her room, having conversations with themselves as if lost in the moment, re-creating their final days. Saying the things they wished they'd had the chance to say in life. It seemed that just being seen and acknowledged was enough for them. Mia didn't know what happened to the people after they disappeared, but she liked to think they crossed over into the afterlife. Every so often, someone would ask her to give their loved ones a message, but usually, the spirit disappeared before she could find out their name and where they had lived. It was as if Mia simply being there to hear their final words of love—or confessions of wrongdoing—was enough to release them from their earthly ties.

///////

Elizabeth had hated being home ever since her husband, Ben, was killed in a car accident when Mia was seven years old. Mia's little sister, Sasha, had been only three at the time. Elizabeth wasn't completely absent from their lives; she just wasn't there as much as a parent should have been. Like the day Mia got her first period. Or the day Sasha fell off the swings in the backyard and broke her arm. Mia was the one waking up most mornings and cooking microwave oatmeal for the girls before they caught the bus to school. The grief had a way of convincing Elizabeth that Mia was mature enough to be the lady of the house for weeks at a time. Little did Elizabeth know that her daughter was just as lost in grief, but the little girl didn't get to escape. The whole situation had triggered a deep loneliness in Mia. She lost the opportunity to feel like a child; instead, she was just a mini adult who no one took seriously.

Elizabeth and Ben had loved each other fiercely, and in the first year after Ben's death, Elizabeth was lost. She had a daughter who could speak to people on the other side, yet Ben never came through. Mia and Elizabeth spent countless nights sitting on the living room floor, the room full of candles, but there was no sign of him. Mia felt like she was letting her mother down. Elizabeth always reassured her that she wasn't, but the frustration was evident in her eyes. Mia and her father had been exceptionally close; if he wouldn't come through to her, it meant he had already passed over. That meant no final words for the love of his life, and it left Elizabeth feeling empty. The way Mia saw it, her father had been free to move on to the next phase of existence, which was a beautiful thing. She wished that her mother could see it the same way. Mia had seen so many spirits lost in all the "what-ifs," the last thing she wanted was for her father to glide around her room, confused and asking questions she couldn't answer. Elizabeth didn't care; she needed confirmation that he was okay. She went as far as waking Mia up in the dead of night during an electrical storm with hopes that the energy in the air would help pull him through.

In the years that followed, Elizabeth often dropped the girls off at Slow Burn, the local hybrid coffee and book shop, on weekend mornings so she could meet with various clients over brunch. She'd kiss them on their cheeks and slip a five-dollar bill into each girl's hand before taking off in whatever fashionable silver sedan she had leased that year. The store was one of several located in an old garment factory. The wooden slats on the floor and the brick walls at the front and back of the building were original; scuffs on the hardwood showed where women had repeatedly pushed back their chairs over the course of a century. Holes in the beams overhead marked where racks had once hung with newly finished blouses and coats.

Every corner of the place smelled musty, and every floorboard was slightly offset from its neighbors. The shop rarely carried new releases, specializing in weird, old books and nonfiction by local authors. It was the kind of place where they wanted you to enjoy a book with your coffee, not feel pressured to buy. Mia loved to pick out a bizarre title and then curl up in one of the overstuffed, mismatched chairs. Her favorite spot was just underneath one of the windows, where a seamstress from an unknown time had scratched *TM+LK* into the wood. The initials were faded, but they were like a secret message from the past, a physical reminder of people who had once walked the floors. That at one point in time, they were the main characters. She loved seeing tributes that showed how even after people were gone, their love could carry on. Sometimes Mia hated how sentimental she was, never wanting to appear too soft.

Mr. Horvath, the owner, had welcomed the girls wordlessly as if it was the most natural thing in the world to have two unaccompanied children spend time with him on Saturday mornings. He would waddle his way down the road and unlock the doors for them, making them a pot of strawberry green tea, or perhaps a nice earthy rooibos, before flipping the sign to Open. Most kids would prefer to spend their weekends with friends, watching cartoons, or scootering around the local strip mall, but not Mia. She was happiest sitting in her chair reading books. She and Mr. Horvath didn't speak most of the time, just existed in the same space until Elizabeth breezed in the door to collect her daughters.

As Mia visited the worlds in the pages of Mr. Horvath's book collection, she found pieces of herself. By junior high, Sasha had outgrown the shop and spent her weekends hanging out with her friends, but by the time Mia could drive, she was working at Slow Burn on Friday evenings and weekend mornings. Mr. Horvath had quickly become something of a surrogate father. His smile reached his ears every time Mia opened the door. His boys had moved away and were preoccupied with their own families and jobs on the east coast. Mr. Horvath was the one who showed Mia how to change the oil in her car and how to save money. School was tedious, but the weekends were less so, thanks to Mr. Horvath and his book collection. Mia's time at Slow Burn seemed to be the only time she stayed out of minor boredom-fueled trouble. She wasn't a delinquent, but when she was bored, she tried desperately to erase the feeling. So sometimes, instead of attending math, she'd end up smoking cigarettes in the basement of her high school, under the science wing. When she was supposed to be in history, she was instead making out with Dylan under the bleachers at the football field, a boy who pretended he didn't even know her when they passed in the hallways. Mia's mother worried, but she graduated on time and without an arrest or even a suspension on her record.

//////

Mia looked at her phone; she had exactly forty-two minutes before she had to be in her car and heading down the lane toward work. She'd planned to work at Slow Burn through college, but the shop had closed down six years ago. Mia didn't want to think about that now. These days, she worked for a bookstore chain, which was the only bookshop in town now. She hadn't known at age eighteen that she'd still be working there at nearly twenty-five. It was the kind of job that was supposed to only fill a gap year between high school and college, that magical year where responsibilities were few and every day was full of a fun part-time job, friends, and drinking, but time just got away from her. After high school, college seemed like a waste of time and money. She had so many dreams and ideas of careers but no idea of who she really was or what she wanted to do with the rest of her life.

After all, she'd peaked anonymously before puberty and was a household name—"Case 37"—in the paranormal community. It was so weird to Mia that she could be so wanted by one community but ostracized by her peers for the same thing. Memories easily flooded back into her mind of moments in the high school halls when spirits as solid as a human being appeared in front of her. Her schoolmates had thought she was crazy since the day they found her in the schoolyard talking to the air—they only found her more strange when she insisted she was trying to tell Maddison Alireza's grandmother that she could move on. Teenagers didn't take easily to things they didn't understand.

//////

Her mother's book itself had become the paranormal community's version of porn. After its publication, Mia started receiving messages from strangers who spent late nights diving deep on the web and using their love for conspiracy theories to connect the dots. Some said they could tell by the way her mother wrote about Case 37 that she had to be her daughter. A few even found her various social media accounts, hoping she could help them contact their loved ones.

Unfortunately for them, she didn't have anything to offer. Her gift disappeared in the rearview mirror along with her childhood. It was as if becoming a woman was the only thing on which her soul wanted to focus. As the curves appeared, the voices and visits almost completely stopped. It left her feeling a bit useless—a one-hit wonder. It wasn't a bad deal, though; a portion of royalties from Elizabeth's book went straight into Mia's checking account, and her mother traveled the world to speak at paranormal conferences.

//////

One of her most vivid memories was The Accident. It was on a warm August morning when Mia was ten years old that her mother explained to both her and Sasha what *bad people* were, not realizing the fear she was instilling in her oldest daughter. That afternoon when her mother left to take Sasha to her dance lesson, Mia swiftly pulled on her red rubber boots and rummaged around in the dilapidated shed that should have fallen summers ago in search of the antique fox trap her father had hidden in the back corner.

Mission accomplished, Mia carried the metal jaws out into the high sun of the afternoon and stood beneath her gabled bedroom window. There was no way to get in without using a ladder. Nevertheless, she bent back the sides of the metal with her tiny fingers, clicking the fastener to the rusty hole.

She placed the trap in the garden under the window and used some leaves to cover any tiny bits of metal that weren't rusted and could potentially reflect the moonlight. She took a few steps back to observe what in her mind was a foolproof plan that would keep her and her little sister safe.

That night as the warm summer breeze rolled over her uncovered skin, she slept deeply and without dreams. The very next morning, she was awoken not by the curtains drifting over her face but by the loudest howl she had ever heard. She flew out of bed and stuck her head through the window; below was Mr. Charles, the gardener, writhing on the ground in agony. The seventy-two-year-old neighbor lived on a few acres of land next door and had been helping take care of the Adair property since Ben died.

"No!" Mia cried out as she saw the trap gnawing at the old man's left ankle like a shark. *How did I forget Mr. Charles?* she thought as she took the stairs three at a time. She had dialed 911 from the hall phone before her mother stumbled out of her room in confusion.

That was the dream Mia woke up with today, the memories of that horrific day—The Accident, as she always referred to it in her mind—living in her head and playing like a movie on repeat.

"Ugh." Mia kicked the sheets off, as the warm breeze already promised a scorcher of a day. She took one step out of her bed to close the window, which made a groan as she struggled to push it into place. As she flipped the latch, she stared down at the spot she had seen Mr. Charles lying on that long-ago morning. She almost expected to see him still lying there, his arms reaching up to the sky as if God himself was about to reach down and help him. Her dream usually ended with Mr. Charles's face blanched in pain, and now her mind forced her to recall the week that followed The Accident. When Mr. Charles's ankle shattered, he fell and landed on one of the fieldstones that rested untouched around the yard, breaking his hip instantly. That morning was the last that Mr. Charles would see anything but the yellow hospital walls.

Mia could see Mrs. Charles from her bedroom window as she walked out her door the first six mornings after The Accident. The old woman maneuvered her arthritic joints into her silver Toyota before backing out of the drive and turning toward the hospital. As Mia tried to force herself to sleep every night, the Toyota's lights would flash onto the wall, and she would get up to watch Mrs. Charles hobble into the house alone. A moment later, she'd see a single light switch on in the kitchen as the woman measured out a half can of food for Roger, their fat orange cat.

Mia had not confessed that it had been she who set the trap. She'd been sure that her mother would have known immediately, but there hadn't been the least suggestion that Mia had placed the contraption. The rusty metal made the trap look as if it had been out in the elements for at least a decade. At first, she had been too scared about being punished to say anything, but once the adults had decided it was an accident, she knew she had to correct them. But how?

For an entire week, she lived with the sickness of guilt eating her alive. She knew the longer this went on, the more trouble she would be in, and that everyone would look at her differently.

The Toyota did not leave the driveway on the seventh day but was joined by two other sedans. Mia already knew why. She had awakened that morning just before the sun was a glimmer on the horizon by a warm hand gently patting her shoulder. Her eyes opened slowly, and she turned her head, expecting to see her mother. It had been her first solid sleep since The Accident. But it wasn't her mother she saw. It was Mr. Charles. Gasping, Mia sat up and looked at his legs. There was no gauze, no crutches.

"Mr. Charles, what are you doing here?" Mia whispered.

"Hello, kiddo," he replied. "I didn't mean to frighten you, but I wanted to see you." He reached out a hand to hold hers, his eyes bright.

"Are you okay now?" Mia's voice broke, and tears started to pool at the corners of her eyes.

"I would say I am better than okay," the old man said, letting out a small laugh.

"I'm sorry," Mia said, relief washing over her. "I didn't mean to hurt anyone. I just wanted to keep the bad people from getting in."

Mr. Charles smiled down at her. "I don't want you to worry about what happened, kiddo. It was an accident. Let's keep this one between us, okay?"

Mia squeezed her eyes shut as tears spilled down her cheeks. "Okay." She sniffed hard, then she glanced back up into his face. He looked a bit wavery, and she blinked her eyes to focus. But it wasn't her tears; Mr. Charles was slowly fading, his kind smile never leaving his face until he was finally gone, and Mia was left holding hands with nothing but the stale air.

"Okay," she repeated to the empty room, her hand falling back to her bedside.

Mr. Charles was not the first spirit to visit her in her bedroom, and he definitely wasn't the last.

//////

Now she stood stretching and looking over the two acres into the forest as she wondered how something that happened almost fifteen years ago could still live so vividly in her brain. Every night she would set an intention of what she wanted to dream about, just like all the books her mother gifted her for birthdays and Christmas said she should. Mia rolled her eyes and headed for the shower, but not before stopping at the full-length mirror that stood angled beside the dark green five-tiered bookshelf that held her favorite books and most precious mementos. Mia took in her frame. Her shape was not skinny but not quite fat. Her gaze shifted to her face. The petite nose and almond eyes were her mother's, but from the pictures that sat at her bedside, she could tell she was practically a carbon copy of her father with her soft chin, dark hair and eyes, and high cheekbones. Mia knew she was average, but she didn't mind. She felt lucky that she didn't hate how she looked, like most of the girls she went to school with seemed to. Her skin wasn't perfect, hormones were always to blame, the curves of her body were soft and smooth, and she had tiny stretch marks in the usual places, but everything looked like it fit her perfectly, as if she had been mapped out and every bulge and mark was preplanned by someone.

As a little girl, she would trace the small pink lines that were scattered across her mother's stomach and thought them beautiful, like shiny ribbons. It blew her mind that society frowned upon them and manipulated women into spending their money and time to erase all the bits and pieces that made them unique. She found peace that she could love herself even if she wasn't the size society wanted her to be. Mia tended to pull away from the women other girls idolized. She got lost in the supporting characters that were full of flaws. She had no issue with people who wanted to change things about themselves. She, too, would love long legs or maybe a smaller nose. But all day at work, she rang up magazines with the same airbrushed models that looked like they were designed by a graphic artist. Girls as young as twelve were buying these clickbait gossip rags. Weekly, Mia saw them change from little girls to carbon copies of the women on the magazine covers.

The only thing that ever made Mia truly insecure was the darkness of her eyes. Her mother and Sasha both shared bright blue eyes and light hair, but Mia's irises were so deep brown that they almost blended with her pupils. The kids at school used to call her "witch" and "demon." Mia had dyed her hair and tried to wear blue contacts for a few years, but the dye job was too time-consuming. Her hair became brittle, and the contacts irritated her eyes, so she eventually cut off her hair and threw out the contacts. She now fully appreciated the woman who looked back at her in the mirror, her nearly black hair pooling around her shoulders. Even the twenty-five pounds she'd put on since high school had settled on her body in a way that she liked. *If only we could have the same confidence in our teens as in our twenties*, Mia reflected.

She flipped her head over and twisted her hair into a bun on top of her head, then gave herself a wink and headed for the shower. It was time to stop procrastinating and get back to her mundane life. She had to open the doors of the bookstore before her manager, Mark, lost his bananas.

As her hair air-dried, Mia did her makeup at record speed: a sharp winged liner and maroon lips. She opened her closet and looked for a decent outfit for the day. Most of her clothes were in earthy tones: greens, browns, and blacks. She also had a great collection of dresses, some bodycon, punk plaids, and turtlenecks. Chunky shoes were an essential part of her wardrobe. She decided on black opaque tights and her favorite black day-or-night dress, then adorned the outfit with a monogrammed necklace that said *Daddy*. Sometimes people thought it was a sexual innuendo, but Mia didn't care. The only other item of jewelry she wore was a simple silver band around her right ring finger.

The first time she had felt the smooth metal of her father's ring was from the outside of a small manila envelope. Four days after her father's accident, Mia woke to her mother sitting on the edge of her bed, facing the wall. She didn't stir for what seemed like ages, and even then, only after Mia's small voice broke the air. Elizabeth turned as if in shock, as if she was so lost in thought she had forgotten where she was. Once she recovered, she pressed the envelope into Mia's hands, telling her it was hers. She had hung it from a chain around her neck until she was a teenager, when her mother took it in to be sized. Now that it fit perfectly, she hadn't taken it off in years.

The steps were cold as Mia made her way to the kitchen. She could smell the burnt Pop-Tarts before she saw Sasha's face.

"Morning, baby girl!" Mia called out to her sister, who was sitting at her computer typing furiously.

"Ehhhhh," her sister grunted before looking back at her keyboard.

"Wow, is the world going to end?" Mia laughed as she grabbed an orange and began to peel it. Sasha slammed the laptop shut.

"I think I give up. I'm not kidding!" Sasha stormed. She was twenty years old and had her sights set on law school. She felt she needed to always be the best at everything. It had been easy for her in high school when she was mixed in with a group of kids from every walk of life: kids who wanted to be anything from doctors to hairdressers, and even the ones who seemed to think smoking pot was a full-time job. It was so easy for Sasha to stand out and be the best back then. But now she was in a cornucopia of overachievers, where everyone had been the best of the best in their own school, and she was competing with students who were as ambitious as she was and got the grades to match. The past two years had been a dose of the real world, and Sasha had been slowly spiraling, working harder than ever before to pull in the same top grades that had once come so easily to her. All this school year, she'd complained about how everyone in her class was a major asshole. All lawyers were assholes. That even she was becoming an asshole.

Mia tousled her sister's blond hair and pulled the glasses off her face. "Sash, you look like you haven't slept a wink."

"No, I did last night. I mean, the night before last night." She squinted at the clock above the kitchen nook window. "Wednesday night."

"It's Friday morning," Mia said, laughing but observing the bags under Sasha's eyes. "You need to go to bed."

"But I have class at 10!" Sasha protested.

"Not today, you don't," Mia replied firmly. "You can afford to miss one lecture. I want to have some fun tonight. Hit the bar. Dance! For that, I need *you*, not whatever zombie you're going to be by then. GO!"

Sasha looked at the top of her laptop in defeat. "Okay."

"Good." Mia gently pulled the laptop toward her while her sister eyed it as if contemplating a final grab for her overheated piece of metal and plastic.

"Keep an eye out for Cooper," Sash grumbled as she trudged into the hallway. "He wouldn't come in after breakfast."

It was normal for the seven-year-old golden retriever to disappear for hours at a time. He loved the fresh air and sniffing out rabbits and squirrels and always had to be coaxed back into the house. Cooper loved being free.

Mia grabbed a few granola bars and plucked her keys from the rack.

"Oh yeah," Sasha called over the banister. "Tell me if that weird girl comes into the store today and what she buys."

"Ha, will do!" Mia gave her sister a thumbs-up and headed out the door.

CHAPTER TWO

After her short delay in ordering Sasha to bed, Mia was lucky to make it to the bookstore just in time to open.

She pulled her 1998 Honda into the parking lot. It had been her dad's, and even though she took care of it as best as she could, the green paint was starting to lose its battle with rust. It was old, but it never failed to start. And maybe it did smell like old muffins, but there was something comforting and reliable about that scent.

Mia climbed out of the car and hefted her bag onto her shoulder. As she closed the door, a black sports car pulled into the spot across from hers. Squinting her eyes, Mia saw the familiar hue of bright blue hair that belonged to one of her regulars in the passenger seat, but in the driver's seat sat a white woman she didn't know. Her curly blond hair was chin-length and matched the paleness of her skin. The blonde flicked her gaze to the rearview mirror, making eye contact with Mia. Suddenly flustered, Mia averted her eyes and made her way to the store without looking back.

Sasha and Mia had a long-standing tradition of gossiping about what certain people bought from the bookstore. It was sometimes hilarious to see what kinds of people came through the door and what kinds of books they liked. There were a few longtime customers who had surprising taste in literature.

Ace was a massive biker dude who wore nothing but leather and bandannas, but over the years, he had purchased an outstanding number of coffee table books featuring cats. Then there was the old, widowed Mrs. Ancaster, who was pushing ninety and came in monthly to buy a good supply of fetish magazines. Each time, she claimed she only bought those magazines because they had the best crosswords in the back, then winked and cracked a tiny, toothless smile. Mia always nodded, even though she had snuck a peek once and knew that there were no crosswords at all in *Bondage Boys Monthly.*

Recently, the store had gained a few new customers. The bustling beach city of Cedar Hollow was only a forty-minute drive away, so many of the store's customers were on day trips or just passing through the small town, and the recent influx of regulars was a bit odd. These folks stuck out because they frequented the store every few days, but each time, they simply browsed. When they first started hanging around, Mia thought they were casing the store and kept a close eye on them. Once they entered through the door, they split up, occasionally making eye contact with each other as they glided through the aisles in silence. After fifteen or twenty minutes, they would merge back into one group and leave without having made a purchase.

The blue-haired woman had come in at least three days a week for the past two months. She appeared to be the same age as Mia and had a nervous air about her. She wandered the aisles for at least an hour every time she came in, breaking spines of bestsellers and discounted books alike. She would stare at a page and seem to take it in quicker than the average reader, and unlike the other new regulars, she did leave with a new book every time she came in. Once she made her selection, she would linger near the counter, pretending to be absorbed in a display until all other customers had paid and left. Then she would approach the counter, eyes down. The front of her hair was dyed a bluish teal that framed her face and lit her ice-blue eyes on fire. She always paid in cash, and her purchases felt random. Once it was *Catcher in the Rye*; another time it was *How to Preserve Almost Everything*. The woman's most puzzling pick so far was *The Goblet of Fire*, as Mia was convinced she hadn't purchased the first three Harry Potter books.

Each time she arrived at the counter with a book in her hand, Mia would try to make small talk just as she did with every customer, but the woman never responded. She only shook or nodded her head.

It was a spring day around noon when the woman with the teal hair finally spoke to Mia. After her usual hour of browsing, she finally sidled up to the counter with *The Virgin Suicides*.

"This book is my favorite," Mia said as she turned the hardcover edition over in her hands. She'd only just finished it for the umpteenth time earlier that morning, closing the worn cover with the missing corner and tucking it safely back onto her shelf. She rang up the woman's purchase and slid it into a plastic bag. "That will be $22.83."

The woman handed over a few bills then did something unexpected. She looked up, right into Mia's eyes.

"If everything ended today, would you be okay with that?"

Mia recoiled a bit in surprise. The woman's eyes were practically boring into her own, and she felt like she couldn't pull away. "Uh . . . I don't know. I've never really thought about it."

"Sorry," the woman replied, and glanced away. She looked wildly uncomfortable. Mia blinked a few times, then quickly opened the cash register and handed the woman her change. She ripped off the receipt and thrust it into the bag, holding it out.

The woman had cast her eyes down to the floor again, and she let out a sigh as she took her purchase and turned toward the door. Just as she pushed it open, though, she turned back.

"My name's Cordelia, by the way," she said with a new air of confidence that didn't match her demeanor of the moments before.

Then she was outside and gone.

Mia's confusion over the odd question quickly turned to curiosity. She'd rushed to the door and looked up and down the street, but there was no sign of blue hair anywhere.

Cordelia had continued her trips to the bookstore, and

she'd remained as silent as ever; she was back to only nodding in response to Mia's words.

///////

There were few customers that morning, and Mia found herself glancing toward the parking lot every few minutes. The black sports car hadn't moved.

"Hey."

Mia jumped. It was Shelly, her washed-up, chain-smoking, alcoholic coworker.

"What's wrong with you today?" Shelly leaned against the counter and absently flipped through a stack of greeting cards. Mia caught a whiff of liquor on her breath. She hated how Shelly could act so disconnected but somehow also read the room perfectly.

"Nothing," Mia replied as she caught movement out of the corner of her eye. The doors to the black car were opening. Shelly followed her gaze.

"That your girlfriend?" she asked. Shelly lived for drama and gossip and always made the dumbest comments. Mia ignored her as Cordelia and the other woman made their way up to the door.

Just like every other day, Cordelia began to browse the aisles. Her head turned downward, slowly scanning titles in the staff picks section, not looking up to meet Mia's eyes.

"That girl comes in here a lot," Shelly observed, a little too loudly.

Mia refused to rise to the bait and instead turned to her computer, pretending to look something up in the inventory. However, whenever she thought Shelly was too busy to notice, she glanced surreptitiously at the two women. The blonde was stunning. Her skin was flawless, her makeup perfect. She wore tight black jeans and a flattering crop top that showed off her figure. She seemed bored and tapped her fingers impatiently along the top row of books. Mia lost sight of both women when they wandered into the far section of the store.

A few customers had just checked out their purchases when Mia looked up to see the blonde standing in front of her. She placed an imitation leather-bound journal on the counter.

"Nice choice," Mia commented casually, scanning the barcode. The scanner was having issues, and as she rescanned the journal, she glanced up to see the woman was staring at her.

"I need to write my days down, or I forget," the woman said without breaking eye contact.

"Yeah," Mia responded as she latched on to the woman's blue eyes. They were the color of the ocean and almost as deep. "Of course."

The blonde suddenly tossed her hair and looked away, and Mia realized that she had accidentally rung the journal up four times. She quickly turned to the computer and began to void three of the scans.

"I haven't seen you before. Are you new to town?"

"Yes, I'm Kris. I'm just visiting for the next month," the woman replied. She nodded her head at Cordelia, who was now standing behind her.

"Oh, you know Cordelia." Mia pushed the journal into a purple plastic bag.

"Yeah," Kris said. "We're kind of family. Or, at least, the

only family we need." She pulled a pair of oversize black sunglasses out of her bag and slipped them on.

Mia nodded. "Your total is $18.67." Kris put a twenty on the counter and took the bag before walking away, Cordelia on her heels.

"You forgot your change," Mia called. Kris kept walking, but Cordelia glanced over her shoulder and shook her head. Mia was surprised to see the glassiness of tears in her eyes.

Mia's curiosity quickly turned to concern. Why did Cordelia seem so unhappy? She tried to think back to all the posts she'd read on the internet about how to spot a potentially abusive situation, but she couldn't recall anything specific. She grabbed $1.33 out of the register drawer and slammed it closed.

"Hey, Cordelia!" she shouted, running out of the store as Shelly watched with fascination. Mia caught up with the women in the parking lot.

"Here. My cash drawer will be off otherwise." Mia shoved the change at Cordelia with awkward force. "I like when you come in," she continued in a low voice as Cordelia pocketed the change. They were the only words she could find to say. She hated how flustered and awkward she sounded.

"Thank you," Cordelia said, so quietly that Mia barely heard, then got into the car with Kris.

Smooth one, Mia thought as the sports car pulled away. She didn't want to be awkward, but she was intrigued by this blue-haired woman, and she couldn't bear to see her looking so sad. She hadn't realized until now that Cordelia's appearances in the bookstore were what she looked forward to the most every day. It was always a strange interaction, but it was a break in her mundane, repetitive life.

Shelly cackled as Mia returned to the counter. "No wonder you don't have friends."

Suddenly fed up, she turned to Shelly. "Mark mentioned that your drawer was off the other day."

"So?"

"He assumed it was an error. I didn't tell him it was your sticky fingers, just like it is every time your drawer is off. Maybe next time I will."

Shelly recoiled, but for once, she didn't have a snarky reply. "I'm going on a smoke break," she muttered, storming off.

"Careful you only light the cigarette, and not your breath," Mia called after her.

///////

The day wore on, but Mia barely noticed the customers she assisted. Something about the women coming in had put her in a strange mood. Somehow their visit had triggered her feelings of aimlessness. She felt disappointed and angry that there was nothing she felt passionate about. Her mood matched the weather as a steady rain began and showed no sign of letting up. Her town's weather changed faster than the hands of the clock, turning from a day blanketed in dry heat to an afternoon of humid rain.

As the rain chased away the afternoon's clientele, Mia's thoughts returned to Slow Burn.

///////

On a Friday, two weeks before Mia turned eighteen, everything had changed. She'd gone to bed late that night, having stayed up to watch videos on the internet and going down a rabbit hole about Sasquatch. She had just begun to relax when there was a sound at the bedroom door. Sitting up, Mia squinted into the darkness. She saw that the door was open a good four inches, even though she always made sure it was tightly closed before she crawled into bed. A figure seemed to be standing in the hallway; perhaps her mother was having trouble sleeping.

"Mom?" she whispered as a hand pushed the door open farther. It wasn't Elizabeth, but Mia recognized the friendly face. She had most recently seen it smiling at a customer from behind the counter at Slow Burn. Mia blinked, and the figure was gone. She swallowed. It had been so long, nearly a decade since a soul last passed through her doorway, years upon years since she had seen a ghost. From some of his comments, Mia knew that Mr. Horvath was closer with her than he was with his sons; it only made sense that he would visit her on his way to the next life. But Mia refused to believe it could be his time. Her mind had to be playing tricks on her in the dim light; she was tired and had stayed up too late.

She swung her legs over the side of the bed and stood, never taking her eyes off the door. Pulling it all the way open, Mia peeked out into the hall. Both her mother and sister had their doors firmly shut, and there was no one else in sight. Sighing, she closed the door, wiggling the doorknob this time to make sure it wouldn't open of its own accord. Mia felt a boulder forming in her gut, but she tried to convince herself that she'd been seeing things.

Mia crawled back into bed and attempted to fall back to sleep, but her mind was racing. She could lie here for the next few hours until the sun rose, but she knew her anxiety wouldn't let her. The unwarranted panic started to settle deep in her abdomen. The all-too-familiar feeling, a rooted seed of "knowing something was wrong" started to grow. After only a few minutes, she sat up. Her legs flew over the side of the bed, her feet making a loud thud as they made contact with the cool hardwood floors. Mia pressed her eyes shut hard, holding her breath as she listened for someone stirring. There wasn't a sound. She slipped into the leggings she'd left on her dresser and reached into the closet to pull out a hoodie. Silently, she tiptoed down the stairs and grabbed her car keys off the rack by the front door. The front door closed with a creak. Her movements picked up speed as she took the porch stairs two at a time. She hated the sense of urgency. She would rather convince herself it was a dream. That it was something the nocturnal hours and her brain's chemistry somehow concocted. But as she shut her driver-side door, she could feel it. One single tear had pooled in the corner of her left eye. She blinked, her back pressed too hard into the seat. The tear fell, its trail leaving a cool line down her cheek. With one twist of the key, her old car started.

The drive felt like it took forever. Mia was lost in her thoughts. She was rotating between playing memories in her head of Mr. Horvath and the sweet way he cared for her. Then she would switch to the thought that everything was fine. That she was just making sure. The truth was that Mia didn't know if she could really handle this.

When she finally turned onto the main strip, Mia slowed down. As she pulled up in front of the store, she felt a wave of panic: the lights in the shop were on. Mia looked at the clock on her dash, where the glowing blue digits read 4:54 a.m. Mr. Horvath always turned the lights off before he left. She parked as quickly as possible and jumped out of the car. Goose flesh prickled all over her body. The planted seed in her stomach started growing quickly into a pine tree, tearing her heart open as she ran for the front door. She grabbed the shop's door handle, and to her surprise, the door swung open. Choking back a gasp, Mia took a moment to steady herself, then slowly eased herself into the store. She took a few cautious steps forward, noting that everything seemed to be in order; the rows of books looked the same, and her chair was still in the same place she had left it just a few hours ago. She glanced at the counter and saw that the accounting book was open, a pencil laid carefully in the open spine. Glancing around, Mia continued to inspect the shop cautiously. Taking such small steps she was barely moving forward.

The shiny brown toe of a dress shoe poking out from behind the counter quickly caught her eye. The toe pointed toward the ceiling.

Mia felt the flush fill her face and heard her blood start pounding in her ears. "Mr. Horvath?" Her broken voice didn't sound familiar to her. There was no response. Reluctantly, she moved forward for a better look, taking small soft steps, holding her breath.

Mr. Horvath lay flat and straight on his back. His skin was no longer a soft beige but held a gray tint; his vacant eyes looked milky, and pale purple pooled in his skin where it met the floor.

Though Mia had seen countless spirits throughout her life, this was her first experience with a dead body. Of course, she'd seen her father laid out in his casket at the funeral home, but that was different. He'd been dressed up, and the makeup had made him look like he was asleep. Mr. Horvath was almost grotesque in death. In life, he had always been the person who held the warmth of the sun. Just eye contact from him filled you with a sense of well-being; this body didn't even look like Mr. Horvath.

Mia closed her eyes and thought back to when she'd left him that night. He'd seemed perfectly fine then, but he could have passed mere minutes after she left. He must have, she thought to herself.

She used the shop phone to call the police. The receiver felt heavy and ice cold. As she pushed the numbers in, she started to feel the tears filling her eyes and softly spilling onto her cheeks.

The young deputy who arrived first asked her some pointed questions about how she'd come to be in Slow Burn at five in the morning. She wasn't entirely sure how to answer; luckily, the police chief arrived shortly after, having been pulled from his bed by dispatch. "This girl sees ghosts," he told the skeptical young man as EMTs examined Mr. Horvath. He said the phrase as if it was common sense. No one questioned him. "There's no sign of foul play, so he probably died of a heart attack or stroke." Mia was allowed to leave, though she couldn't help but linger outside the shop as the medics wheeled her friend's lifeless body into the ambulance. He'd always been there for her, and now it was her turn to return the favor, even though he was gone.

Mr. Horvath's two grown sons didn't want to take over the store and had no interest in its inventory, so they paid a company to board up the windows and doors and left it as it was, all the stock sitting in the cold, empty rooms. Years went by, but the landlord couldn't find a new renter for the location. Mia often stopped to peer through the tiny slits between the boards. Now, six years later, the shop was still the same as it had been the night Mr. Horvath died, save for a thick layer of dust and cobwebs. Its unchanging walls were almost a comfort to Mia, but they too closely resembled her own stasis. Just like the old, unwanted shop, she was going nowhere. She had exchanged one bookstore for another.

////////

When her shift ended, Mia was out the door before realizing that Mark had called goodbye. Sometimes she was too lost inside herself to acknowledge the world spinning around her.

CHAPTER THREE

Mia was braking for a red light halfway home when she noticed the black sports car behind her. Though both of the visors were pulled down so that she could only see the bottom half of the occupants' faces, she could tell it was Cordelia and Kris. The light turned green, and Mia hit the gas, her wheels sliding slightly on the wet pavement. The road curved up, and as she crested the hill, she glanced in the mirror again to see if the sports car was still there. It was, and behind it were nearly half a dozen more. *Strange*, she thought, a bit unnerved. It was unusual to see so many cars on this particular road, even at this time of day. The windshield wipers were fighting hard against the heavy rain.

She was only a mile from her driveway when she looked in the rearview mirror again to see if the vehicles were still behind her. Suddenly, she caught a movement out of the corner of her eye. A rabbit was dashing across the road not far ahead, and close behind it was Cooper, her golden retriever. Mia slammed on the brakes and swung the wheel to avoid the dog. Keeping her eyes on him, she saw that he had safely made it to the other side of the road. Mia looked forward again just in time to see the hood of her car dip into the ditch past the shoulder. She tried to regain control, but the road surface was slick from the worsening rain, and the car slipped over the ground as if on ice. Mia didn't have time to react as a maple tree rushed up to meet her.

///////

She didn't feel anything. There was no white light. There was nothing but darkness. She wasn't aware of her body, only a loud buzzing noise and then the sickening sharp scent of gas. After a few moments, Mia realized she could see, and she blinked something sticky out of her eyes. Hot liquid was pouring down her face. As her vision slowly came into focus, she found she was slumped against the steering wheel, a scary amount of blood and tissue smeared across the horn.

She was so unaware of her body. There was no pain. Was this shock? Darkness had once again begun to set in around the circle of her vision. The weirdest thing of all was that she didn't feel fear. She didn't think of her mother or sister. The only thought in her mind was that her father had also died in a car accident. That's what had to be happening now, right? She had spent so many nights crying, thinking of the pain and fear he had felt as he hung suspended upside down while he bled out. *This isn't too bad,*

Mia thought dreamily. She saw someone through the shattered passenger-side window. It was a beautiful woman with straight red hair. She was approaching the car as if in slow motion. Behind her were Kris and Cordelia, and at least ten others flanked them. No one made the slightest attempt to reach her.

Mia suddenly felt a sharpness in her head, but she couldn't move. She tried to speak, but the most she could manage was a pathetic groan. There was no reaction from the group at the side of the car. The red-haired woman simply took a step closer as if to see her better. *Why aren't they helping me?* Mia tried to move her arms, but they wouldn't budge. Now she saw that many of the strangers had smiles on their faces. Panic grew inside her chest as she frantically tried to push herself away from the steering wheel. She tried to scream, but her mouth wouldn't open. She realized then that she was paralyzed; her body wasn't reacting to the movements she wanted to make.

Despite her struggles, her eyelids grew heavier and heavier until they drifted closed. The last thing she saw was Cordelia moving toward the car, putting her hands on the bottom of the shattered window. Mia stared at her through half-open eyes. She knew this was the end; she could feel it, feel whatever "soul" was separating from the skin she had finally grown to love. A lightness crept into her consciousness, and she felt acceptance.

"I'm sorry. We'll talk soon." Cordelia's voice was a quiet echo as she pulled something shiny out of her breast pocket. It was a syringe full of dark fluid.

Talk soon? Mia barely registered her confusion.

The needle entered Mia's chest easily; she didn't even

feel the spike that had glinted in the rain. Her vision spun into silver flakes, then faded into static. She trained her eyes on the small silver ring on her right hand. Everything inside her was shutting down, and she could feel it. She didn't want to fight it; right now, she was content to die on the roadside, surrounded by strangers.

"She's gone," a lovely voice said far off in the distance as static filled Mia's ears. "Are you sure?" another answered, even farther away.

There was a substantial pause. "I'm sure," Cordelia replied.

"Perfect. Call 911."

The words and sounds around Mia trailed off as the light of the world did, too. It was soft, and she felt warm.

Then it all went black.

Only Cordelia, Izzy, and Kris stayed.

CHAPTER FOUR

The rest of the group had swiftly moved back into their assortment of sports cars. They had all done this kind of thing before, and there was a perfect plan in place. Weirdly, though, this time the air of difference was palpable: Mia was different. Every time Cordelia had seen Mia's face from across the bookstore counter, she could feel cool sweat at her temples. They had all watched, and they had waited on Mia for months, because one of the Family's only rules was that they could never, ever, under any circumstances, take a life for gain. So, it was simply a waiting game. And now, anxiety bubbled in the three watchers. They had all known something was going to happen, but not what, or that it was going to be today.

Cordelia, Kris, and Izzy were to be the passersby who

saw it all happen, three young women heading home, only to be caught up in a tragedy of epic proportions. The police car arrived first, flashing lights bouncing off the tall pines. The officer passed the three women and ran toward Mia's car before calling, "Are you okay?" Kris looked toward the ground, an almost imperceptible soft slip in her usually strong personality showing through. The officer thrust his arm between the gaping, twisted metal that framed Mia's body, his fingers pushing into bloody skin trying to find a pulse. He held his breath as if the lack of his own sounds could help him find life, could ensure that Mia still had a future and dreams. His head stayed still for a whole thirty seconds before he looked over his left shoulder and made eye contact with Cordelia.

"She's gone," Cordelia said to the man, her voice cracking in the night air. "I checked."

The officer, an older, heavyset man, stood and brushed the dirt from his knees, keeping his eyes averted from the headlights of Mia's car that intertwined with the branches of the tree that had taken her life. Kris then walked forward with intention, her black leather pants making a brushing noise, and pulled down the sunglasses that she still wore even though it was dusk. When the officer met her eyes, he stopped moving immediately.

"She swerved to avoid a dog, overcorrected into the ditch, and died on impact." Kris's words were firm.

The man blinked twice. "She swerved to avoid a dog, overcorrected into the ditch, and died on impact." The words flowed out of his mouth monotonously.

Kris pulled her glasses back up and turned, smiling as she walked back to the other women.

"God, she is *such* a badass," Izzy murmured, pulling on Cordelia's sleeve. Cordelia didn't respond. She wasn't like the other two. To them, Mia was simply an object, something that would only be a benefit to them. This wasn't a game to Cordelia. She had been pulled into this life selfishly and without warning when she was far too young to understand. But Izzy had been with the Family for a couple hundred years and barely had any memories of who she had been before. Kris had always wanted this life; she never could understand how anyone wouldn't. She was strong, and she thrived.

The officer was still staring at the place Kris had been standing, then as rapidly as he'd fallen into her gaze, he quickly snapped back out of it. "Looks like she swerved to avoid a dog, overcorrected into the ditch, and died on impact," he repeated in an authoritative voice, looking back at the accident. "Do you know her?" Mia's body sat unmoving in the seat; if it hadn't been for the shock of the red, she could have been mistaken for a prop with her white skin, her open and unseeing eyes.

Cordelia looked at the two other women. Kris was now preoccupied with her phone and Izzy was staring at the officer with a giant stupid grin on her face, as if she was excited to be a part of Mia's death, the drama. Cordelia understood that to them, this was an opportunity to look good in the eyes of the Families. Any change was fun and good to them. She, though, was a healer, someone who wanted to remove the pain of others and couldn't stand those who reveled in destruction.

"No, we don't know her," Cordelia responded after realizing the other two wouldn't. "We were behind her when she drove off the road and crashed."

"Yes," the officer said, nodding. "She swerved to avoid a dog, overcorrected into the ditch, and died on impact." Cordelia closed her eyes and gritted her teeth at this repetition. She knew Mia would wake up in a couple of days, but she also knew the devastation that would consume her family.

The ambulance's scream pierced the air, coming closer and closer. They pulled up on the road and turned off the siren, but the blue and red lights continued to flash, adding a new layer of horror to the rapidly darkening scene. The first responders used large flashlights to go about their work of wrapping caution tape around trees to cordon off the area. A stream of cars had begun to take turns passing in the left lane, drawn like moths to the flame of the flashing lights.

Cordelia joined Kris and Izzy in the warmth of their car, a mere twenty feet from the accident, while the first responders gently extracted Mia's body from the wreck. She knew why they had to stay: Kris was waiting for the coroner's van so that she could exert her control over him, telling him exactly what she needed him to do. Cordelia had never got used to the fact that one person could hold so much power. With just one push of energy, Kris could make someone do almost anything. That was terrifying to Cordelia.

As a healer, putting her energy into others could wipe her out for days. When she was still human, people would come from far and wide to meet her. She had been scared of her power then. When she was only six years old, the neighbor's daughter had been diagnosed with an aggressive skin cancer. The look of it was angry, but that didn't keep Cordelia from reaching out to it, her small hands emanating heat. The little girl had cried out for her mother, a religious, superstitious woman who had seen the concentration in Cordelia's eyes. She placed her hands on top of Cordelia's and the energy she felt filled her eyes with tears. The energy spread until the whole room seemed to crackle with it. Suddenly, Cordelia had fallen back onto the hardwood floor, and just like that, the energy was gone. A perfect outline of Cordelia's hands lingered on the toddler's body in the shape of a heart, the skin perfectly healed. Just hours earlier, the child's mother had been told there was little to no chance her daughter would live another year. But now . . . now . . . The doctors ran new tests and shook their heads with amazement as they told the mother that her daughter showed no signs of cancer.

That's where it all began. As Cordelia's talent grew, so did the underground knowledge of her gift, and people would come from all over the world to seek her help. She saw elderly parents with dementia who barely knew their children; she would touch their soft faces, and memories that had drifted away suddenly returned to them as they looked at their children in recognition. People with debilitating diseases visited and left without the pain they'd suffered for years. Those who had been told they had no hope to see their next birthday celebrated many more after only a touch from Cordelia's hands. But after every time she helped someone, she would lie in bed in a deep sleep for days. She could heal everyone but herself.

///////

Cordelia was jerked back to the present as the coroner's white cube van pulled up, crunching over bits of Mia's broken vehicle. Kris was out of the car in one smooth movement.

"I'm going to do this Veil quick, so hurry up." Cordelia opened her door and ran to Kris's side as she stepped in front of the coroner. "Hello, ma'am," Kris said, blocking the woman's path. "I'm Kristina Bellamy and this is Cordelia Sutton. We're from the National Union of Coroners." The woman stopped, confused, and Kris continued. "You'll remember that we've been sent to monitor your handling of this case." The woman seemed about to challenge the information, but then suddenly she smiled and relaxed.

"Of course," she replied in a calm voice. "I've been expecting you." Cordelia relaxed as well. The thing about Veils, which Kris was incredibly talented in casting on humans, was that they had to match reality in some ways to work. The human brain was so much smarter than most people thought, and it could find the smallest wrongs and make the connections.

"This is a classic auto versus tree fatality," Kris said as the coroner opened the back of the van to pull the stretcher out.

"Yes," the coroner agreed.

As the wheels hit the ground, the air was broken by a scream. Through the headlights, Cordelia saw the legs of a tall woman running fast toward them. *Shit*, she thought, and saw Kris frown slightly. If only the accident hadn't happened so close to Mia's house! She wasn't sure she could handle Elizabeth Adair's pain.

"Mia!" The word was piercing, and even Kris flinched.

A young officer managed to intercept Elizabeth. "Ma'am, please. This is an active crime scene. I need you to stay back." Elizabeth's eyes were trained on the wreckage of her daughter's beloved Honda.

"You let go of me, you shit! That's my daughter!" She

ducked low and shot out from behind the officer, moving fast. The man turned and threw his hands up in defeat.

The rain was now falling heavily, and the sheet that had been pulled over Mia's body was flapping in the wind, giving glimpses of her soft, broken body. Elizabeth sank to her knees in the mud beside her daughter. She was sobbing now, her voice cracking as she called Mia's name over and over. Cordelia moved quickly, the healer inside her taking over. As Elizabeth's hand reached out to pull the sheet from Mia's body, Cordelia caught it in her own. Elizabeth glanced up in surprise and met Cordelia's steely blue gaze.

"You don't want to look. You don't want to remember her like this." Elizabeth slumped over, and Cordelia pulled her into a hard embrace. They both collapsed to the ground as Cordelia felt the weight of Elizabeth's grief emanating from her. It was a force Cordelia had never felt in her entire life. It flooded her with ice and fire all at the same time.

"She's dead," Elizabeth sobbed over and over. "My girl is dead!"

"Shhh, shhh," Cordelia murmured, knowing that nothing would settle this kind of pain. The two women lay there like that for what felt like hours as Mia's body was loaded into the coroner's van and emergency crews began to clear the scene. Cordelia's arms were tightly wrapped around this crying woman who had lost most of the people she loved. Cordelia cried, too—with Elizabeth, for Elizabeth, and for herself, for all the times she'd had to be the one to take all this on. She used her healing ability to flood the woman's body with endorphins that would sedate her.

She heard footsteps approaching; it was Kris. "I could help her, you know," she whispered as she bent down, her knees settling into the wet mud. Normally Cordelia would say that was out of the question, but this time was different. No matter what, a Veil felt unnatural, but the emotions in Elizabeth were like a fire set to a hole in her heart that had already been burnt beyond repair. Cordelia knew that Mia had a sister who would need her mother now more than ever.

"Mrs. Adair, I need you to sit up," Kris said firmly. The woman pulled away from Cordelia and used her hands to shift her weight onto her knees; her mud-spattered coat hung heavily around her as it trailed in a puddle. Kris put her hand on Elizabeth's chin and tilted the woman's face up till their eyes met and locked.

"I know this is hard," Kris whispered into the air between them. "I know you've seen this all before, but like before you *will* pull through, and this time you will be stronger."

"I'll be stronger," Elizabeth repeated.

"The next day will be hard, but you will be proud of yourself when you see how well you're dealing. You know Mia is in a better place; she was too good for this world. Yes, you will be sad, but you won't wallow in your grief."

"She has a sister," Cordelia whispered. Kris nodded.

"You will be strong for your other daughter. She cannot lose you, too. The funeral will be a celebration of Mia's life, not a time to fall apart. Then you will think of her often, but you will move on, and you will help your daughter to move on, too." Cordelia watched as Kris stopped talking but kept staring at Elizabeth.

"I am going to take her home," Kris said, standing Mia's mother up. Elizabeth stood there in the shock and daze of both her loss and the Veil. Cordelia looked up the road. A yellow porch light shone in the dark as if it were a beacon of hope in the distance. Mia's sister would be there, Cordelia realized, and she would have no idea what had happened. Kris would take care of that.

The noise of an engine starting caught Cordelia's attention. The coroner's van was leaving.

"What about the coroner?" she said to Kris.

"I've taken care of it. The Veil will last until I can get to her later. You and Izzy go, and I'll meet up with you at the morgue."

CHAPTER FIVE

Cordelia gave Elizabeth's hand a final squeeze, then ran to the car and jumped in the front passenger seat. Izzy gave her an exasperated look as she pulled out onto the road behind the van. The ride was short, and only a few minutes later they arrived at the morgue parking lot. The coroner nodded to Cordelia as she walked up, but she didn't seem to notice Izzy. That was probably for the best, as Izzy was wearing a light blue dress with an insane amount of lace that was in vogue a few centuries ago. Cordelia wasn't sure why the Bellamys had sent Izzy along; she was the least inconspicuous of them all.

The coroner quickly removed the gurney from the van and wheeled Mia's body into the storage chamber. Hours went by as the woman undressed Mia and washed away the blood and mud, then re-covered her in a clean sheet and rolled her into one of the cold chambers.

Izzy spent most of her time examining the different parts of the morgue, which she found fascinating. "I still can't believe they cut people up after they die," she whispered to Cordelia at one point. "I'm glad Kris made sure they won't do that to her."

When Kris showed up, the coroner greeted her and went back to her work documenting Mia's injuries.

"Everything's set with Elizabeth," Kris told Cordelia and Izzy. "She agrees that it's best to hold the funeral as quickly as possible—"

"*Agrees*," Cordelia snorted.

"Yes, she agrees with all of my suggestions," Kris continued, unfazed by Cordelia's outburst. "She's going to take care of everything tomorrow. Luckily, there's only one funeral home in town, so we don't need to spend any more time with the Adairs, just watch to make sure everything's carried out accordingly."

"How was Sasha?" Cordelia asked.

"Who?" Kris frowned. "Oh, the sister?" She waved her hand dismissively. "About as good as she could be under the circumstances. She was grateful for my help."

///////

The three women watched from the parking lot the next day as Elizabeth and Sasha visited the morgue to confirm Mia's identity. Cordelia ached to comfort them, but it was best they remained out of sight unless necessary. The more people involved in a Veil, the more details to keep straight, and the easier it was for it to fail.

The funeral director was next, and once again, the women followed the hearse to the Riddley Funeral Home. It was located in a massive Gothic revival mansion.

Cordelia had kept vigil over dead bodies before and knew what directions Mia's mother would have given to the director. They would leave Mia's body in a natural state and not embalm it or introduce any chemicals into it. Over the next few days, the change Mia was to go through would be the opposite of decay. If embalming fluid coursed through the body, the results would be disastrous. After the funeral, the body would be scheduled for cremation, at which point members of the Family would take possession of the body while disguised as cremation employees. The ashes returned to Elizabeth and Sasha would be those of some unfortunate Jane Doe that the Family would claim from a morgue hundreds of miles away.

For that day and the next, Cordelia and Izzy sat in the parking lot and watched florists come and go. Elizabeth and Sasha arrived with the clothes Mia was to be cremated in, and Cordelia fidgeted with guilt to see that they seemed shrunken in their grief. While the Adairs met with the funeral director, a member of the Sutton Family picked Kris up in her Cadillac to go through Mia's wardrobe and possessions; none of the other Family members showed up. That wasn't so strange. They weren't needed until the end, and too many people would draw attention. So much relied on everything going according to plan.

So much would go wrong if *Mia* went wrong.

Not long after Elizabeth and Sasha left, their arms supporting each other, Kris returned.

"We've got a date. Tomorrow afternoon. Bellamy Cremation will be retrieving the body that evening." Winking, Kris leaned against the door and commenced devouring a pack of Cheetos. "God, you two must be so bored. It won't be long now, though."

//////

The next day was dark and rain fell hard from the sky, just like it had the night Mia died. Elizabeth and Sasha arrived early, and not long after, the Families' cars pulled slowly into the lot, each taking turns to back in side by side. One by one the darkly tinted windows slid down until the row of a dozen cars had a perfect pathway to gaze through to the funeral home entrance. There was no conversation, just small movements as the occupants leaned forward to watch as Mia's friends and family arrived. Cordelia could feel the nervous energy that slid between the cars. By three o'clock, the parking lot was full. Groups of people dressed in black made their way slowly into the building, many hand in hand. Only fifteen minutes before the service, the Families began to leave their cars in pairs, moving slowly inside to pretend to pay their respects, telling Elizabeth and Sasha made-up stories about how they knew Mia, like a well-rehearsed play, recycling the stories they'd perfected at other funerals.

Whenever they attended a funeral, members of the Families spread themselves out around the chapel, acting like old friends of the deceased. Most pretended to have been her customers at the bookstore, as it seemed the least likely to be questioned. Several didn't even bother with the reception line, just hovered in the back trying to blend in. Just earlier that morning, Cordelia had heard Alexander rehearsing his "sad" voice. She cringed every time he broke out laughing, and finally had to tell him he wasn't allowed to talk at the funeral.

In reality, they were there to deal with any potential problems should they arise. But it also meant they had to watch the actual family and friends grieve in real time. Pretending to share their sadness didn't seem right to Cordelia. Still, there was little else they could do without drawing unwanted attention to themselves.

Cordelia and Kris were the last of the Families to enter. It shook Cordelia how silent the room was considering that easily a hundred people filled the chapel. She realized that most of these people had likely been here over a decade ago when Mia's father had died. Mia would have walked the same garish pink carpet to say her final goodbyes to her father, who would have lain in the same state on the same dais that Mia herself now rested.

A few of the employees from the bookstore were in attendance, including the one who always smelled of alcohol. They looked bored, which gave Cordelia a quick flash of anger. Mia had deserved better than these people. Looking around, she made eye contact with Sasha, who stood alone in the reception area. Mia's sister looked smaller than the times she had watched them throughout the past few months, secretly and from afar. Sasha had always seemed so animated then. Now, the slim blonde woman's arms were wrapped tightly around her waist like she was trying to pull herself into a cocoon. Cordelia could see Sasha's unpainted nails clawing deeply at her sides. She wore little makeup, and her eyes told the story that she had not slept in the forty-eight hours since her sister's death; the purple darkness let the whole world know that she had cried more tears within these past two days than she might ever again. The stains on her cheeks looked like soft pink scars.

Cordelia walked over, her feet feeling like lead as they pulled heavily against the carpeted floor. The stare from the woman was too strong, it held too much pain, so Cordelia trained her eyes on other parts of the room, like the crown molding, and the bits of Victorian-style wallpaper that had started to peel from the corners.

"Hello, I'm Cordelia," she said, offering her hand.

"Cordelia . . ." Sasha said slowly and quietly as she tried to place the name. "Oh wow!" She lifted her hand and made contact with Cordelia's, shaking it warmly. "You're her—the woman from the bookstore!"

Cordelia nodded as she dropped her hand back to her side.

"Mia finds you interesting." A small awkward laugh left Sasha's thin lips, but her eyes glazed with tears. "I mean, she *found* you interesting, and not in a bad way." Sasha's head turned, and Cordelia followed her gaze as both their eyes fell upon the open casket. Mia lay there peacefully, her hands folded neatly on her ribs as if she was only asleep. "It's going to be hard to change the way I talk about her," Sasha said faintly into the air of the room.

"I understand," Cordelia said, not knowing what else there was to say.

"I just—I don't know, I thought she was going to . . ." Sasha's voice faded.

Cordelia was intrigued; it felt like a thought that needed to be finished. "Going to what?" she asked.

The woman's eyes shot to Cordelia's, but they were not soft and full of sadness like the moments before—they were on fire. Sasha was angry. Cordelia could feel the heat penetrating her own skin. "Make history, you know?" The force of the words made Cordelia take a step back. *If you only knew*, she thought. "It's not fair that she was taken from the world so soon."

"I'm truly sorry for your loss," Cordelia replied uneasily. She turned, hoping to break the intense energy radiating from Sasha. "Where's your mother?"

"Wherever the pills have taken her. Mom is a pill popper when she can't deal." Sasha seemed almost ready to laugh at the end of her sentence, but instead she turned and gestured to the other side of the room. Elizabeth Adair, the usually pulled-together woman, was leaning hard into one of the funeral employees. A glass of red wine dangled from one of her hands. "Make sure you go say hello." Sasha excused herself to speak with someone else who had just arrived.

Before Cordelia could take a step toward Elizabeth, she felt a cool hand grab her wrist. It was Luca, one of the members of her Family. "Best if you don't," he said in his raspy English accent. His brown eyes penetrated hers with purpose. "I already tried. Honestly, whatever world she's in seems much better than this one, and it'll break your heart." Cordelia knew he was right. Luca was the closest thing she had to a brother, and he knew her better than anyone else.

//////

Together, Luca and Cordelia scanned the room for their Family members. The two Families were split, each group clinging to a different side of the open room. Even though they occasionally spent time together, it was mostly frowned upon, and they had to be on their best behavior today. Mia's actual friends and family were scattered throughout the middle of the room or grouped around the casket. Cordelia realized with a frown that almost everyone here was older, closer to Mia's mother's age, though there was a small sprinkling of young people that stood in the back, away from the sight of Mia's body.

Luca knew Mia hadn't had many friends. In reading her journal, he'd gotten to know an isolated young woman who loved nothing more than to curl up alone with a good book. These young people might have known Mia in small ways, might have been acquaintances, but they couldn't be her friends.

He had seen this before. He glanced at Cordelia, letting her know they were sharing the same thought. So many people who barely knew the deceased always showed up, as a way for them to gain attention. Most times, they never went up to see the body, as if they knew they were cowards and what they were doing was wrong. They wanted to be seen in mourning, often to receive a bit of sympathy themselves. Too many people lived in the thought that they were the main character, but went on to live the most mundane lives.

Pathetic, Luca thought to himself as he and Cordelia made their way up to the casket. It was jarring to see Mia lying there. Like the rest of the Family, he had taken his turns over the past few months to watch Mia, waiting for the moment her fire would be blown out. He had not minded in the least; she was beautiful, though the last time he'd laid eyes on Mia, her features were scrambled within the mess of blood, plastic, and wires. Now he looked down into her glowing face, which most would chalk up to the funeral director's talent with cosmetics but was really due to the fact that her body was healing. She was wearing a black dress that clung to the curves of her soft body. As he leaned forward, a twinkle caught his eye. She was wearing a necklace that said *Daddy*. He chuckled softly. He couldn't believe that she was being buried in her favorite jewelry. It was so inappropriate for a funeral, but after the days he'd spent watching her, it seemed right.

"She was fun like that." Luca pulled back quickly and glanced to his side. It was Sasha. "We used to talk about dying a lot, ever since Dad's accident. Honestly, I would say it was almost an obsession." Luca didn't know how to respond, but Sasha kept speaking. "On my nineteenth birthday I had the flu and couldn't go anywhere, so instead we pretended the power was out. Mom was out of town as usual, but Mia lit candles around the house, and we sat at the table and planned our funerals. I know that sounds fucked up, but she knew that was exactly what I would want to do instead of playing Monopoly." Luca laughed as he felt a lightness come into the conversation. "She told me that night that she didn't want Mom to put her in some bright outfit so she stood out. She wanted to look like everyone else." A tiny second of a smile passed Sasha's lips.

"And the *Daddy* necklace?" Luca asked, staring at Mia's neck.

"She loved that thing. It made people uncomfortable. She knew a funeral is always already awkward, so she wanted to make it even spicier." Luca watched as Sasha's face started to drop again. He didn't know what had caused the shift. "My mom absolutely refused, so I brought it with me anyway and put it around her neck. I didn't want to disturb her, so I didn't clasp it in the back. But I made sure she would be wearing it, just like she wanted." Luca saw the color draining from the woman's face and realized she was about to faint. He took her by the shoulders and sat her in the easy chair closest to the casket. "You smell good," Sasha said dazedly just as the funeral director called for everyone to take their seats.

The service itself was simple and fast. It felt too small for Mia, but it was apparently what she had wanted. After the short service given by the director, Sasha stood up and walked slowly to the front of the room to address the mourners.

"My sister was incredible," she began. "The world is a darker place now that she's no longer with us. She had so many dreams. There was so much she wanted to do with her life, but she never got around to doing any of it. Some people probably thought she was quiet or unmotivated, but I know the truth: Mia wanted to do so much that she didn't know where to start. She was afraid of making the wrong choice, so instead she didn't make any. And now she'll never have a chance to do any of the things she wanted to do. Don't wait on your dreams. Live like there is no tomorrow. Live for Mia."

Sasha returned to her seat numbly, and Elizabeth reached out and embraced her. When the director nodded, Elizabeth stepped up to the casket. She placed her hands upon her eldest daughter's folded hands for a moment. Her breath caught in her throat as she said her final goodbye to her child for the last time. With the funeral director's aid, she closed the lid. Elizabeth bent forward and pressed her lips to the soft cherrywood, her rings clacking against it. She had been here before; she knew this was the last moment she would speak to her daughter, the last moment she could pretend it was all a dream before she went home and had to walk past a bedroom full of memories. It was just Sasha and her left in this world.

//////

The room slowly emptied as Elizabeth stood unmoving in front of the casket. Almost half an hour passed before the funeral director took her hand and asked her if she would like a final look. "No," Elizabeth said loudly before stumbling quickly down the aisle. Sasha had been sitting in the armchair waiting for her mother, and she silently stood and followed her out.

Cordelia watched from the lobby, completely unseen by anyone other than the Families. She knew that the funeral director was now operating under Kris's Veil and would meet the cremation company in the viewing area soon to hand over the casket. At the approved time, members of the Families, dressed in the uniforms of Bellamy Cremation Services, noiselessly made their way back up the stairs and into the building. Anxiously they awaited the moment they would explain everything to a woman waking up to a world she'd never known existed.

CHAPTER SIX

This is ridiculous. Something must be wrong." A tall, stunning woman with warm brown skin paced back and forth in front of the casket that held Mia's body. She reached out toward it, but a musical voice that spoke with authority made her hesitate.

"Step back, Gianna." Elenora's soft words carried through the room. "No one bothered you when you were waiting to rise. This will be just as shocking for her as it was for you. Let her be."

Gianna turned in frustration, yet she dared not challenge Elenora, so she trudged the few steps back to the front row and sat heavily beside Margo.

The room was cloaked in darkness and silence, with the two Families sitting on each side of the aisle. The pink paisley wallpaper looked like sepia maps scratched into the walls, as if the grief that had been felt in this room over the past century had left tiny notes on how to move on. Margo stared at the markings hard with the hope she would find some kind of recipe to cure her heart. It had been almost two hundred years, and she still thought daily of the causes and actions that led up to the moment she had died. She'd thought they would fade with time in the same way a tattoo bleeds from the fine lines set with intention, but no. As each day, month, year, and century passed, she was surer of what had happened, where she'd gone wrong.

"It's twenty minutes past midnight. There has to be something wrong; I know it." Gianna was back up near the casket again, her impatience permeating every corner of the room.

"Jesus Christ, G. Sit down!" Kris leaned forward and pulled on the hem of Gianna's pink bodycon skirt, forcing her back into her seat.

//////

Inside the casket, Mia's eyes opened. She wasn't sure if she was dreaming, but she was hyperaware of the pitch darkness and the hard surface beneath her. She moved her hands but found they would only lift a few inches before being met with silky fabric. Blinking, Mia tried to remember where she had fallen asleep. As a child, she would crawl under the bed in her sleep, as if she subconsciously wanted to meet the monsters that lived there. Was she under her bed now? She reached out to her side in an attempt to slide out from beneath the mattress, but she found more fabric, behind which was something that felt like a wall.

She blinked again, still unsure if she was dreaming. Not only was she unable to place where she was, but she also couldn't remember going to bed. As she tried to feel the space around her body, she realized she was trapped in some sort of box. The air seemed stale and hot, and she couldn't move her legs any more than she could her arms. "What's happening?" Mia croaked loudly, her throat dry and sore. She swallowed, and the muscles of her throat reacted slowly.

A muffled voice came from her right side. "I think I hear her!" The voice seemed familiar, but she couldn't quite place it. Suddenly panicked, Mia banged hard on the walls that held her. A moment later, she heard clicking noises, the ceiling above her rose, and cool air flooded in. Mia's eyes took a moment to adjust from the pitch-black and acclimatize to the dim room. A blurry face peered over the sides of plush walls.

"Cordelia?" Mia rasped in disbelief.

"Hey, Mia." Cordelia reached out both hands to help Mia as she struggled into a sitting position. The world was starting to spin, but a moment later, Mia felt a blessedly cool glass of water being gently placed in her hand. She took a large gulp. Though her stomach immediately wanted to reject the water, it brought relief to her dry mouth.

"Where am I?" Mia said in a clearer voice, her fingers wrapping around the glass as if she was trying to ground herself.

"Well . . ." Cordelia replied hesitantly, then gestured to the room.

Mia looked around, her vision still a bit fuzzy, then rubbed her eyes, and the memories flooded back. She recalled Cooper running across the rain-flooded road, then the tree, then all the people just standing there as she felt hot blood pooling around her. Then the memory of a burning in her chest before falling fast into a pit of pure darkness. And then . . . nothing.

The room was completely still, but as Mia's eyes cleared, she could make out the forms of the people who sat in chairs around the room. They were the same people who'd stood and watched her while she sat injured in her car. Glancing around, Mia realized she knew where she was. She knew this place better than she would have liked. She'd been here just six months earlier when Brandon from her twelfth-grade science class died after a tree fell on him at work, and before that, she had stood in this very room for hours as she greeted and shook the hands of her father's friends and colleagues. She had never seen the room from this perspective, though. She looked down at her legs and the silk that surrounded her.

Mia was the one in the casket this time. Looking up, she saw the concerned expression on Cordelia's face.

"I need you to listen to me, okay?" Cordelia said gingerly in the same way Mia's fourth grade teacher told her class how the hamster had gotten out of his cage and was gone.

Mia nodded her head slowly. "Okay."

"Three nights ago, there was an accident."

"Is everyone okay?" Mia blurted out.

"Everyone but you, honey!" The loud exclamation came from the back of the room, where an athletic-looking Korean man stood with a grin on his face.

"Not the time, Oscar," a woman in the front row admonished in a cool voice. Oscar looked for a moment like he wanted to make a retort but then crossed his arms and shut his mouth.

"You passed away that night, but just for a little while," Cordelia continued. The words hung heavily in the air, and Mia turned to face her again.

"Excuse me—" she pushed the word from behind clenched teeth "—but that's impossible."

"I assure you, not only is it possible, it happened."

"If I'd been dead, and now I'm not, I would be in the hospital, not the Riddley Funeral Home." Mia grabbed the side of the casket and started to push herself up. There had been some massive mistake. The thoughts in her head felt scrambled.

"No, hang on—" Cordelia began to say, putting her hands on Mia's shoulders.

"You're a bunch of crazy people!" Mia continued to push herself up. "You've drugged me or something. You're probably in a weird cult, sickos who kidnap people and try to convince them to join your wacky religion."

Mia felt like her emotions weren't in check. The words were flying irrationally from her mouth. These people had triggered her fight-or-flight, and she just wanted to get home. She'd managed to work her right leg out of the casket. Someone in the room snickered, but she ignored them.

"Listen, Mia," Cordelia begged. "Just hang on a second."

"Mom!" Mia called out as she heaved herself over the edge of the box. With a thud, her body hit the floor. She tried to pull herself up, but it was as if a ton of bricks was on top of her. Her arms and legs felt incredibly heavy, and her joints were stiff.

"I was trying to tell you; you need time to adjust."

Cordelia put her arm around Mia and held her in a bear hug. "I know this is a lot to take in, but you need to trust me."

"Trust you?" Mia snorted. "I don't even know you."

"I know," Cordelia replied quietly. "I'm sorry, but I'm telling the truth."

Oscar, the man who'd laughed earlier, was suddenly beside Mia, helping her into a chair. "Just listen," he said.

Cordelia knelt in front of Mia and held her hands. "It was raining. We were driving behind you, and Cooper ran across the road. You swerved to avoid him." Mia gasped a little. "Don't worry, Cooper is fine. But the road was washed out, and you skidded into a tree. You hit your head hard, and you broke your neck. Mia, you died."

"That's impossible," Mia said again. "If I died, how am I sitting here talking to you?"

"Because we brought you back."

"If you brought me back, did someone call my mom to tell her I'm okay?"

"We can't do that," Cordelia replied softly. "No one can know."

"But if I'm not dead anymore, then I want to see my mom! I want to go home!" Mia felt tears in the corners of her eyes.

"I'm sorry. You can't ever go home again." Cordelia's eyes were also brimming with tears. "That's part of the deal." She knew this was all so blunt and final, but there was no other way.

So many thoughts were running through Mia's head. Was this heaven? Or hell? How could she have died and then woken up in a casket, not dead anymore?

"Stop beating around the bush, Cord." Mia turned and, through her tears, made out the form of Kris, the other woman from the bookstore. "You're the one who didn't want to upset her, but it looks like you need to rip off the bandage."

"What?" Mia said angrily. "What's more shocking than being told you've died?"

"Mia—" Cordelia began, but Kris cut her off.

"You're a vampire."

Mia gaped at Kris for a few seconds, then started to laugh. "Oh my god, you're insane!"

"We're all vampires," Cordelia continued.

Mia's laughter faded away as she realized that everyone was staring at her, their expressions grave. "You're insane," she repeated as she attempted to stand up. "You're all insane, and I'm going home." Her legs were too weak, and Mia sank back onto the chair in defeat.

Two people in the back row stood simultaneously, a man with dark hair and bright eyes and a woman with striking red hair. They both appeared to be around thirty years old. They walked down the aisle with an air of superiority.

"Hello, Mia. My name is Elenora," the woman said before nodding her head and moving to stand in front of the chairs to Mia's left.

"And my name is Eli." The man moved in front of the chairs on the right as if executing a planned dance routine. Each of the two looked at the people who sat in the rows behind them.

"This is Sutton Family," Elenora said, smiling and making a graceful sweeping motion over the crowd in the chairs.

"And this is Bellamy Family," Eli said softly, placing a hand on Kris's shoulder.

Elenora moved toward Mia so gracefully that she almost seemed to glide. "I know this is terrifying and strange, but please understand that each and every person in this room has been right where you are." She folded her hands and stared at a spot on the floor. "Just like you, few of us had a choice in this outcome. It is understandable that you find this hard to believe. To you, vampires only exist in films and books. Let me assure you that not only are vampires real, *we* are vampires, and you are now one of us."

The woman's presence was soothing, and Mia found herself willing to believe her. "I don't understand," she said, looking over the room of people. Some were now smiling, though some still held an uncomfortable grimace. All she could think at this moment was that there had been a terrible mistake or that she was in a dream.

"I think I'd remember getting bitten by a vampire." The words sounded ruder than Mia meant them, and she covered her mouth with her hand.

Cordelia spoke gently. "Your injuries from the accident were too severe, and you would have been dead for good, so I used this." She pulled a metallic syringe from her breast pocket, and Mia recalled the silver flash before her world went black. Cordelia saw the understanding in her eyes.

"This contains a mixture of all our vampire blood." Cordelia held the syringe out, and Mia took the object, the silver plating cool in her hands. "When it became clear that you were going to die, I injected the contents of one of these syringes into your heart. There was no need to bite you or do anything else that legend says is required to turn a person into a vampire."

Mia felt dizzy, and she handed the device back to Cordelia. How could this be true? Vampires weren't real. But if it wasn't true, then why was she in the funeral home? Where was her mother? Mia thought back to everything Cordelia had said, but the only explanation that made any sense was that she had been kidnapped by a cult, and they had drugged her and stuffed her in that horrid box. If that was the case, who knew what else they were capable of? It was best to play along.

"Okay, I'll give you the benefit of the doubt that you're all vampires. But I still don't understand how that is even possible."

"I will explain in better detail," Elenora solemnly replied, standing up. Even in the room's darkness, the woman's brassy head seemed to shimmer. She started to walk in a counterclockwise motion around the room. "I was born in the early 1700s. When I was sixteen, my family and I left the city to return to my mother's childhood home. That's where I met Eli."

Elenora's eyes drifted over to the dark-haired man on the other side of the room. They locked in on each other intensely, the way eyes do when they are about to cry. But Eli broke the gaze quickly and stared at the window. "We were in love for a decade," Elenora said. Her eyes dropped to the floor as if the following words still brought her pain.

"One day, the river dried up, and the land suffered a great drought. We were starving, so we packed up and began to make our way to a town that was rumored to have been spared. The trip did not last long; everyone fell ill and died until Eli and I were the only ones left. We thought we had avoided the sickness, but one morning I awoke to find Eli so sick he could not move." The reflection of the tear in her eye caught Mia's attention. She had been listening so intently that the words were playing out like a story in her head.

"At that moment, I knew I could not live without him, so I decided to take my life. I would have most likely died of the sickness anyway. Before I could follow through, a woman found me, a witch. Her name was Thea. Both she and her son had been alive for well over one hundred years. She gave me a potion that she said would save us both. I drank. I did not ask too many questions; all I could think about was getting the potion to my husband as quickly as possible. I ignored the hot metallic taste. The second I poured it into Eli's mouth, her son attacked him with a knife before stabbing me to death."

"I'm Mr. Stabby-Stab," a voice shouted, then gave a deep belly laugh. Mia looked up to see a man who gave off the look and attitude of an old drunken sailor. He was dirty; his chestnut hair pooled at his shoulders. He held a bottle-shaped brown paper bag in one hand with fingers covered in oversize rings. "My mumsy turned them both," he said before taking a swig. The English accent made Mia crack a smile.

"Alexander, please," Elenora snapped before nodding her head apologetically at Mia. "He is . . . not quite right." She pointed to her head.

The man leaned forward and placed his chin on the chair in front of him. "I think we're going to be the best of friends. I am Alexander—Sir Alexander if we are being formal about it." Alexander let out a laugh and slumped back into his chair. A few others let out muffled laughs, but most rolled their eyes or otherwise looked annoyed.

"In any case," Elenora continued undeterred, "Eli and I both awoke a few days later as if nothing had happened to either of us. Just like you, we did not believe what we had become, but here we—" Elenora took a long pause and stared at the old carpet "—still are." She clasped her hands in front of her.

"Alexander's mother was a vampire?" Mia asked, looking at Alexander. But Elenora took the lead.

"She was when she found me, but before that, she had been a witch. When Alexander was a child, he was terribly ill, and she was able to keep him alive using her knowledge of herbal medicine. Eventually, his disease became too much for even her skills, and she made a deal with a creature to save him. Miraculously, it worked, and he was never ill again, though he immediately began craving blood as his only source of food. They lived in a secluded cabin in the woods, and Alexander would prey on passing travelers.

"After he grew into a man, Alexander seemed to stop aging. Thea believed she had discovered the secret to eternal youth, and one night she drank his blood before slitting her wrists. She, too, stopped aging, and today she still appears to be as old as she was when she drank Alexander's blood, though she has become somewhat frail as of late. She believes that because she was a witch, the purest form of nature, she too will naturally die." When Elenora paused, Mia noticed the other vampires exchanging glances, though Alexander kept eye contact with her. She had the feeling that there was more to the story of this strange witch-turned-vampire.

"That is why she could not be here today to welcome you into the Family. She tires easily from her responsibilities these days. Because she turned the first vampires in our Family, she is our matriarch, and she protects us and rules us."

An eerie quiet fell over the room. Mia struggled to understand what this woman was explaining.

"So, do you all drink blood?" Mia finally asked.

"Well, yes," Elenora replied.

"Animal blood or human blood?"

"Unfortunately, only human blood can satisfy our hunger."

"Do you kill people to get it?"

"Not anymore. It was an unfortunate requirement in the early days, but we have been able to evolve with technology. We follow certain rules now and consider human life precious. In the past, we would use our powers to hypnotize our suppliers—we call it a Veil—but that is a talent that only a few like Kris have either been born with or mastered through intense study. Those who are less proficient in casting a Veil can inadvertently cause strange side effects in our suppliers that draw too much attention. Luckily, the recent prevalence of blood banks has made it possible for us to live more normally. These days we Veil humans for when we prefer a little variety in our meals, but when we do, we only take a small amount of their blood."

Weirdly, the talk of blood was causing Mia's stomach to gurgle. She wanted to change the subject. "Why me?" she asked, glancing at Cordelia. "Why did you make me into a vampire?"

Elenora dropped her arms to her sides. "All of your questions will be answered in time, but we must finish this first night's task before dawn."

Mia bit her lip. "Is that because you'll turn to dust when the sun rises?" she asked.

"No," Elenora replied coolly. "It's so no one notices that we've been here all night." She gave the tiniest of sighs as if exasperated with Mia's questions. "Originally, Eli and I were part of the same Family, but we eventually split into two separate families. Mine is the Sutton Family, and Eli's Family is Bellamy." The respective Family members gave small waves at their mention. "We are still technically considered to be of the same Family since Thea turned us. There are more Families, but not many. Some vampires choose to live in solitude and blend with the humans. For now, though, it is enough to know that you will eventually be living full-time with either the Suttons or the Bellamys, though you, of course, may interact with members of both Families. Before you are required to make that decision, you will have—shall we say—a brief trial period with each Family. But first, the Families will introduce themselves to you."

With that, Elenora sank back into her seat.

CHAPTER SEVEN

Mia adjusted herself in the chair, her body starting to feel a bit more like normal, and she cast a suspicious eye over the dozen or so people scattered around the room. A strange feeling was growing in her chest. Whether it was excitement or fear, she didn't know; she just knew she had lived a mundane life since she lost her Gift. She craved to be someone or something, but she could never have expected this. Was it a coincidence? Fate? She packed the questions deep inside herself as some of the people began their introductions.

"I'm first!" A pretty blonde woman with a fair complexion popped up from behind Elenora. "Hey, babe! I'm Alyssa Sutton; I was turned back in 1992 when I was twenty-two years old. Picture it—Paris fashion week! I got to walk for

Chanel, my favorite. It was a dream come true! Margo saw me there." She pointed to a dark-haired woman sitting in the second row on the other side of the aisle. She waved at Mia, who strained her eyes to focus on the woman named Margo. The second their eyes met, a feeling Mia couldn't explain came over her. Margo smiled back. Alyssa's voice snapped Mia out of it.

"We became fast friends; Margo was a bit of a lush and felt terrible that I was going back to Arkansas to wait tables. She wanted to show me the better side of life. I didn't believe her at first, but it beats looking old!" Alyssa laughed and took her seat.

Next, a short, slim white woman with a blond pixie cut stood with a sigh. She kept her eyes on the floor, and her depressed tone matched her words. "I'm Isla. I was an artist, and alcohol was slowly killing me. I was thirty-nine the night I passed in 1899, and Elenora was a nurse at my bedside. She had seen my work and wanted to preserve my talent. I didn't ask to be saved." The woman didn't look at Mia once, slumping back into her seat tiredly.

There was the sound of a throat clearing, and a lanky man with deeply tanned skin stood at the back. He pushed his curly locks to the side of his face as his blue eyes connected with Mia's. "Hello, I'm Luca. I was turned in 1901 when I was twenty-eight. I had been traveling the country to procure investors for a new business venture. A rogue vampire turned me." Mia could tell he had kept the story short for a reason. Mia eyed his slow movements—he was stunning. He winked before sitting back down like she was supposed to "get it." She didn't ask any questions but watched as he sat, while another rose.

The next person to introduce himself was a short Black man, his fingers constantly working over a smooth, oval stone. "It's so nice to meet you," he said, nodding. "My name is Miles. I—I had lived with a traveling circus in the 1930s. Um, they gave me my own show because I knew a lot of facts and could solve any math problem quickly." The man's eyes drifted quickly to the floor.

"But—but they were not nice to me. If I didn't answer as fast as they thought I should, they would hurt me. Elenora came to a show and saw how they hurt me. After she confronted them, they hurt me real bad. Then I woke up, and Elenora had me in a nice place, a safe place. And now I have a family I never thought I would have, and I don't have to answer questions at all if I don't want to." He sat down. He'd said the words so fast, but his eyes had never left the floor. His stutters filled the room with a nervous energy. Mia wanted to stand and hug him.

As Mia absorbed the horribleness of the story, the loud man from before stood and tripped, falling against the chair in front of him.

"We meet again." He laughed, though no one else did. "I am what the kids call an 'OG.' I like to call myself the GOAT. I live in Sutton House because the food is good, but I'm a free man. My mumsy talked to the dark man and poof! Here we all are." He staggered, then sat hard against his chair, letting out a groan.

The woman beside him patted his shoulder before she stood. She cleared her throat before attempting to smooth down her curly, mousy-brown hair. In a soft voice, she uttered quiet words. "My name is Annie. I was nineteen years old in 1830. Scarlet fever had infected many of us. I was so ill that my parents knew I wouldn't survive, so when I fell into a deep sleep, they put me out with the dead. That's when Eli found me." The woman's eyes traced the crowd until she found Eli. She looked at him for what felt like too long. Mia watched the exchange. Eli finally broke eye contact and trained his eyes on the floor, but Annie seemed to address her final words to him.

"He heard my heart beating, so he took me back to the house and tried so hard to save me. The moment my heart stopped, he changed me." The room fell silent until Cordelia's voice broke into the room.

"I am also a part of Sutton House. I was turned in 1990. My story is a bit different. I was born different. When I touched people who were sick, I would heal them with my energy." Mia saw redness pool in Cordelia's cheeks. "I lived with my mother and brother. People used to come from far away so that I could help them." Cordelia put her hands on her cheeks to calm the redness, then glanced over her shoulder at Isla, the woman who had seemed so depressed. "Isla had heard through the grapevine about what I could do. She came one evening, hoping I could heal her mind. My mom had sensed something wasn't right but let her in anyway." Cordelia's voice broke; her gaze was full of emotion. Mia lifted her eyes to look at Isla, who was staring numbly at the wall. "She was the first person I couldn't help. I was only nine. When my mother went to bed that night, Isla took me. Children are rarely turned, but she thought that if I were a vampire like her, then I would be able to fix her." The words ended abruptly, the way all electrical noises ceased when the power got cut during a storm. Mia easily saw and felt the pain in Cordelia. When she pictured it in her mind, it all played out like a horror movie.

"I'm sorry," Isla said under her breath. "I thought it would work. It has before."

"It didn't, but it was a long time ago, and you were desperate," Cordelia said kindly as she walked over to Elenora and sat down beside her. Elenora gently moved a lock of Cordelia's hair over the woman's shoulder. "Elenora raised me as her daughter. Just like Alexander, I continued to grow into adulthood, but I stopped aging around my twenty-fifth birthday." Cordelia looked to be roughly the same age as her adoptive mother. It was hard for Mia to picture Elenora raising Cordelia; they looked like sisters or friends, not mother and daughter.

Movement caused Mia to shift her gaze. A beautiful woman directly in front of Mia stood up; she was white, her long brown hair lay in soft curls against her chest, and in the dark room, her eyes looked almost black. She was short but curvy and dressed sharply in a box-cut black dress and platform-heeled boots. Her lips looked as if she had been chewing on them out of nervousness, as they glowed a soft pink. She had a look in her eye that hinted she was always up to something sneaky. "I'm Margo," she said with a slight accent that Mia couldn't identify. "Eli found me and turned me. I was his first. I started my new life in 1829. I was a twenty-seven-year-old spinster—" she rolled her eyes "—and the daughter of a powerful man. He wanted me to marry someone who would benefit him, a blending of families, you could say." The woman made a twirling motion with her fingers. "I had never even met this man, but what did it matter? Many people then were married simply to increase their fortunes or gain power. I didn't agree to the marriage; I had already found the love of my life." Margo abruptly paused as if at a loss for words, a panicked look spreading across her face. The others seemed startled by the sudden change. "I am, or I was, um—"

"It's okay; you don't need to say it. You can tell her about it later if you want." Kris grabbed Margo's hand and pulled her down, then stood straight and spoke loudly and confidently as if to draw attention away from Margo.

"We've already met, so you know I'm Kris." She pulled her dark glasses down to reveal piercing blue eyes, then winked. "I'm new to the Family—well, newish. I was turned in 2008 when I was twelve. I was obsessed with *Twilight*. You might have heard of it?" She grinned.

Mia drew a half-cocked smile. "I was more of a *Vampire Diaries* girl myself," she said, looking down. A small awkward laugh escaped her open mouth before she realized it. "Will I run into Damon at some point?" she added, trying to mask the sound.

Kris adjusted her sunglasses firmly against her nose and quickly interrupted. "The Bellamy Family was living near me in Vancouver at the time. I'd heard rumors that they were like a real-life Cullen family, and I decided to find out if the rumors were true. I broke into their house when they were out. Long story short, I found an ornate box—opening it, you could smell the blood. It was in the same metal vial we used on you, but there was no needle attached like we used on you. I drank it, and somehow had the guts to jump off a cliff near my house. In all vampire movies, you have to die to complete the transition, you know? I tried to go home, but shit hit the fan. Eli heard about a rabid kid in town and went to investigate, and of course, he found me. I've lived with the Bellamy Family ever since. And, like Cord and Alex, I stopped aging." She looked around the room. "And I wouldn't have it any other way," she declared as she sat back down and nudged the woman beside her.

"Hey, hon. My name is Gianna." The woman stood tall and brushed her waist-length hair behind her shoulders as she adjusted her posture. She wore skintight clothing, with flashy bangles around her wrists. "I started my life as a vampire in 1922, but back then, my name was George, if you catch my drift." The woman's squinted eyes peered hard into the darkness where Mia sat. "In those days, the world expected girls to be girls and boys to be boys, but I knew I wasn't a boy. There was only one safe place in town where people like me could go to have fun." Gianna bit her lip. "One night, word got out about our safe place. Some men came in with baseball bats. Most of my friends were able to get away, but they caught me. They took turns beating me. I lay in the street, and people passed by me like I was a pile of dirty laundry in the gutter. No one did anything to help. Night had just started to turn into day when Margo found me with only minutes to spare. She fed me her blood, and when I passed, she held me." Gianna looked back at Margo, who returned the fierce gaze. "I woke up at Bellamy House, and she helped me become, well, me. And I finally didn't have to hide who I was anymore."

Mia nodded at Gianna as she sat back down. The story resonated with Mia; she had spent all four years of high school watching her friend Katie transition. She'd seen firsthand how terribly some people treated her just for being her true self.

The next to stand was a short, squat, awkward-seeming woman. "Hello, love. I am Izzy. I was turned in 1792 when I was twenty-nine. Alexander over there and I were lovers."

The man's loud voice boomed out from across the room. "You know you will always be the one!"

Izzy shook her head. "He truly is an absolute arse. But I was in love, and I loved being the life of the party. Now I am the death of the party!" She laughed a little too loudly at her joke as she sat back down. None of the others looked at her, and Mia thought she saw a few of the Suttons roll their eyes.

A handsome black-haired man in the front row was the next to rise, stuffing his hands into his pockets as he stood. He slouched a little as if self-conscious about his height. He appeared to be in his late twenties. "Hey, I'm Toby." He ran a hand through his tight Afro and smiled at Mia genuinely. "Gianna turned me in 1974. All things beautiful are born out of a love story, are they not? The '70s were a wild time of love and fun. I had moved to LA, and love was like my drug." Toby winked. "I went from boyfriend to boyfriend and finally discovered the love of my life in Anthony. We had only been together for six months when I found him in bed with another man. After that, blow replaced love as my drug of choice. I tried only to use as much as I needed to dull the pain, but that kept requiring more and more, and one night I went a bit too far. Gianna happened to be there."

"Vampires metabolize—er, illicit substances—better than humans," Gianna explained. "The '70s were an amazing time for us."

"She found me and offered to turn me. It was either let the party stop or go vamp. You know what I chose." He smiled. "The best part is that I got to watch that asshole Anthony grow old and die." Mia surprised herself with a laugh. Toby grinned and flopped down in his chair, his perfectly straight teeth shining amid the dark walls.

The athletic-looking man seated behind Toby stood. "Hey, girl, I'm Oscar." Mia remembered someone—she thought it might have been Isla—calling him that earlier. "I was turned in 1997 after I dove into a lake without checking the depth. I hit my head on a rock just under the surface. My friends pulled me out and called for an ambulance, but I had already suffered severe brain damage. Eli was at the hospital getting blood when he overheard my family crying and trying to decide whether or not they should remove me from life support. They were so conflicted—I have so much regret for putting them through that pain." Oscar's voice thickened with emotion. "He decided for them."

Eli looked at Oscar with a small, sad smile. "It was the kindest thing I could do for them and you." Oscar blinked back tears as he nodded and took his seat once more.

Mia couldn't help but think that even the stories that weren't so sad still felt tragic. She thought of her own. How she'd tried not to hit her dog, but in making that choice, put her own life on the line. She was just about to speak when she saw someone stir behind Oscar. Almost hidden by his enormous frame was a petite, young-looking woman wearing beaded earrings. Her long, black hair was plaited into braids that beautifully framed her face. When she spoke, Mia had to strain to hear her.

"I'm Talli. It's short for Tallulah."

With that, she sat down. Mia waited for her to add more, but the woman was finished. Talli quickly glanced at Elenora, and then turned her head sharply to stare straight ahead again. Mia saw that Elenora was concentrating her stare on Talli, who shifted as if trying to avoid pain. An uncomfortable silence fell over the room, and the very air seemed to shrink from Elenora's glare. The only sound was the staccato beat of raindrops that fell on the windows.

Mia blinked back tears, but she still wasn't convinced that this wasn't all a dream or a kidnapping. All these people were telling her their stories, and none of them sounded made up. She saw the truth in their eyes; she felt it in their words. What reason did they have to lie to her? Could vampires actually be real? All she knew for sure was that she wanted to go home; alive or dead, she needed to see her mother and sister. Whatever was going on, her best course of action was to play along.

"Wow," she said. "This is all a bit overwhelming." She gingerly moved her legs. "I'm just like all of you, then?" she asked, not expecting an answer, and indeed not getting one.

"You will begin with the Bellamy Family." Elenora sat back in her chair and tucked a strand of hair behind her ear.

"We are going to have such a great time, babe!" Toby gave Gianna a high five.

Mia's head was swirling with the information, and a cool sweat was pooling in her palms. Everything was happening so fast. She looked down at her hands to escape Elenora's unsettling eyes. She was surprised to see that she still wore her father's wedding band. She traced it with her finger, wondering why her mother hadn't removed it. But it gave her an idea. "I don't have any of my things," she said.

"You must cut ties with your old life," Elenora replied. "We will give you new things."

"But I—"

"No."

Mia swallowed hard, unsure of what to do. "I'm not going with anyone until you prove to me that I have no other choice."

The people all looked to Elenora, who nodded. As one, they opened their mouths wide to reveal sharp, pointed fangs.

Mia fainted, the truth causing her to fall heavily to the floor.

CHAPTER EIGHT

Mia was woken by the heat, though it didn't bother her as much as usual. She lived for the cold; summers were a dreaded nuisance that left her feeling drained. How could anyone say they loved summer when it was three months of endless boob sweat and sunburns? Spring and fall were much better suited to her. Nothing compared to waking up early on a Saturday morning and making the drive into town to Slow Burn. She snuggled into her comfy chair next to the carved initials and opened her book, but stirred as the sunlight fell through the window and onto the musty pages. Something was wrong.

She wasn't sitting in Slow Burn; she slowly became aware of a smooth surface beneath her cheek. Mia ignored the sensation and focused on the coffee shop, envisioning the stacks of books and Mr. Horvath making someone a cappuccino. She could almost believe that she was there as if experiencing some kind of astral projection, but of course, that was impossible.

A jarring movement and a pull to the left caused Mia to open her eyes ever so slightly. She was in a car with black leather seats. Jolting up, Mia looked around in terror.

"Hey, you're up!" Kris, who was sitting beside her in the back seat, patted her hand. "You just needed some more sleep." Margo drove, and Toby was in the front passenger seat.

"Where are you taking me?" Mia said in fear. The car turned off the pavement and onto a gravel drive. She sat up straighter and saw a black iron gate in front of them and, beyond that, a massive midcentury modern house. Margo reached out the window and punched a code into a pin pad. The gates ground apart, and as the sports car passed through and continued up the drive, Mia heard several other vehicles crunch across the gravel as well.

"We're just outside Cedar Hollow," Kris replied. "This is Noir House. You're going to be staying with us tonight."

They turned toward a garage the size of a small airplane hangar, the exterior of which was covered with ivy. The doors opened simultaneously, and the car smoothly pulled inside, cool air meeting them as they entered the dark space. All along the garage, more black cars entered and parked.

"Welcome home, Mia," Margo said warmly, her voice sounding musical.

Kris pulled herself out of the back seat and within seconds was yanking Mia's door open. Seeing the woman's tidy blond hair, Mia self-consciously brushed her own unruly hair behind her shoulders.

"Jump out, girl. I don't have all day! Let's get those legs moving." Mia shuffled her still-stiff body so that she could step out of the car without too much trouble. She didn't want to see what would happen if she pissed off this stern-looking woman.

Mia took a few tentative steps out of the garage and looked around the property. The two-story house was built of glass windows framed in wood. The black roof was set at interesting angles, and columns jutted from the right side of the house. Although it looked like one of the fancy houses featured in free architecture magazines that littered the entrances to grocery stores, it complemented the forest behind it beautifully.

"You live here?" Mia said with a bit of a frog in her throat.

"The Bellamy Family does," Toby replied as he pulled a bulky bag from the trunk. "We come and go with the seasons."

"Or years," Kris added.

"There are eight of us—Eli, Kris, Toby," Margo chimed in, counting on her fingers, "Gianna, Izzy, Oscar, Talli, and of course, me." She placed a hand on Mia's back, guiding her toward the house. "And hopefully, you." A coy smile played on her lips.

Mia suddenly felt a warmth in her chest, but she couldn't fight the feeling that she needed to get away. She wanted her family to know she was okay. She'd watched them live through her father's death, and she couldn't imagine how her mom and sister were handling her own supposed passing. She knew that of all people, her mother would be aware if vampires were real or not, and if so, how that was possible. Maybe if she explained that to her captors, they would let her go home. For now, she would continue to play along; if all of this turned out to be true, she would stay with the vampires. Perhaps once they got to know her and trust her, she'd find a way to sneak home and see her mother one last time.

"Babe, you forgot your purse." Toby threw a Gucci handbag to Margo, who caught it with precision. He also removed a black-and-white gift bag before shutting the trunk. "This one's for the new girl, isn't it?" he asked smugly as he jogged up to the three women.

"Not to butter you up or—god forbid—to pressure you into choosing us, but after your funeral visitation, I just knew this would look killer with your death dress." Margo suddenly started laughing hard, turning away and putting her hands on her knees to catch her breath. "Wow, I didn't realize how fucking dark that would sound!" She wiped her eyes. "Sorry, I get a little slaphappy after turnings."

"You'd think with all the people you've turned and the hundreds of years under your belt, you would know how to approach this better," Kris said, shaking her head, hands on her hips.

Instead of delivering the gift bag to Mia, Toby peeked inside. "Yes, perfect choice!" he gasped, yanking out a leather purse. Mia prickled a bit over the fact that she didn't even get to open her present, but Toby was right; the black leather gleamed in the early-morning light, and the gold chain made a pleasant tinkling sound. Toby looked up and took a few steps to close the distance between them, then looped the chain over Mia's shoulder.

"It makes your eyes pop," he said approvingly. Mia looked down and stroked the leather. Unexpectedly, she felt a twinge of happiness that began in her chest and flowed to every inch of her body. The faces before her now were so beautiful, so eager, so alive! Even if this was all bullshit, no one had seemed this excited to be around her in years. She couldn't help but feel a little sad; she had never in her life had real friends. If she did, they felt temporary. They came in strong and tried to hold on but slowly curled in on themselves before drifting away like autumn leaves. Mia always thought it was because she was too passionate and jumped into friendships before the other person was ready, but that was the kind of person she was: all in or all out. Casual just wasn't her thing. Now, as she moved her eyes over the three people in front of her, she felt a pang of regret. Even though they'd kidnapped her, they were being nicer to her than most people she'd spent time with during the past few years.

Mia suddenly realized she must have looked crazy to them, just standing there staring wordlessly, taking them in. She felt awkward, but no one else seemed to feel that way.

She looked down at the purse, then back to them. For some reason, she was struck by the fact that she knew Toby was a good person, the kind of person who would stand up for what he believed in and had his friends' backs. But how was she so sure of this? It was as if she could see small frames and pictures of Toby in her mind, like she could feel his heart.

"Thank you," Mia said softly. "But why?"

"The night of the accident . . ." Margo trailed off.

"Your bag didn't make it, either," Kris said bluntly as she turned and walked toward the house. "Let's get a move on. Everyone else went inside ages ago."

Margo let out another laugh, but this time it was noticeably awkward. She followed Kris, and Mia was left to trail the others into the house. They clearly assumed that she would do whatever they wanted. Perhaps escape was more accessible than she'd initially thought. She looked longingly at the black gate, but it was firmly shut and looked impossible to climb. Reluctantly, she entered the giant house.

The rest of the Family mingled inside, their soft voices echoing down the front stairs. Mia was the last one in, and the door closed behind her. Margo turned and grabbed her hand.

"We're going to have breakfast. Are you hungry?" Her words triggered an audible gurgling sound from Mia's abdomen, and she looked down at her body in horror.

"I guess that means yes!" Margo grabbed her hand and pulled Mia into a long hallway; it had a marble floor and giant tinted windows that flanked either side. On the other side of the passage was a spacious room with a twenty-foot ceiling. A massive cobblestone fireplace climbed up the far wall, in front of which were a rose-chintz couch and several overstuffed chairs arranged in a semicircle. A taxidermy goat kept guard in one corner while an ornately carved grandfather clock stood in another. An onyx-black table stretched along one side of the room, and various paintings of different styles adorned the walls. Ornate vases and modern art alike were arranged on end tables. A record player in an enormous stand sat against one wall next to several shelves of vinyl records. The odd mix of decoration struck Mia, especially since it all somehow looked perfect together, but as people began to enter the room, she realized that the objects must have been curated from the different time periods the vampires had been alive.

Mia felt disconnected; she was still looking aimlessly at the art collection and worldly items while the others took seats at the table. Kris gestured to the bamboo chair she had pulled out between her and Margo. Embarrassed, Mia made her way across the black shag carpet and lowered herself onto the chair. She was slightly disconcerted to see that all eyes were on her.

"Good, everyone is here," Eli said as he rounded the corner, a silver tray in his hands. He moved swiftly to the table and started lifting clear bags filled with red liquid off the trays and placing them on plates in front of everyone, Mia included. Then he took his seat at the head of the table. "We are glad to host you for the night, Mia. I want to say that I am sorry for the reason you are with us, but I hope that you embrace this life the same way most of us have."

Talli hung her head, and Mia wondered again about the mysterious woman.

"It is not easy for anyone to learn they have become a vampire," Eli continued, "but whether you decide to become a Bellamy or a Sutton, you will always be part of the Family. Do not let anyone try to influence you into joining one Family or the other; you need to decide for yourself. Being a vampire is all about perspective. I have been around for centuries, and while I still find myself in love with the idea of this life, I do wish I had been allowed to die in certain moments. Alas, that was not my choice. This was not your choice, either, but hopefully you will not resent that we decided to turn you."

Eli took a deep breath. "Whew. I have not made that speech in a while." He glanced at Oscar. "It has been twenty-eight years, has it not?" The man nodded.

"Do you feel like a new dad?" Oscar said, grabbing his bag and shaking it. Mia felt slightly sick at the sight.

"A little bit," Eli agreed, picking up the bag in front of him. He pointed to it. "As you can guess, Mia, this is indeed blood." A ringing sound started booming in Mia's ears, and she momentarily felt like fainting again. "That is about the only thing that the myths and legends have right."

"Except that we also kill babies," Kris chimed in. Mia gasped.

"Kris, don't do that." Eli shook his head and pushed back his hair. "We do not kill anyone."

"Unless they deserve it," Kris corrected.

"Unless they deserve it," he agreed before looking at Mia. "But that is incredibly uncommon. We generally only collect blood from blood banks or hospitals, but Kris over there will occasionally Veil someone as a treat. When we do that, we only take a little sample. We prefer to coexist peacefully with the rest of the world. We try to only turn people if they are going to die otherwise, and we think they deserve a second chance at life." He glanced at Talli. "Usually. There have been times when we turned vampires for our own gain, but we are constantly revising our rules to change with the times. You will be learning about what those rules are and why it is so important to adhere to them."

He looked around the table. "That is enough talk for now. Please, enjoy your meals." Everyone reached for the bag in front of them, though they all seemed to be waiting for Mia.

She took a deep breath. Gingerly, she stretched her pale hand out toward the bag of hospital blood. A Cedar Hollow General Hospital label was plastered to the front; the stated blood type was A+. She hesitated; cult or not, she wasn't sure if she was up for this. There was going along with these freaks to stay on their good side, and then there was drinking blood like a lunatic. Feeling a bit nauseous, she ran her finger across the bag and looked at Margo's, which featured the letter *B*.

"A+ is really smooth," Margo assured her. "It's a great one to start with; it tastes like a tender steak."

"Why is it warm?" Mia asked.

Gianna laughed. "We microwave them—can you believe these bags are microwave safe? It beats the old days when we had to warm blood in boiling water."

"Try existing before there was refrigeration." Izzy giggled.

"We warm it to 98 degrees so it tastes like it's straight from the vein." Mia grimaced as Margo picked up her bag and tore off the corner, squeezing some of the red liquid into her mouth. Immediately, Margo's eyes turned jet-black.

Mia pushed back her chair in alarm, but instead of moving a few inches, she instead found herself hurtling backward as the chair tipped, sending her sprawling on the floor.

"We probably should have warned you." Oscar appeared at her side, his eyes as black as Margo's. He held out his hand, but Mia shrank from him. "You're a lot stronger than you were before," he explained, righting the chair instead.

Everyone at the table was looking at her; they all had black eyes now. Izzy was the only one ignoring her, her mouth plastered to the side of her bag as she drank. Mia began to panic, her chest heaving with every breath.

That's when she smelled it: the scent of a rare steak. She found she could think of nothing else, and as she searched for the source of the heavenly smell, she saw that she had knocked over Kris's bag, and its contents were dripping onto the table. Mia was ravenous, and the liquid was suddenly more appetizing than she would have ever imagined.

Margo rummaged inside her purse and pulled out a small silver compact. Opening it, she handed it to Mia. "Look."

Mia hesitated, then took the compact. She gasped as she viewed her reflection in the mirror. Gone were the color of her irises and the whites of her eyes; they had turned completely black.

"See? You're just like us," Margo said. "Our eyes turn black whenever we smell or consume blood."

"Is that why Kris wears sunglasses?" she asked in a trembling voice.

"No." Using her finger, Kris wiped the spilled blood from the table before licking it off. "I wear sunglasses so that I don't accidentally Veil everyone I look at."

"Oh."

Mia slowly stood and resumed her seat. Placing the compact on the table, she picked up the plastic bag in front of her, contemplating its contents. Once again, she felt the gaze of the other vampires in the room. They were smiling encouragingly.

"You've got this," Kris said.

"The first time is the weirdest," Toby added, "but it gets easier."

Running her tongue over her lips in anticipation, Mia noticed that her canine teeth felt different. They were sharper, but they didn't seem much longer than normal. Looking once more at the bag in her hand, Mia bit into it with one swift movement. She'd expected to taste copper, like when she'd accidentally bitten her lip in the past, but the liquid was salty and rich. It was precisely like the steak Margo described, but better. All previous reservations gone, Mia pulled the bag from her mouth and heaved in a gasp before draining it completely. Looking at Margo, she realized that she was more alert than she'd ever been before. She could make out the sound of every movement around the table; she even heard a fly buzzing somewhere in the room. She was hyper-focused on the noise, like a fox on its prey. She felt like herself, but better.

"How do you feel?" Toby asked eagerly.

"I feel *good*," Mia replied as she scanned the table; everyone looked pleased. Feeling a tickling sensation on her cheek, she put her hand to her face and realized there was blood smeared around her mouth.

"Can I go to the bathroom?" she said, embarrassment reddening her cheeks. She used her hand to cover the mess.

"I don't know—can you?" Kris snorted.

Eli calmly lifted a hand and pointed down another breezeway. "Last room on the left."

Mia turned swiftly and didn't look back as she raced for the heavy black door at the end of the hall. She scooted into the room and closed the door behind her. Flipping the light switch, she turned to find that she was in the most enormous bathroom she'd ever seen.

The room was lined entirely with marble, and two

chairs were placed next to a stout table. A lavatory was set apart with a separate door, and there was a giant mirror covering the expanse of the entire left wall. It only took her a second to reach it, and when she saw her reflection, she staggered back.

It was her, but not her. Recovering her composure, she slowly walked forward and pressed her hand against the mirror. She gazed at her face. Her skin looked softer, smoother. Her dark hair was thicker and shined with a luster she would have never dreamed possible. She didn't look like she'd just died; she looked amazing. Mia continued to absorb the unfamiliar reflection for a few moments, then searched for a tissue. She found a box of them on the sink and wiped the blood from her face with a shaky hand.

She felt like she was floating, like the time she'd had her tonsils out and the doctor gave her round white pills to deaden the pain. She didn't understand why she felt so euphoric, but she didn't care; she liked it.

Mia didn't know how long she stood there, but gradually she saw the blackness fade from her eyes. She put the tissue up to her nose and inhaled, filling her nostrils with the aroma of dried blood, then looked back in the mirror. Her black eyes had returned. Mia opened her mouth, and her tiny fangs glinted in the luxe lighting of the bathroom. They stood out only to her, to a stranger they would look normal. She tentatively felt their points with her tongue. Her reflection looked like she was ready for Halloween.

One thing was for sure; vampires were real. And Mia Adair was one of them.

CHAPTER NINE

Three short raps on the bathroom door broke Mia's focus.

"Are you okay?" a musical voice asked softly. Before Mia had a chance to answer, the door swung open, and Margo entered. Seeing how Mia was entranced by her reflection, Margo came up to her side and looked at herself in the mirror, assessing both of them with a steady gaze. The two women didn't look too much different. A light smattering of freckles covered Margo's nose bridge and cheeks, but her hair was a rich brown, lighter than Mia's. Margo's cheeks were rosy, and her skin warmer than Mia's golden hues. She was about five foot five, so she was only a bit taller than Mia's five-foot-three-inch frame. The two of them standing there looked powerful. Like if they entered a full restaurant, they would have eyes straining to look at them—not even for their looks, but for their power.

Mia could feel it as her eyes scanned Margo. The woman exuded confidence in a way that Mia had never seen from anyone around her age. The rich perfume Margo was wearing filled the room, and the heaviness of it had stolen Mia's words. Margo was the kind of woman she had always wished she was. Margo looked effortless, cool, calm, and collected. Mia blinked hard and reminded herself that Margo wasn't at all her age. She was a mirage. The woman beside her could be hundreds of years old. It was crazy to think of everything the woman's hazel eyes had witnessed over the centuries. Her own eyes pulled away from the mirror to look at Margo's profile when it hit her. She looked back into the mirror and realized she, too, wouldn't have an "end."

"I look different," she said.

"We always look like we just had a good spa weekend," Margo replied. "Our cells regenerate faster than a human's."

A thought struck Mia. "Why can I see my reflection?" Margo laughed and pulled her away from the mirror and over to the chairs under the window.

"I guess this is as good a time as any to discuss the details of being a vampire," she said, plopping down on the cushioned seat. "There are a lot of misconceptions about us. We're surprisingly similar to humans—we breathe, our hearts beat, we sweat." Mia made a face at the latter but moved her hand over her heart. She could feel it there, beating steadily as always.

"We feel the heat and the cold, but not as extremely as humans do. We have reflections; we go to the bathroom. A stake to the heart won't do anything but hurt. We can drink, we can eat regular food—it's like candy to us. It doesn't sustain us, but we enjoy it."

"So, we aren't dead?"

"Elenora found a scientist willing to study her years ago. After vampire blood enters the system, it causes cells to change. They replace themselves at a high rate of speed, healing the body incredibly quickly. Think of it almost like a mutation. We're still alive, but we have different needs and abilities. After we die, it takes about forty-eight hours for our hearts to start beating again to fix the death that had settled in our cells."

"Does that mean we can't die?" Mia squinted her eyes.

"Oh, we can still die. Thea used to be able to do it with the snap of her fingers."

"Thea? The one who turned Elenora and Eli into vampires?"

"Yes, Alexander's mother. Thea was kind of like a kill switch for us. Because she created our line, she is our matriarch, and she had the unique ability to end our lives with only her power. A matriarch from another Family wouldn't have the same ability over us. Recently, though, she has weakened to a point where she can no longer . . . end . . . anyone." Margo shifted uncomfortably in her chair.

"Anyway, we're powerful, but we are not indestructible. New vampires are particularly vulnerable—sorry—and we can die if we're stabbed in the heart with a big enough quartz crystal. Something about its natural properties is like oil and water to our hearts, so I avoid New Agey shops." Margo rubbed her hands together hard. "And even though I've already hit the two-century mark, if a tank ran over my head, it would pop like a balloon. We tend to avoid situations like those." Margo laughed and pulled away, a weird look crossing her face. She recovered only a moment later. "It's fun to party as a vampire because we can't die of overdoses, we can't reproduce, and we don't catch diseases of any kind. And no more periods!"

Mia smiled. "If that gets out, you'll have women the world over begging to be turned!" She grew serious again and contemplated Margo's words for a few moments. "This is real, isn't it?" she asked softly. "You didn't kidnap me? This isn't a cult?" Mia felt like a child asking the questions when she knew the answers.

"It's real. Sorry." Margo's eyes lifted warmly to Mia's.

"Then why can't I go see my family?" The words hung in the air between them.

Margo leaned over and held one of Mia's hands between hers. "I know it's hard," she said quietly. "We've all been where you are. We all wanted to go home. Some of us tried, and it didn't go well." She dropped her eyes to the floor and absently began to stroke Mia's hand. "Your mom and sister already said their goodbyes. Think of how much it would hurt them to see you now."

Mia thought back to the days after her father's accident when she would have done anything to see him again; even if he'd come through the front door broken, dragging himself across the floor like a zombie, she would still have run to him. But Mia knew that if she pried too much, there would be no chance she could sneak out later. A few moments of silence bounced between them as they sat holding hands.

"Why me?" Mia finally asked. "Eli said you turn people to give them a second chance. What have I ever done to deserve that?" Mia silently scanned over her entire life in her mind, thinking back to all the events of her life, all of the unremarkable moments, looking for one reason they would want her to be a part of the Family. She thought of the time she keyed Adam Ross's car when he cheated on her. The time she tried to save that baby bird after a hawk dropped it from its talons.

Margo flinched and glanced away before gently pulling her hands back into her lap. "Right place, right time," she said, standing up and moving to the mirror. She made a show of checking her makeup.

Mia narrowed her eyes. It was a reasonable question, so why was Margo acting so jumpy and nervous? She stood up and joined Margo at the mirror. "I remember before the accident, I saw the line of all your cars behind—"

Margo clamped a hand over Mia's mouth, cutting her off. Mia's eyes widened in alarm.

"Right place, right time," the other woman said again, louder this time. Margo's eyes burrowed into Mia's like daggers. "What did any of us do to deserve this fate? You heard our stories: suicides, illnesses, accidents. Most of us are not extraordinary, though there are a few exceptions."

Margo's words cut off quickly; she dropped her posture but held her penetrating stare. She stepped away slowly but didn't look away, her concentration playing like a movie on her face. Mia's mouth fell open for a moment, but she was lost for words. She could feel something in the air now, but she couldn't place it. Mia took two steps forward with new confidence and reached out to Margo.

"Are you okay?" Mia asked, taking the woman's wrist.

"I was just trying to see if you could read my mind."

"Excuse me?" Mia asked.

"One fun thing about vampires is that if you had some kind of Gift in your human life, it amplifies after you die. Most of us don't have any Gifts, but some of us were turned because of them. Talli and Cordelia, for example. Both are valuable to the Family." Mia pictured Talli, the diminutive woman with braids. And, of course, Cordelia, the blue-haired woman she'd obsessed over for months. The woman who had turned her into a vampire.

"Once you died, I googled you," Margo said bluntly. "I read about your mother and your Gift. Honestly, I went to your store and bought the book. Talking with the dead, huh? That's a pretty unique talent. In fact, it's something that I'd never heard of before. At least, not as a real Gift. I thought if you could read spirits in life that maybe you could read vampires' thoughts because we are, you know . . ." Margo paused and took a breath. "Kind of dead."

Mia frowned. What was Margo getting at?

"Most people who claim to be mediums are either fakes or have a bit of telepathy. They're just picking up on what their clients are focusing on, which would be their dead loved ones. That's why I was wondering if you could read my mind. That would be a far more valuable talent for the Family."

"How did you know I was the girl in the book?" Mia asked. As far as she'd known, only internet weirdos had figured it out.

"Talli," Margo said, deadpan. "Her Gift."

Mia felt her face grow hot. "I don't read people's minds," she responded angrily. She turned to leave, but Margo grabbed her arm. Fuming, Mia faced her again.

"I'm sorry," Margo said. "I was just wondering. But perhaps it wouldn't matter anyway. Your mom's book said your Gift disappeared a couple of years after your dad died?" Mia hated how personal this all felt. Margo knew so much about her, but she barely knew anything about this pretty, slightly mean woman. She usually hated being challenged, but something about Margo made her like it.

Mia relaxed a little, though she still felt guarded. "Yes, it just kind of faded away, like a scar."

"A scar?" Margo pulled a gold tube of lipstick out of her pocket and leaned toward her reflection to apply it. "You didn't consider it a good thing? Being able to talk to the dead?" She made eye contact with Mia in the mirror.

"I guess I never thought about it as a good or evil kind of thing," Mia admitted. "It was just there."

Margo closed the cap on the red lipstick as she turned and leaned back on the counter. "You'll learn soon that in this world, everything is either good or evil." She casually bit her lip and looked Mia up and down. "It's probably a good thing you can't read my mind."

Mia took a self-conscious step back. "What?" The words left her mouth unexpectedly as a shiver ran up her spine.

"Ignore me; I'm a flirt." Margo laughed and grabbed Mia's hand, pulling her toward the door. "Let me show you your room."

Margo led Mia down the hall past where everyone had been sitting at breakfast; they were all gone. As they made their way through the house, Mia was taken aback by how the entire place was constructed of white and black slabs of marble interspersed with golden wood. It was gorgeous.

"Do you all live here full-time?" Mia asked as she glanced around.

"We do at the moment. We tend to move around every few years before people start asking too many questions. And sometimes we split up for a few months. Some of us like the heat, and others prefer the cold. But both Families do tend to find homes in the same area. It's been safer the past decade or two."

Mia had already seen that around the corner from the great room was another vast, open room with a staircase lining each wall. The marble stairs were covered with black carpet runners, and the walls were adorned with paintings.

"Do you know any of these people?" Mia asked as they climbed one set of stairs, pointing to the faces that littered the walls, her fingers softly tracing gilded frame edges. Margo jerked her chin toward an enormous portrait that hung above the landing. A woman sat elegantly on the edge of a velvet chair; she wore a massive, intricately embroidered ball gown with sleeves puffed at the shoulders. Margo ran up the stairs and mimicked the woman's serious pose. Mia peered at the portrait for only a moment before she laughed. "It's you!"

"Yes. Eli had it commissioned after he turned me; he wanted to commemorate the occasion. Times were so different then." Margo smiled.

"You look stunning." Mia looked into the portrait's face and then back at Margo.

"You look stunning, too." Margo reached out and lightly touched the ends of Mia's hair. Mia's hand rose to graze her fingertips. A strange vibration seemed to pass between the two women.

What am I doing? Mia thought to herself. She wasn't about to kid herself; she knew exactly what this feeling was. She broke her gaze from Margo's and looked back at the painting. She had only just met this woman—no—*vampire*.

"What's taking you two so long?" The voice broke the tension, and both women glanced to the top of the stairs. Kris stood there with her hands on her hips.

"Just pointing out the decor," Margo said, letting out a coy hum and heading up the stairs.

Mia hated fitness of any kind, and stairs usually had her immediately winded, so she was pleasantly surprised that she could bound up this staircase like it was nothing. She followed Kris and Margo down a hallway, passing many doors until they came to the last one at the very end. Mia gasped as Kris led them through the open doorway.

"Wow," she said, taking a few steps into the room. Like the rest of the house, the room was decorated in a combination of marble and wood. A bookshelf covered one entire wall, with two cozy chairs parked in front of it, along with a small table. The ceiling towered fourteen feet high, and despite the summer heat, a fireplace crackled welcomingly on one exterior wall. The oversize bed was across from it and covered in a white duvet thicker than any she had ever seen and enough pillows to cover half the bed—black, of course. One door was closed and appeared to lead to a closet. A second door stood open, revealing a bathroom. The other exterior wall was a mass of floor-to-ceiling windows. Her bedroom must have been at the back of the house because it was evident that they were on a hill. From these windows, she could see the town of Cedar Hollow and the beach that lay beyond it. The town had a year-round population of fewer than ten thousand, but during the summer months, it would increase to many more times that.

"This is all for me?" Mia asked, stepping up to the window.

"Bitch, yes!" A clear voice rang through the room. Mia turned to see a slim woman wearing nothing but a baby blue string bikini.

Kris sighed. "Alyssa, it would be great if you said 'hi' first."

The new woman rolled her eyes. "Hi, bitch!" She shot a nasty look at Kris.

"What Alyssa means," Kris retorted, "is that you're immortal now, and you deserve to spend it in comfort." Kris rolled her eyes and fell backward onto the bed.

"Alyssa purchased your wardrobe," Margot said with a smile. "Even though she's a Sutton, she insisted on getting your clothes in order."

"I might not model anymore, but I still keep up with fashion," Alyssa said, tossing her blond hair over her shoulder.

Mia scanned her eyes over Alyssa. She was afraid to look in the closet. The look on her face must have been obvious because the blonde rolled her eyes again. "Oh my god, seriously? Unlike you, I have taste."

"Alyssa went through your closet while your family was making your funeral arrangements," Margo explained.

"Your new clothes should fit your aesthetic," Alyssa added, "but they're from high-end retailers."

"Alyssa only buys the best," Kris said, exasperated.

"That's why you look so good, baby!" Alyssa winked in Kris's direction.

Mia peeked her head into the closet and looked around. The color palette of the clothes did match the look of her usual wardrobe; the dark hues of blacks, maroons, and greens triggered a pang of homesickness in her belly as she reached forward and touched the soft fabrics.

"You really should change out of your, um, death clothes," Alyssa said delicately as she reached in the closet and pulled out a black top and sage leggings. "It's a nice dress, but let's not be morbid." Pushing a sliding door to the side, she uncovered dozens of shoes from which she selected a pair of black platform sneakers. "Try these on."

Mia accepted the outfit awkwardly; she wasn't used to so much attention, but she didn't want to hurt Alyssa's feelings. She noticed that the others were watching her as if they expected her to strip in front of them. She wasn't ready for that, so she headed into the bathroom to change. Closing the door, she took a moment to settle her nerves. She slipped the dress off over her head and pulled on the leggings and top. Admiring herself in the mirror, she realized that they flattered her in a way none of her clothes ever had. She could tell they had all been expensive—the fabric told that story. What a difference expensive garments made. *And it might have something to do with the fact that you're a vampire now*, she thought. She shook her head, still confused by it all.

Her hands went robotically to her neck to adjust her *Daddy* necklace, but she found nothing but skin. She searched her bra to see if the jewelry had fallen, but it was gone. Feeling sick, Mia opened the door. "Has anyone seen my necklace?" Margo stood quickly, reaching into the pocket of her dress and pulling out the gold chain.

"Oh. Thanks." Confused, Mia reached out, but Margo walked behind her.

"May I?"

Mia nodded and stepped back to let the woman into the bathroom. She turned to the sink and lifted her hair from her neck. She watched Margo's arms rise and the necklace go past her eyes, then felt a breath on her neck. She met Margo's eyes in the mirror; there it was again, that weird spark. The warm air tickled the soft baby hairs at the nape of her neck, causing them to lift and goose bumps to rise. She knew Margo noticed. She felt the shift, and then Margo's warm exhalation on her neck.

"Don't do it, Margo," Kris called from the other room.

"I'm not doing anything," Margo replied with a scolding look through the open doorway.

"What?" Mia asked.

"Margo is a giant fucking flirt," Kris said, confirming the feeling Mia had fluttering in her stomach.

"I was just helping her with her necklace," Margo said with nothing but innocence.

"And how did you end up with it in the first place?" Kris snorted.

"They didn't have it fastened on her neck, and when she came out of the casket, it fell off. I didn't want her to lose it," Margo protested, but Mia wasn't listening.

She was thinking about the last time a woman gave her goose bumps. In the eleventh grade, she'd made friends with a new girl who had moved from California. Amber's skin was tanned, and her hair fell in perfect curls on her shoulders. They used to skip classes and hide in the meadow behind the school. Amber had always talked about her boyfriend, Josh, back home, but one day she accidentally said the name Jessica instead. When Mia questioned her, Amber's face went bright red, and she admitted that she'd been in relationships with girls. She explained to Mia that because she moved a lot, she found it was easier to be normal and pretend she dated boys. She'd had bad experiences in the past with people finding out she liked girls. "Normal" wasn't something Mia ever clung to, and she assured Amber that she didn't have to pretend around her. Secretly, she was intrigued by Amber; she'd had crushes on females before she'd discovered boys. In tenth grade, she'd awkwardly lost her virginity to a boy and had set out on the journey of dating different types of guys: the jocks, the normies, the Goth wannabes. She didn't want to lie to herself; she admired both guys and girls. She hadn't yet tried anything physical with another girl, though. It still felt taboo in her conservative town, and she hated that it held her back for even a moment.

The two girls grew closer in the days after Amber told Mia she was gay. Friday the thirteenth was approaching, so Mia invited Amber over for a horror movie marathon. They squealed and clutched at each other in terror, and before long, they were holding hands.

And then Mia's mother walked in on their very first kiss.

Elizabeth apologized for not knocking and shut the door. Amber's hand flew to her mouth, and Mia's stomach flipped upside down with anxiety. Excusing herself, she ran down the hallway and found her mom putting a giant bowl of popcorn on the counter. Before she even opened her mouth, her mother turned and looked at her.

"I was just coming to let you know I made you more popcorn," she said. "Don't worry; we're not going to have one of those moments."

"What do you mean?" Mia asked, digging her nails into the palms of her hands.

"You know I believe that everyone should do whatever makes them happy in this life." She took a deep breath. "Before I married your father, I was in love. Her name was Ashley."

Mia was speechless. She'd never seen this side of her mother before. Elizabeth swung around and pushed the bowl into Mia's hands, then turned and left without another word.

Mia and Amber had the best time that night; they laughed and kissed and threw popcorn into each other's mouths.

Come Monday, though, things had changed.

Mia waited at Amber's locker, but when the girl saw her, she shouted, "Stay away from me, you dyke!" Mia was stunned into silence as people snickered at her from up and down the hallway. The memories of Friday played in her head. *Dyke?* What was Amber doing? She wanted to ask for an explanation, but instead, Mia just turned and fled. She never spoke to Amber again.

For that whole year, Mia's life was a mess. She had found Amber so soft, inviting, and fun; she set Mia's soul on fire. Mia found herself overcompensating at parties just to show everyone how much she liked boys. Which she did—she just *also* liked girls.

Last year, Amber had sent Mia a message on Facebook. She apologized, explaining how her family didn't accept that she was gay and had moved away from California due in part to her relationship with Jessica. Amber had panicked, thinking Mia would go public with their relationship and was afraid that her parents would find out. In college, she had broken ties with her family altogether and had recently married a wonderful woman. Mia was happy for her, but she was still heartbroken that someone she'd trusted would treat her like that. It was a betrayal that was difficult to forget.

And now, here she was, barely knowing Margo and having the same pangs in her chest that Amber had given her. She took a breath and stepped back into the bedroom.

"You look amazing if I do say so myself," said Alyssa as she admired Mia's new outfit. "I gotta go, but I'll see you soon!" She flounced out without waiting for a response.

"She's always like that." Kris sighed, typing on her phone. "I'm just glad she's a Sutton. We have enough drama in this house."

"Where do they live?" Mia asked curiously. "The Suttons?"

"They're in Cedar Hollow, too. They rented out a wing of the Bruce Hotel."

Mia knew of the Bruce. The Adairs had stayed there after Sasha finished her first year at college and Elizabeth had treated them to a rare family weekend at the beach. Once a health resort for the ultrarich, the entire place was full of old-time charm. The enormous brick expanse and meticulously landscaped acres were famous. It was the kind of place where anything was just a phone call away. Thinking of Elenora, Mia could perfectly picture the elegant woman strolling down the red-carpeted hallways and climbing the carved staircases.

"Why are there two Families?" Mia suddenly wondered out loud.

Kris glanced at Margo, who turned her attention to the bookshelves. "Eli and Elenora were married. I guess you can only be married to someone for so long before you get sick of each other."

"None of us knows why they hate each other so much. I think she broke Eli's heart," Margo said. "She still speaks tenderly of him, but whatever happened, he generally won't talk or look at her. They only come together when there's a new vampire. *We* don't even see her outside of that. Which is sad because she seems really sweet."

"Why did you both choose the Bellamy Family?" Mia asked curiously.

"We were both turned by Eli, so you could say it was loyalty," Margo replied.

"Sutton Family is kind of strict," Kris added. "They live very much in a routine, and to be honest, Elenora weirds me out. There's something about her I don't like."

Margot shot a nasty look at Kris. "Don't you say that. Elenora would do anything to protect any of us."

"We have very different philosophies on how vampires should act. That's why we give you a chance to learn about all of us, so you don't get stuck for eternity with someone who's not a good fit," Kris explained, shooting a strange look at Margo. "You'll spend a night here and a night there. After that, you can choose your Family."

Mia trained her eyes on the floor as she pictured her mom and Sasha. *I already have a family,* she thought to herself. "What if I don't want to choose either the Bellamys or the Suttons?"

The two women exchanged glances. "When vampires go solo, it usually doesn't end well," Kris finally replied. "We don't recommend it. It draws so much attention that getting your 'supplies' can be hard."

"You're going to like one of the Families," Margo insisted.

The words didn't bring Mia peace; they just made her more homesick.

"I know your first night is going to be hard. We're going to make sure you have a fantastic time, though. We're going to take you to our favorite place in town."

"There's a storm rolling in." Kris stood and pointed to the heavy clouds.

"Are you going to be okay with the storm?" Margo asked anxiously. "The night you died—"

"I'll be fine," Mia said. Her words felt small in her mouth. The flash of the memory of that night played in her head: the rain, the smell of her blood mixed with the car's oil.

Margo looked relieved. "If you need anything, I'm the next room over. We share the bathroom. Take your time settling in," Margo said. "You may want to squeeze in a nap so you feel fresh for tonight."

"I forgot to tell you. When I took Alyssa to your house, we managed to sneak back a few things that hopefully won't be missed," Kris said as she strolled out of the room. "We'll come to get you later."

Margo opened her Gucci bag and removed two bags of blood. Mia's mouth started watering immediately. "The first days are the thirstiest, so I grabbed these from the fridge. Let them come up to room temp before you eat."

"Thank you."

"I think we're going to get along great." Margo winked and walked into the bathroom, opening and shutting the door that separated them. Mia walked to the windows and gazed over Cedar Hollow, the people looking like ants from this distance.

"Oh, how breakable you all are," she whispered to herself.

CHAPTER TEN

To her surprise, Mia ended up taking a four-hour nap the second she lay down, the stress of the day shutting her mind right off. After she woke up, she decided to investigate her new belongings. She started with the closet, where she made a thorough search of its inventory. There were more Gucci handbags on a shelf, though she thought the one that Toby, Margo, and Kris had given her was more her vibe. Several pairs of luxury shoes lined the shelves, including Louis Vuittons and Manolo Blahniks. Though she'd never enjoyed wearing heels, Mia slipped on a pair. She gasped at how comfortable they were, so completely unlike the inexpensive shoes she'd purchased at department stores.

Testing out the pumps, Mia walked over to the bookshelf and examined the titles. *The Virgin Suicides* popped out at her, and as she pulled it off the shelf, she realized it was her own copy with the torn corner. It must have been one of the tokens they had brought from her home. She was touched that Cordelia had remembered their short conversation about it in the bookstore. Mia noticed what seemed to be a wide bookmark placed in the pages halfway through, and when she opened to it, she found it was a photograph. Her own face, Sasha's, and their parents' grinned up at her. Mia blinked back tears. She placed the book back on the shelf and then gently propped up the photo on the bedside table. Slowly, she removed the expensive pumps from her feet.

She missed her family. All she had left of them was a photo and her father's wedding band. She removed the ring and ran her finger around the edge, a movement that had always brought her comfort. She turned the ring in her fingertips and watched how the light from the dying fire caught the metal. It was silver except for a black line that ran along the ring's interior. She assumed it was a result of how the band had been made; it was centuries old. Her father had told her it was his great-grandmother's.

Mia remembered sitting with her dad on the floor in front of the fireplace on Christmas Eve, family albums strewn all over the carpet. When he opened a crumbling book full of black-and-white photos, Mia's young chubby finger had pointed to a man who looked just like him, the curly hair and thick glasses peering out of the page at her. Her father had told her that the man in the photo was his grandfather, her great-grandfather. Then he pulled the ring off his finger and held it against the image, lining it up with the one on the man's finger.

"Mia, this ring has been passed down for generations. The eldest child passed it on to his eldest child, and so on. My father received it from his father, who had been given it by his mother. I'm not sure who had it before then, but one day, it will be yours." When Mia first understood that she had actually died, she was upset to realize the ring was still on her finger. Her mother should have removed it and given it to Sasha.

Now, though, she was grateful that she still had something of her father left.

There was a box of jewelry on the dresser containing gorgeous necklaces, earrings, and bracelets. Mia absently played with her father's ring as she looked through them all. She was surprised to see a few of her own pieces mixed in with the more expensive items.

Mia also noticed a folded piece of paper with her name scrawled across it sitting on top of the dresser. As the rain began to beat the expansive windows, she unfolded the note carefully to find that it was from Eli.

Dear Mia,
In the top right drawer of the dresser, you will find a Visa Black Card and cash. I have invested in many businesses and ventures. The fashion industry has been very lucrative over the past century and our pockets are deep, so don't be afraid to spend. The tap won't run dry.

Eli Bellamy

Mia put the note down and pulled open the drawer. A credit card and a crisp white envelope were its only contents. Mia folded back the paper carefully and pulled out a stack of hundred-dollar bills. She counted them.

It was $10,000.

She dropped the money back into the drawer and shut it quickly, taken over by the feeling that she had found something she wasn't supposed to have.

A sudden pang in her stomach had her turning to the bags of blood that Margo had left for her. It was strange that she didn't crave the usual strawberry salad or fries; they had no appeal now. Instead, she craved the rich liquid she'd first tried only a few hours ago.

The bag felt heavy in her hands. She looked up at the reflection above the dresser and turned away uneasily. A part of her felt humiliated, but another part was afraid to see the black eyes and the shine of pointed teeth. Facing the window, Mia bit into the bag. The liquid slid smoothly down her throat and tasted even better than before. As blood poured into her mouth, she could almost feel the shift in her eyes, as if a film had slid across them. Though it was still foreign, she was becoming used to the sensation. Mia finished the first bag and then tore into the second. After she finished, she dropped the bags into the garbage. She felt more awake, more alive, as if this random person's DNA had wiped the cobwebs from her mind. She didn't feel satisfied, though; it seemed the more she drank, the more she wanted, and she wished there was an endless supply. She also hated how aware she was of everyone in the house. Her new vampire senses were heightened, and she could hear the others moving around. As the electricity of the storm built and the thunder started, it thankfully masked the sounds of the Family.

A flash of lightning drew her attention to the windows, and Mia glided over to watch the storm. That's when she saw it—a fire escape ladder just to the left of the window. Mia glanced again at the photo of her family. Maybe she could go home quickly and let them know she wasn't dead, that it had all been a terrible mistake, but that she couldn't stay. She would tell them that she would check in. It was unfair that they had to suffer. And if her mother tried to force her to stay, Mia would tell her the truth. For all she knew, her mother had already come across vampires in her line of work.

She worked at the unfamiliar latch on the pane before figuring out how to unlock the window, which slid softly to the left without making a sound. As Mia peered down at the thirty-foot drop, anxiety filled her chest. She reached out to the ladder; it was cool to the touch and slippery. Mia craned her neck to see if the ladder was in front of any windows, but it didn't look like it. She didn't think anyone would see her if she climbed down.

Pulling her wet head back into the bedroom, she moved silently to the dresser and withdrew four hundred-dollar bills from the stack in the drawer. Then she reached into the closet and riffled through the clothes until she found some coats; there was one covered in a rubbery material. Yanking the black jacket off the hanger, she shoved her arms into it, the fabric hugging her curves as she zipped it up. Grabbing a pair of sturdy sneakers, she closed the closet door and looked around her room to make sure it was tidy.

Mia glanced over her shoulder at the bathroom; she hadn't heard any sound through Margo's connected door.

With the thunder, Mia couldn't tell where the other Bellamys might be. While she didn't think she was strictly confined to the house, she also doubted anyone would be thrilled if she left, even temporarily. She tiptoed through the bathroom and put her ear softly against the opposite door. There was no sound.

"Just there and back," she whispered to herself as she stepped out of the bathroom and closed the door slowly before locking it.

Mia poked her head out the window. The storm had passed, but a light rain continued to fall. Her foot felt like lead as she swung it out and it made contact with the metal ladder. Grasping the top rung tightly, she shifted her weight and put the other foot on the ladder. Looking over her shoulder, she could see the town of Cedar Hollow in the distance. If she ran through the forest, she could probably be there within a half hour. She moved fast and almost slid down the ladder. Her feet hit the lush lawn within seconds, and she didn't waste a moment. Like a frightened rabbit, she ran through the forest.

She looked down with shock as she ran; she was moving faster than she ever had. Her breath was quick but steady, and she wasn't fighting for air. The journey she'd thought would take a half hour took only ten minutes. Mia broke out of the brush and was shocked to see how busy the streets were, even in the rain. Across from the forest was the main strip, and between the stores, she could see waves of water lapping at the sand. Looking up and down the road, she saw a sign for Willies Wet Bar. Laughing to herself at the name, she walked through the front door and up to the bar.

The blonde woman working there took one look at her and stole a surprised step backward.

Fear rose in Mia's gut, and she looked down, covering her face with her hands. Were her eyes still black? If they scared her, how terrifying would they look to a normal person?

"Honey, are you okay? Your makeup is a mess. If you've got a guy after you, I'll call Chuck, and he'll break his legs." Her Southern accent rang loudly.

Mia lowered her hands and caught her reflection in the mirror behind the bottles of liquor. The mix of rainwater and speed had caused mascara and eyeliner to flow freely over her entire face. She laughed shakily. "I'm fine. I got caught in the storm. Could you call a cab for me?"

"You got it, baby doll," the pretty bartender cooed.

Mia ducked into the restroom to tend to her face, then walked back outside and sat on the bench to wait for the cab. Everything felt so strange to her. Tourists milled about like normal, but the past twenty-four hours of Mia's life hadn't been even close to normal. Just a few days ago, she was living a mundane life full of routine. She had died and become a vampire, and now she was trying to escape and get back home so she could tell her mom she wasn't dead. She wondered if anyone here guessed how close they lived to over a dozen supernatural beings.

A silver car pulled up, and a fat, gray-haired man stuck his head out the driver's window. "Hey, girlie, you call about a cab?" Mia nodded and opened the back door.

Most of the car ride was silent. The driver had introduced himself as Gary, then tried to make small talk, but after giving him the address, Mia became lost in her thoughts. They were sitting at a stoplight when she noticed a ring of laminated paper hanging off the passenger seat. She absently reached out and flipped through the papers, seeing that each was a picture of a young person. The word *MISSING* was written in red ink above each photo.

"What are these?" Mia asked.

"Ah, those are all the people who've gone missing from Cedar Hollow," Gary replied. "Haven't you heard about them?"

"I'm from out of town." As she studied each photo in turn, the smiling faces stared up as if trying to tell her their stories. Each person was unique in their own way.

"Yeah, I guess it's kind of our dirty secret. Everyone comes here for a good time, but not everyone leaves. A few are local, most are tourists, but all are young." He shrugged. "Maybe they got inspired by this place and decided to start fresh. Or maybe it's the work of a cult." The words made Mia uneasy. "No one knows. They just disappear without a trace. I'm around all hours of the day and night, so I like to keep a record if I see anyone." Gary glanced in the rearview mirror. "You're not a missing girl, are you?"

"No," Mia said softly. *If only he knew.*

It wasn't long before they were turning onto Mia's road.

"Can you stop here?" she asked.

Puzzled, Gary pulled over onto the shoulder. "We're more than a mile away. Wouldn't you rather I take you straight up to the house?" he asked.

Mia shook her head. "I'll be fine. Can you wait for me? I'll be back in twenty minutes."

"You've already run up quite a bill, missy," the cabbie warned.

"I can pay."

Gary nodded, and Mia climbed out of the cab. She jogged down the road, trying to keep herself to what she thought was a humanlike pace. She'd only gone a hundred yards when a sick feeling hit her in the stomach. Looking down, she realized why: she was in the spot of her crash. A few slivers of brake lights were mixed in with the churned-up gravel on the shoulder. Mia dropped to her knees and reached out, collecting the plastic fragments. She looked to her right and made out the damaged trunk of the maple tree she'd impacted, the marks her car had left etched into it like art. A forgotten piece of caution tape beating the air.

Mia was overcome with the memory of that night. The flash of her dog in the road, the lurch as the car left the pavement, the last moment when Cordelia stabbed the metal syringe into her chest. The trees seemed to close in around her, and Mia set off toward her house at her new pace with a burst.

The familiar porch light shined like a beacon, lighting her way to the steps. She slid to a stop in a shadow twenty feet from the door, gazing up at her home with longing. The house felt like an old memory, a place she'd last been years ago instead of merely days.

Now that she was here, Mia didn't know what to do. Knocking on the door seemed wrong. Besides, what would she say? Composing herself, Mia cautiously began to walk the perimeter of the house. She looked up at her bedroom window, which was dark and shut tight. She didn't know what she'd expected to see, but it made her feel cold and uninvited. Still, she supposed leaving it open made no sense, especially in this weather.

Continuing around the house, Mia saw that every window was just as dark. Maybe Elizabeth and Sasha weren't home. She'd just rounded the corner when she saw a soft glow emanating from the family room. Mia crept silently through the bushes beneath the window and peeked in. The couch was directly under the window and faced the television, which was on and illuminating a scene Mia hadn't witnessed in years.

Her mother was curled up on the couch, Sasha beside her with her head on Elizabeth's shoulder. Her mother stroked her hair as they watched a rerun of *The Golden Girls*. Mia pushed her hair behind her ears and concentrated on listening; they were laughing. She swallowed the dryness in her mouth. It had been years since she'd seen her mother on that couch, almost a decade since she and Sash had had a quiet moment together.

Mia backed away from the window and shoved her hands in her pockets. Her fingertips grazed the plastic pieces she had taken from the road. Her undead heart started to pound. How had her death made them closer? When her father passed away, everyone had been pulled apart. But now, her mother and sister seemed to find comfort in each other.

Finally, what Margo had said made sense; she couldn't go home. Right now, they knew where she was—her body was about to be turned into ashes and dust. If Mia burst inside and told them she was a vampire and that she couldn't stay, she knew they would either go insane or lie awake every night wondering where she was, if she was safe, and whether or not *she* was insane. Or she could be safe in an urn beside her father's on the mantel. Tears ran down Mia's face, hot against the cool rain. As she cried, Mia realized she wasn't just sad; she was washing away all the parts of her that had belonged to the Adairs. It wasn't until this moment that she understood their lives would move on without her. Her life would go on forever, but her mother and Sasha would be gone in a few decades. She owed it to them to let them live the rest of their lives in ignorance. "How could I be so selfish?" Mia whispered to herself. She fell forward onto her knees and stared up at the window.

A low growl came from her left side, and she turned her head. It was Cooper, the reason she had lost her life in the first place. She was so relieved that he had escaped the accident unscathed that she wanted to gather him up in her arms and give him one last embrace. Mia's tears came strong now. "Come here, Cooper," she called quietly. The canine took a step back and bared his teeth. In her confusion, Mia stopped crying. She'd always been his favorite, and Cooper didn't have an aggressive bone in his body.

Mia stumbled to her feet. Cooper stepped forward again, his growl turning into a snarl. "Cooper, no," she whispered. It was no good. The dog barked fiercely and then lunged, connecting with her arm and tearing. Mia choked back a scream. The soft glow of the television burst white as the family room lights went on. She knew she had to get away now, before it was too late. Wrenching herself away from Cooper, Mia fled across the lawn holding her bleeding arm. Luckily, the dog didn't show any desire to chase her past the driveway; she was fast, but not that fast. She had just burst through the tree line and onto the road when Mia heard the front door click open. She turned and saw Cooper run to her sister, who was standing on the porch.

She froze. She knew that Sasha wouldn't be able to see her through the pine trees, and she wanted to take in this final glimpse of her family. With an aching heart, she fastened in her mind the image of the place she'd once called home. Sasha looked around the yard for a few moments before letting Cooper into the house and closing the door. Reluctantly, Mia sprinted back to the cab and ripped the back door open so fast that it almost came off its hinges. She didn't know what she looked like, but Gary didn't say a word, just pulled onto the road and sped off in the direction they'd come. Mia stared at him through the mirror, but his eyes were set hard on the street in front of them. She swallowed a sob and let the darkness and heat from the vents swallow her whole.

The gnawing pain in her arm where Cooper had latched on worried her. She could smell her own blood, a scent that was nauseating rather than alluring. She was afraid to look, but she knew she had to assess the damage. There was a push light on the ceiling, and she turned it on. A yellow hue filled the back seat, and Mia glanced at Gary. He was still giving his full attention to the road. Mia gingerly pushed up the sleeve of her jacket, and blood smeared onto her fingers. She inhaled sharply—her skin was unbroken. The only signs that Cooper had torn into her were soft pink lines, like scars faded by the passage of time. She ran her fingers over the lines, and something stirred in her. She was healed.

It was her turn to be the main character, her turn to make something of her life.

"What the hell is that?"

Lost in her thoughts, Mia was startled to hear Gary speak. She'd nearly forgotten he was there. A moment later, he slammed on the brakes, and Mia was flung forward into the back of the passenger seat. She struggled back up, then peered out the windshield. Gary leaned forward as well, then hit the high beams.

There was a mass in the road. Mia sucked in her breath. Something wasn't right. The shape in the road looked like a person lying there, wearing a beige trench coat. Red hair pooled in the road.

"Wait here, darling," Gary said, reaching for the door handle.

"No, don't!" Mia called as he stepped from the car.

"I have to see what's going on. There might have been a hit-and-run." Gary passed an anxious glance at her before slowly walking toward the body in the road. Instinctively, Mia reached up and turned off the light.

"Hello, do you need help?" In the headlights, Gary's hand looked porcelain white as it reached out toward the figure. Mia dug her nails into the soft leather of the console.

It all happened so fast.

One moment Gary was reaching out; the next he was slammed into the windshield. The glass shattered, and Mia shoved herself down behind the passenger seat. She covered her mouth with her hands, trying to be as quiet as possible. Gary's body rolled off the hood of the car, and he cried out in pain as he landed on the pavement.

Mia peeked out the window. The crumpled body was no longer on the road. A dark figure in a black dress swept up to the back door of the car. Red hair spilled out from beneath a black hood.

"Get out!" Elenora boomed, her milky white arm pointing directly at Mia.

Mia didn't need to be told twice. She scrambled out of the car and onto the road. She smelled it before she saw it: Gary's blood. She walked around the open door and knelt in front of Gary. She could hear his heart beating, slowing with every breath; she knew it was too late to save him. The pungent scent of blood was overpowering, and Mia swallowed hard, trying to ignore her instincts.

Elenora leaned over her with black eyes. Her trench coat was covered in Gary's blood. "Don't fuck this all up," she snapped before shoving Mia toward the cabbie.

"No!" Mia called to the woman who stood over her as still as a statue. She knew what was going to happen next, and she wanted to fight it. But as a baby crawled to its mother's breast, Mia was drawn to the vein weakly pulsating on Gary's neck. Despite the kind moments they'd shared, he was no longer a person to her. She wasn't a person anymore, either. She was an animal, a monster. The moment her fangs touched him, his heart stopped. Seconds felt like hours, and a familiar euphoria washed over Mia.

"Mia." The familiar voice snapped Mia out of her bliss. She looked up to see three figures illuminated in the headlights. Margo, Toby, and Kris stood gawking, and one of the Bellamy cars was parked a few yards away.

"Thank god we found you before something bad happened," Kris said dryly as she walked up to the car and cut the ignition.

"Bad?" Mia repeated drunkenly as she looked down at Gary's corpse. "This isn't bad?" Mia swung her head in every direction looking for Elenora, wanting to ask her why she was there, what was happening.

Toby had his arms crossed and was shaking. Was he

laughing? Margo pulled Mia up from the ground and put an arm around her.

"It's dangerous for you to be out here."

"You need to tell her what's up," Toby said. "You can't coddle her. If you don't tell her, then she has no reason to stay. Do you want her to leave again? Jeopardize us all?"

"Do you really think that's a good idea?" Margo snapped.

Mia felt kind of drunk and confused; she'd just consumed liters of blood all at once, more than she ever had. It'd caused a rush that felt the same as drinking seven beers. "What are you not telling me?" She glanced at Margo, who looked more beautiful than ever. "God, you're pretty," she blurted out before slapping a hand over her mouth.

"Yeah, I don't think we have a choice," Toby said. She heard Gary's car start and then crunch down into the ravine. "Let's go," Toby called behind her.

CHAPTER ELEVEN

The effects Mia felt from Gary's blood had diminished by the time they returned to Noir House, but she still felt woozy. Upset by the evening's events, she practically had to be carried up the stairs before she collapsed onto her bed. Kris, Toby, and Margo spoke quietly before a knock at the door startled them, and Toby threw glances at the others before cracking the door two inches.

Gianna shoved her way into the room. "What the fuck is happening?" she demanded before sitting on the bed and patting Mia's leg. In a kinder voice, she said, "You scared the shit out of us, babe."

"We found her ten miles north. She ate Gary." Kris drew her finger across her neck before taking off her leather jacket and sitting down.

"Jesus Christ!" Gianna exclaimed. "I loved Gary!"

"How do you know Gary?" Mia asked dazedly.

Gianna laughed. "There aren't too many people in Cedar Hollow year-round, so we tend to know the locals." She grew serious. "You'll have to learn how much you can take from humans before you go too far and they die."

"Rookie mistake," Toby said.

Clearing her throat, Mia sat up. "I didn't kill Gary. Elenora did." The others exchanged concerned looks.

"You were alone when we found you," Margo said gently as she opened her bag and rummaged for a moment before pulling out her phone and scrolling.

"Gary was driving me back to the house. Elenora was lying in the middle of the road, but we didn't know it was her. Gary thought someone had been involved in a hit-and-run. When he got out to see if she was okay, she slammed him into the car. He was dead before I drank him."

The room was silent as Margo checked her phone. "I don't have any messages from her. Are you sure it was Elenora?"

"Yes." The others looked skeptical. "I'm not lying! I wouldn't lie about killing someone."

"I believe you didn't kill Gary," Margo said without hesitation.

"We're just saying it might have been someone else, babe. Elenora would never kill a person. Honestly, there's even less of a chance she would be out in the rain. Elenora preaches the importance of human life so much it's annoying. You're confused." Gianna pushed her hair over her shoulder.

"I know it was Elenora. She spoke to me and made me get out of the car." Mia put her head in her hands. The group exchanged looks that told Mia that Elenora couldn't have been the one she saw. "I feel so bad that Gary is dead; I don't know what came over me. I didn't want to drink his blood. It was like she made me."

Kris looked at her sharply. "Are you saying that Elenora Veiled you? I didn't think she had that power."

"I don't know," Mia admitted.

"Well, don't feel too bad," Gianna said, rubbing Mia's back. "Gary's had three heart attacks in the past two years. He was running on borrowed time." The three were giving each other side glances.

"What were you doing out there, anyway?" Kris demanded. "We *told* you that you can't go home."

Mia hung her head. "I just wanted to see them one last time," she replied. "But you were right—it wouldn't have worked."

"What happened to your arm?" Margo asked, pointing at the ripped coat.

"My dog bit me. He—he didn't even recognize me."

"You smell different," Kris explained. "At least maybe now you'll realize that we're telling the truth."

"Margo, why did you say it wasn't safe for me?" Mia asked, ignoring Kris's blunt tone. The others again exchanged uneasy looks. "I can tell you're keeping something from me. I don't know what, but I'd like to know."

Margo touched Gianna's shoulder, and the woman moved off the bed. Sitting down, Margo looked straight into Mia's eyes. "We didn't have a plan yet on how much we should tell you." The other three vampires arranged themselves in front of her like they were about to tell her Santa wasn't real.

"Mia, things have been weird for us vampires lately and it's getting worse," Margo began. "As Elenora told you at the funeral home, we're only two of the Families. There are others, but we pretty much keep to ourselves. And there are rules about turning people. Everyone follows these rules so we aren't discovered. As Eli said, we're peaceful, and if everyone follows the rules, there's a slim chance of being outed as vampires. As you can imagine, that wouldn't be good for anyone." She laughed shortly. "In the past five years, there's been a population growth—an unsanctioned population growth. And we haven't figured out what's going on. Someone is creating vampires and not documenting it, and these new vampires aren't being brought into any of the Families."

"They're like nasty stray cats," Toby said grimly. "Well, until they randomly disappear."

"Disappear?" Mia asked slowly.

"Every one of these new, unruly vampires causes a bunch of shit, and then just—*poof*—gone." Toby shook his head.

"It's not only that. Other things have been happening, too. Thea, the woman who started our lines, began to lose her powers on February 22, 2001." Margo looked pointedly at Mia, who frowned.

"That's my birthday," Mia said.

Kris turned and started examining the books on the shelf as if she hadn't heard Mia. "The story goes that on that day, Thea heard a deafening crack, and a white ball of light shot out of her body. For years she didn't know what it meant, but her powers began to dwindle."

"That wouldn't mean much to an ordinary vampire, but Thea is special," Margo continued. "She's our matriarch, and as I told you earlier, she's one of the only vampires with the power to kill other vampires. The white light that left her was the source of her power, including the ability to destroy us."

"Isn't that a good thing?" Mia asked in confusion.

"Well, no," Toby said. "Vampires are intended to live in family groups, but sometimes a person doesn't fit in anywhere, so they head out on their own. They still need to follow the rules, but more often than not, they go rogue. When that happens, their matriarch deals with them."

"You see, Mia," Margo said, moving her hand onto Mia's knee, "Thea realized that losing her power to terminate vampire life was her final notice from the universe. Not only have her powers weakened, but so has her body." She paused. "Do you remember Talli?"

"Yes."

"The way Talli came to be with us was . . . horrible."

Toby made a choking sound and turned to the wall, his hand over his mouth. "It was the worst day," he murmured, then abruptly went into the bathroom and closed the door.

Margo stared at the bedspread. "In 1985 the Families had a problem. Someone killed Grace and Noah from Sutton Family. Because they had been recently turned, they were easy targets that practically any vampire could kill. Toby had just broken up with Gianna and was temporarily staying with Sutton Family, so he saw everything that happened. Elenora went on the hunt for someone with the Gift of psychic abilities, hoping she could find someone who could tell her who the murderer was. They weren't having much luck until they passed through a small town in Alabama and caught word of an eighteen-year-old woman named

Tallulah. Elenora went to visit her that night. Talli knew what Elenora was right away. It didn't scare her, but because Elenora wasn't a human, she couldn't read her. That was a problem. Elenora needed someone who'd be able to read vampires."

The bathroom door opened, and Toby emerged, his eyes bloodshot. "I told her to leave Talli alone. There was no reason to believe she'd be able to read a vampire if she was turned. But Elenora didn't listen." A heavy silence filled the room.

Kris walked over to Toby and held his hand. Mia hadn't seen this soft side of Kris before.

"Elenora can be very . . . different; her ideas come from a very primal place to protect us," Kris said, gazing at Mia.

Toby shut his eyes. "That night she drugged Talli and turned her." He paused and swallowed hard. Kris led Toby over to one of the reading chairs as Margo continued.

"Talli woke up three days later, alone and starving. She was confused and disoriented, and she somehow managed to leave the abandoned house where Elenora had left her alone—Talli woke earlier than expected—and then she went home. Her grandmother and brother were the only ones there, and Talli couldn't help herself." Margo took a deep breath. "She murdered them and drank their blood before Elenora found her. She managed to steal Talli away before she could do any more damage. Talli's mother arrived home to a ghastly scene: her mother and son dead and her daughter missing. She's never stopped looking for Talli. Once Talli became a vampire, her Gift was stronger. I suppose if it hadn't been, Elenora would have killed her on the spot. Talli lives haunted by what she did. Anyway, she was able to show us who had killed Grace and Noah. It was a rogue vampire with a god complex, thinking he could destroy vampires without being a matriarch. Thea took care of him."

"Talli served her purpose," Toby said bitterly. "Elenora wanted to keep her around because of how valuable she was, but she didn't count on Talli knowing what had happened to her. After that, I left the Suttons' and brought Talli here."

"Elenora's success with Talli is what inspired Isla to turn Cordelia," Margo added. "Except it didn't work because it turns out that Cordelia can't heal depression. Talli's also the reason we found you tonight. She knew you'd gone out to visit your family, so we were on our way to stop you. She can't see everything, but she could see you."

Kris picked up the story from there. "Three years ago, the Bellamy Family had another member, Alison. One night, a few months after she was turned, she went out on her own, and she never came back. A few days later, we found her body in the forest: it was completely drained of blood." She paused, a troubled look on her face. "That brings me back to the new vampires showing up. We don't know who is creating them; not even Talli knows. A lot of these new vamps are locals or tourists." Mia thought back to the laminated flyers in Gary's cab.

"They hang around for a few weeks before disappearing," Gianna said. "Some have turned up, though—drained of blood."

Margo held Mia's hand tighter. "The first five years of a new vampire's life are different. They can't turn anyone, and their lives are as delicate as baby birds. It's the only time someone other than a matriarch can destroy a vampire."

"Why didn't you tell me it wasn't safe for me to be out?" Mia pulled her hand from Margo's and slapped it on the bed in frustration; she knew they were avoiding something.

"Would it have made a difference?" Kris snapped. "We told you not to try to see your family, but the first thing you did was run away."

Margo held up her hands. "More importantly, the blood of a new vampire is different—it's incredibly potent. We only found out by accident that it heals anyone who uses it, vampire or human. We think a rogue is creating vampires and then killing them for their blood."

"The life cycle of a human is sacred," said Gianna. "Imagine what the world would look like if no one died, or if we decided who lived and who died? This is putting us at risk of being found out, and if humans knew about us, vampires would be kept in labs, hooked up to machines. I would sell my soul not to end up like that. Metaphorically speaking, of course, as we don't have souls anymore."

Mia broke into the middle of Gianna's sentence: "We don't have souls anymore?" The thought scared her.

"When Talli looks at a human, she sees their soul in the form of their aura," Margo explained. "When she looks at us, she sees emptiness. She calls us the Hollow Ones."

Kris had been staring at the window, and now she turned her face toward Mia. "To be a vampire is to be hollow." The room grew quiet for a moment, the air heavy.

Even though Mia wasn't sure she believed in souls, the thought that anyone, even a vampire, could exist without one felt cold.

Toby spoke, changing the subject. "Talli's the one who

told us that you speak to ghosts. When was the last time you saw one?"

Mia thought about the night Mr. Horvath died and how his eyes had locked with hers from the doorway. "It's been just over six years."

"Have you seen any of the ghosts of the vampires who have died here?" Toby asked.

"No."

Gianna fidgeted uncomfortably. "Sorry, babes," she said, "but this is getting too heavy for me. We'd planned on showing you a good time tonight, not discussing serious matters." She stood up and stretched. "I don't know if you're into partying, but partying as a vampire is the sickest thing you'll ever do. We only get one night with you, and there's no chance we're sending you to that uptight Sutton Family without showing you what Bellamy is all about!"

"Well," Kris asked, "what do you say? Are you up for having the best night of your life?"

"So far," Toby added, a crooked grin spreading over his face.

Mia felt uncomfortable at how they had shifted the conversation so quickly from talking about the darkest parts of their history to partying.

She thought for a moment before answering, overwhelmed by everything she'd just learned. Part of her wanted to hide under the blankets. On the other hand, this was the first night of her new life.

"I'm in."

CHAPTER TWELVE

The Bellamys practically flew around the room as they helped Mia prepare for her first night out as a vampire. It was as if until this moment, every one of them had been playing a role, and now they'd all let their hair down. Even their language and their physicality changed; before, they had seemed more human, but now they moved with the fluidity of professional dancers. Margo tugged at Mia, lifting her off the bed and spinning her onto the stool in front of the makeup table. She already knew from her earlier exploration that the drawers were full of new products perfectly matching her skin tone. Mia noticed Gianna admiring her in the reflection of the mirror.

"Are you the one to thank for this?" Mia called out to her.

Tugging on the ends of her blond hair, Gianna grinned. "Yes! I love this time in the world. There are just so many choices when it comes to makeup. When I first came out, there was only Sears and Mary Kay." Gianna mimed gagging.

Despite her dramatics, Mia thought she was one of the most beautiful women she had ever seen. Her mouth was a perfect pout, her skin shined as though gold ran through her pores, and her blond waves looked like the beach air had tossed them all day. Gianna slinked over to the closet where Toby had been pulling out various wardrobe options. The bed was littered with dresses Alyssa had thoughtfully picked out, but Mia would never feel comfortable wearing most of them. She hoped she would be able to go out shopping with the money Eli had left and pick out clothes on her own; she'd even visit the "high-end retailers" that Alyssa preferred.

Mia glanced over the choices: a slippery black mesh number with opaque panels cut into curves that only covered the important bits, a white ruched minidress with a corseted back, something made of either leather or plastic, and a tight tube dress. Gianna leaned forward and grabbed Toby's ass, which took Mia by surprise. Toby turned around with a smile on his face and met Gianna's gaze.

"Are you two together?" Mia asked the question before she realized how rude it sounded. That was one thing about this new life: she said things that she didn't mean to say, as if one or two of her filters had been obliterated. She turned to the mirror on the desk and saw her red-cheeked reflection.

"Aw, she thinks we're in love!" Gianna grabbed the white dress off the bed and walked to the mirror, pressing it against her body.

"Yes, I am madly in love with Gianna," Toby said, "just as I am with Margo. I think I'm starting to love you, too." Mia's insides immediately warmed. "But when it comes to the bedroom, I'm all about the boys."

"Toby loves men, all the men," Gianna said, spinning to her. "Do you mind if I wear this one?"

Mia shook her head, amused.

"When I met Margo and Gianna, Gianna was still George."

"Barf!" Gianna cackled. "You see, Mia, it took me quite a few decades to embrace who I am. Like I said before, I was born in a time when these things weren't accepted at all. As a vampire, time seems faster; it's weird. In some ways, it was hard for me to see the world becoming more accepting—I have so much jealousy that I didn't experience that kind of acceptance when I was alive. It hurts to remember a time when I had so few allies, especially now that I know how amazing it can be. I know the world has so much further to come, but I'm not as scared anymore." A smile pulled at Gianna's lips before she turned to Toby. "And stop using my dead name, or I'll feed you poisoned rat blood." He winced and nodded, a coy smile pulling at his lips.

"You've also had a wicked long time to perfect that winged liner," Kris said from her chair, her phone held up to her face as she scrolled.

Mia sat comfortably as Margo styled her hair, running her fingers through Mia's black tresses. The sensation sent tingles across her whole body. Margo's face was set in concentration as she manipulated the strands of hair into soft curls that bounced around Mia's shoulders. The curling wand gave off a faint heat that matched Mia's cheeks. She found herself wanting to reach out and stroke Margo's wrist just to feel how soft the skin was. Earlier, when she had grabbed Mia's hand, it was electric.

Once Mia's hair was done, Gianna spun her around and started on her face with the soft makeup brushes and products. Mia took the time to secretly study Margo from across the room under her half-closed eyelids, and she gazed at her lips. A few moments later, Kris coughed loudly, and when Mia looked at her, she was still focused on her phone but had a sly grin on her face. Mia knew she'd been caught. In a way, she didn't mind.

"Perfect, we're done!"

Mia felt the chair spin again and caught her reflection in the mirror. "Wow!" she breathed, admiring the beautiful woman who looked back at her. She had never seen herself like this. Maybe it was the new vampire blood coursing through her veins, or maybe it was the artistry of her friends' handiwork, but she looked stunning. Her hair was voluminous, her eyes were smoky and sexy, and her lips were a dark maroon that complemented her black hair perfectly. She looked how she had always wished she would.

"I think you look drop-dead," Margo said shyly. Mia could see Kris in the mirror shaking her head. She knew Kris read her and the situation perfectly.

"I'm going to get dressed—you change, too." With that, Margo cut through the bathroom and back to her room.

Kris gathered her things and sauntered up to Mia. "She's right. You do look like you fit in." The blonde looked stunning; her lips were bright red, a perfect contrast to her dark jeans and black crop top. Her pale features were shocking against Mia's dark ones. "I know I can come off a little harsh, but it's for the best. I'm not always excited about letting people in." She ran her fingers through Mia's hair before lifting her eyes to the reflection to connect with Mia's gaze. "You seem like someone who sees through bullshit. When you spend time with Sutton Family, make sure you keep your eyes open." She paused. "I promise I'm not trying to convince you to pick us, but something with that Family hasn't sat right with me for the past few years. I don't want you to get hurt."

It felt like Kris had more to say, but the moment was broken as the door swung open. It was Izzy, the bizarre English vampire who definitely had something going on with Alexander.

"Ahh, you arseholes, I knew you were going to ditch me!" she shouted half-jokingly.

Gianna popped out of the closet in the white ruched dress. "Babe, every time you come, you get too fucked up, and shit always happens. We need to have a good time tonight, memorable in the *right* way."

Izzy made a pouting face at Gianna and then looked at Toby.

"Don't do this to me, Izzy baby," Gianna said. "You know I can't say no to those chubby cheeks."

"*Pleeeeeeease!*" she said, forcing the most enormous puppy dog eyes Mia had ever seen.

"Fine." Gianna grabbed her and shoved her toward the door. "Just wear something from this decade—or at least this century."

Izzy looked down at her dress—Mia had worn something just like it in *Romeo and Juliet*, her tenth-grade play.

"This is just my comfy dress," Izzy called as she trotted down the hall.

"You have just made this either the worst or the best night." Toby laughed and held up the mesh dress. "This is it. You're wearing this, with this." Toby held up a black G-string.

"Are you insane?" Mia shrieked. It was apparent Toby didn't know her at all; she could never wear anything like that. She had only ever seen those kinds of dresses on models on those fast-fashion sites, the women with bodies built by doctors. She had never seen it on the body of what America would consider "average."

"Just try it." Toby thrust the dress at her. Mia grabbed it, thinking that she would look incredibly pudgy in such an outfit. Then the realization hit her like a ton of bricks: she would most likely be this size forever. She wasn't sure how she felt about that; she had been fine with it before, so why was she questioning it now? Mia stepped into the closet. The door shut with one smooth motion, and she found herself staring into the mirror that hung on the back of the closet door.

When she held the dress up to her body, she knew it was a size too small, but since she wanted to please her new friends, it seemed like she'd be wearing this or nothing at all. Her clothes fell to the floor, and the mesh felt sleek as it slid in her hands. Mia was starting to fall in love with how aware she was of everything. She'd never done any drugs before, but she had seen what they did to people. Stephanie from history class had loved stroking flat surfaces when she was high, feeling how smooth they were. Mia slid her fingers over her naked hips, feeling the small indents. She made sure to pull on the G-string and pull down the dress facing away from the closet door. Mia could only get the zipper three-quarters of the way up, but she pulled her hair free and spun on her toes quickly. Staring at her bare feet, she grabbed the Louis Vuittons she'd tried on earlier and slipped into the heels.

Mia looked at herself. There was a heart of material that covered her breasts and a single band that went around her hips. She would typically feel too insecure to wear something like this, but to her amazement, she looked incredible.

"Wow." She meant to merely think the word, but it came out audibly.

"Oh, I think she likes it!" She heard Toby's voice echo through the door before he ripped it open. "Turn around," he demanded. She did, and he zipped up the rest of the dress.

"My God, why did you want to cover that?" Gianna pulled Mia out of the closet and fluffed her hair before stepping back and admiring her.

"Are you sure it isn't too much?" Mia felt a touch awkward as she smoothed out the front of her dress. The voice came from the direction of the bathroom.

"No, it's perfect." Margo had one hand on her hip, the other holding her chin. Her eyes were on fire as Mia couldn't help but look over the woman with appreciation. Margo was wearing the same dress but in maroon. She looked stunning, and Mia let out a loud gasp that set Gianna to laughing. Mia looked around the room, her cheeks burning. It was obvious that everyone could see what was happening. The lusty tension could be cut with a knife. Mia walked slowly to Margo since she wasn't used to wearing heels. She felt like a newborn deer and didn't want to trip and look like an idiot.

"Can you zip me up?" Margo spun and pulled her hair to the side, revealing the nape of her neck. Her perfume was sweet, and Mia could sense it on her skin, a mix of amber and plum.

She grabbed the zipper and slowly slid it up, feeling it pull snugly into the curves of Margo's body.

"There," Mia said. "All set." Margo spun and threw her hands around Mia. At first, Mia thought she was coming in for a hug, but no, Margo's arms were quickly around her neck. Mia felt stupid as her hands hung awkwardly in the air; she didn't know what to do with them.

"I was just tucking your tag in," Margo said. All of the blood pulled away from Mia's heart, and the butterflies took over. The door banged open, breaking the spell.

"I look like magic, eh?" Izzy twirled for the others. The black velvet dress was 100 percent from the early nineties, but with the e-girls and hipsters of today, it would be considered a sick thrift find. Gianna let out a short cackle before pushing past Izzy and out of the room.

"She doesn't like me," Izzy said sadly as Toby entered the room. Mia had been so caught up she hadn't even noticed him leave.

Toby shook his head at Izzy's response as he finished buttoning up a pair of tight black jeans. He flattened down his patterned Versace shirt before slapping a hand on Margo's ass. "Okay, gays and dolls, let's go!"

They all met in the courtyard out in front of the bank of ivy-covered garages. Mia passed her eyes over the group.

There was Margo, Toby, Kris, Izzy, Gianna, and her. A few members of the Family weren't present. "Where are Eli and Talli?" she asked Kris.

"Wow. That hurts." The voice had come from the bushes. She saw an ember float through the air before a man with a cigarette stepped into the light of the courtyard. It was Oscar, the handsome, muscular man.

"You got my text, right?" Toby called from the front of the garage.

"You know I'm always down for some fun, but it seems that Mia forgot about me," Oscar replied as Mia blushed. "It's okay, pipsqueak. I can be kind of antisocial. The timing has to be right. Also, Eli and Talli are introverts who don't like to party with us." Oscar reached his arm out into the sky, and Mia's gaze followed his finger, which pointed at the full moon. "It looks so beautiful tonight." He dropped his arm and pulled Mia into a side hug. She could smell the smoke thick on his breath.

The garage opened to reveal two matching cars, one white and one black. Both were Porsche Panameras. Mia's mother had driven one a couple of years back. It was weird that for a moment, Mia had almost forgotten about her other life.

"I'll meet you there," Oscar said. He pulled back from the group and ran into the forest, just as Mia had a few hours earlier.

Mia got into the black Porsche with Kris and Margo, their fragrances mixing like an English garden. They pulled out smoothly onto the cobblestone, and the gate at the end of the driveway opened as they reached it and glided through. The silence in the car was deafening to Mia.

"It's too bad Oscar didn't want to drive with us," she said. "It would be nice to get to know him."

Kris looked in the rearview mirror and made eye contact with Mia. "Oscar doesn't really do cars unless he has to," she said. "He had a full ride to Harvard playing soccer. He was young and thought he was invincible. He drank and drove after partying all the time. One night his luck ran out, and he got into an accident." There was a pause. "That's how his brother and girlfriend died."

"Is that how he became a vampire?" Mia whispered from the back seat.

"No. Things got worse from there. He lost his scholarship; his dad was the mayor and so disappointed. Feeling guilty about causing the deaths of the two people he loved most and with nothing to look forward to, Oscar hit the bottle hard. One day he went swimming at a lake with some of his friends, got drunk, got reckless, and dove in where he shouldn't have. Eli overheard his parents talking about pulling his life support. He said they were certain about their choice—they sounded almost relieved."

Mia recalled Oscar's story now. "Eli turned him at the hospital."

"Yep. It felt meant to be," Kris replied. "It wasn't very often that we were in New Jersey. He still comes out with us, but he doesn't drink anymore, and he avoids cars whenever he can." Mia pictured Oscar's carefree face and realized that a person couldn't judge a book by its cover.

Mia remembered the story he had told about the swimming accident. "But when we were at the funeral home, he said—"

Margo cut her off. "He has been telling that story for

years. I think he's trying to believe it himself. I don't know why he lies."

//////

The drive was short, and the strip of touristy locations came into view within a few minutes. Most storefronts were dark, but bright signs let them know that a good time would be easy to find.

"Neon Viper is the best place," Margo announced as the car slid into a parking spot out front of a building shining with purple and blue neon lights. Mia could already hear and feel the dubstep music penetrating the car. All three of them exited the vehicle as the white Panamera pulled up behind them.

The sidewalk was littered with every kind of person. More than a hundred people stood in a line that snaked down the right side of the building. Mia started to make her way to the back but turned when Margo called her name. "We don't wait in lines."

Kris turned to the big bouncer and lowered her sunglasses. After a moment of quiet concentration, she dropped the glasses back into place. "Ryan, my friends and I want to dance!" The bouncer didn't hesitate as he unclipped the red rope, and they all entered while the queue booed them. The group found itself in a hallway painted with black walls, and little light. They swiftly made their way through; at the end was a room the size of a warehouse where hundreds of dancers jumped and writhed to house music. A light show flashed rapidly, and the beats triggered fog to roll in from all angles.

From the outside, you would have never expected such

a thrilling place. Mia had only been to a rave once, but it was just like this. The vampires peeled off and headed in different directions. Mia started to panic as she looked around and saw no familiar faces. She began to feel out of place in her mesh dress, her newfound confidence fading without the others' presence.

Someone grabbed her hand, their fingers intertwining with hers, and Mia immediately recognized the spark of electricity that she felt whenever Margo touched her.

"Let's get drinks!" Kris screamed over the music.

//////

The drinks flowed, the lights got brighter, and the mingling of all the bodies had Mia rocking to the beat. She was lost in a moment all by herself. She felt and heard the people, but she was swinging her hips in a motion known only to her.

She knew she was drunk; flashes of pictures went off in her mind. Her mother's face, the smear of blood, Margo's smile, blood dripping from her lips, running fast through the woods, then more blood. Mia almost didn't notice the soft touch at first as hands wrapped around her waist. She felt so free that she didn't care what aimless boy pulled her back into an embrace. That's when Mia smelled it: the mix of amber and plum. She spun around, and with her eyes closed, slid her hands down Margo's arms. Swept up in the moment, Mia tilted her head and opened her eyes. The pulsating lights made Margo's every movement look like it was in slow motion. Mia reached out her fingers to wipe a smear of lipstick from Margo's mouth; she pulled back her hand when the whiff caught her off guard.

The red color wasn't lipstick. It was blood. Mia stopped dancing and looked at her in confusion.

"Oh my god, you need to try this delicious little creature," Margo shouted as she grasped Mia's hand and began to pull her through the crowd. They stopped at a recess in the wall, where Kris was standing with a black-haired woman who looked to be in her early twenties. A second woman was standing next to them with a blank expression on her face. Sensing their presence, Kris lifted her head to reveal her black eyes and fangs. Mia staggered back a step and looked around to see if anyone was watching.

"Chill out," Kris yelled over the music at Mia. "It's fine to have some fun every once in a while!"

"I thought we didn't kill humans," she replied.

"Who said anything about killing? A little sip doesn't hurt them," Margo assured her. "They took Molly, and Kris put them under a Veil so we could sample it." The woman with the blank face stepped forward.

"I'm Carly," she said, grabbing Mia's hands. "You look so nice." Margo swept Carly's hair aside to reveal two small puncture wounds just above her delicate gold necklace.

"Try her," Margo urged. "She's fun and tasty." Mia stepped forward uncertainly, and Margo held up her hand in warning. "Just a pull or two, or you'll hurt her."

Mia put her arms around Carly and held her, feeling uncomfortable at what seemed like an intimate moment. The woman closed her eyes and swayed as Mia closed her mouth around the tiny holes in her neck. Carly's blood was different than any of the other blood she'd already drunk. It was almost sweet, as if the rich liquid had been mixed with gummy bears. Mia could feel herself pulling deeply on the vein; in her ecstasy, she couldn't stop herself.

"That's enough," Margo said, placing her hand on Mia's. When she didn't respond, Margo brought Mia's hand to her mouth and bit into the soft flesh between her thumb and pointer finger. The bite didn't hurt, but it was enough to startle Mia into releasing her grip on Carly.

"Hey!" Mia protested.

"She's going to pass out if you take any more," Margo told her. Blood was seeping out of the wound on Mia's hand, and Margo held it up to Carly, who was deathly pale and swaying. "Lick this," she ordered. The woman obeyed, and almost immediately, the color returned to her face, and she smiled.

Mia was startled. "Is she going to turn into a vampire now?"

"No. Newbie blood only heals, remember?" Margo reminded Mia. "You try it."

The small wound had already closed, but Mia lifted her hand to her mouth and licked the remaining blood. It tasted like freshly salted warm pretzels. "Oh wow," Mia said, her eyes widening. "Is everyone's blood different?"

In response, Margo bit the side of her own hand and held it to Mia's mouth. Mia didn't hesitate as she collected a tiny drop on her tongue. The blood was rich and oaky. "You taste like an expensive red wine," she told Margo, who laughed. Mia shook her head violently and pulled back from the moment, realizing at once that she was in a club randomly swapping blood. Why wasn't this disgusting to her? Or at least weird?

"That's me, an old Bordeaux aged since 1829," Margo yelled over the music, bringing her back.

"It was a very good year," Mia replied drunkenly as the effects of the Molly-laced blood began to take effect. It was difficult to picture Margo alive at that time. She pictured the poofy dress Margo wore in her portrait and thought of the things she must have seen: the World Wars, the Great Depression, the Swinging Sixties, Watergate. Mia's head was spinning, and her thoughts were turning into jumbled nonsense, but she felt invigorated and strong. She realized that Carly and the black-haired woman had left, and Kris and Margo were dancing against each other in front of her, lost in their own world. Clubgoers brushed by them on their way to the bar or to find a private nook.

Feeling euphoric, Mia wanted to reach out and touch the bodies of everyone who moved around her. She wanted to shout her secret that she'd got to hit the reset button and been given this wild opportunity to have a whole new life, start again, be anyone she wanted. At that moment, she found peace. She was excited to realize that everything was as she wanted it. And ironically, it was because of her death that she was finally living—a living dead girl.

Her thoughts were broken by the undeniable call of nature. Looking over the crowd, she saw the restroom sign in the flickering light, so she moved through the mass of dancers. Just as she broke out of the crowd, she saw it: a familiar flash of red hair. Elenora wore a black slip, her hair piled on top of her head in an elaborate style. Mia glanced back through the crowd at Margo and Kris, unsure of what to do. She wanted to confront the woman, ask her to explain what had happened earlier with Gary. She only hesitated another moment before she spun and followed the head of Sutton Family at a distance.

Elenora was following someone herself: a tall man and two young women. Mia's heart skipped a beat when she saw that they were Carly and her friend. Adrenaline coursed through her veins, dulling the effects of the Molly. The group was headed down a dark hallway and then through a doorway into another area of the club. Mia waited as they all entered, then poked her head around the doorframe. It was a room full of smoke and dark silhouettes. She caught a glimpse of red hair and quickly slipped between the smokers to catch up with the woman.

Mia watched as Elenora and the people she was following exited the smoky room through a door in the back wall. She opened the door a few inches to see that it led to a dank, filthy stairwell. The floor was littered with cigarette butts, drug paraphernalia, one discarded black heel, and empty red cups. It reeked of urine, and Mia cursed her heightened sense of smell as she covered her nose with her hand. Grimacing, she removed her heels and held them in one hand. She crept down the stairs barefoot, trying to avoid the worst of the mess, and listened for any indication that Elenora knew she was being followed.

The steps terminated at the basement level; all signs of the party were long gone. Only the rhythmic thumping of music penetrated the walls in an unsettling manner. The floor was damp from a leaking pipe that dripped water in an annoyingly steady beat. Mia peered into the darkness and concentrated on her hearing; there were quiet voices coming from the other side of the basement. She followed them until she arrived at a hallway with storage off to either side. She took her steps slowly, and toward the end of the hall, she saw a faint light spilling from one of the doorways. Mia held her breath and peeked in as much as she dared.

The two women were lit up by the light of a cell phone Elenora was holding. Mia could only make out the silhouette of the man's shape. He clutched the black-haired woman's face to his arm, which dripped with blood. The woman drank eagerly as she stared trancelike into the phone. Carly stood motionless; blood was smeared across her lips and chin.

"That's enough," Elenora said. Releasing the woman, the man stepped back from the circle of light and melted into the darkness. Elenora took a step forward. One hand whipped out so quickly that Mia barely saw the movement, but she did see what happened next. Red lines appeared on the necks of Carly and the other woman, blood spilling out as they collapsed to the ground. Mia suppressed a gasp, then shot back against the wall with her hands pressed tightly over her mouth.

"Put them in the closet," Elenora commanded. "We'll deal with them in the morning." The man didn't say a thing. Mia desperately looked for a place to hide. Glimpsing a mass of pipes in the opposite room, she ducked through the doorway and squeezed herself into a corner. She could hear the man shuffling as he dragged the women's bodies.

"Have you heard from the Darwrites?" she heard Elenora ask.

"Not yet."

The name sounded familiar, and Mia only had to focus for a moment before she realized why she knew the name. The Darwrites were one of the oldest, richest families in

America. What could Elenora possibly have to do with them?

"Let me know when you do. And clean this up." Elenora's shoes echoed as she made her way back down the hall. Mia heard a sweeping sound as the man cleaned the floor before he too left the basement. She waited a few more minutes just in case, but they were gone. As Mia's fear subsided, the booze and drugs began to take over once more. She stumbled down the hallway and then up the stairs, keeping a lookout in case Elenora was lying in wait. Once she'd weaved through the smokers, Mia rushed back to the main dance floor and frantically looked around for Margo and Kris. Spotting them dancing with a group of men, she pushed her way into the circle and dragged them both to a secluded corner.

"What the hell?" Kris protested, ripping her arm out of Mia's grasp.

Mia pushed her hair off her face. "Elenora is here. She and some guy took Carly and that other woman to the basement."

"Why were you in the basement?"

"I followed them," Mia said impatiently.

Kris's eyebrows shot up in surprise. "This isn't really Elenora's scene." She looked over the crowd.

Margo opened her compact and started to touch up her makeup. "Good for her, though. She could use some fun."

Mia shook her head violently. "No, that wasn't it at all. She had them drink from the guy's arm, and then she slit their throats."

Margo's compact snapped shut with a loud sound.

"Wait, what?" Kris said, shaking her head in bewilderment.

Mia hurriedly explained. When she finished, Margo didn't say a word; she just turned and marched down the hallway. Mia took over when they reached the smoky room—she led them down the stairs and into the lower level. Everything was as dark and quiet as it had been earlier.

"Elenora told him to put them in the closet," Mia said. "They must be somewhere down here."

The women searched the basement, but there was no sign of the two humans. When they reached the room at the end of the hall, a faint odor of blood lingered in the air. Kris pulled out her cell phone and flashed it around. Mia looked at the ground. There was a drain on the floor, which had been washed clean.

"Are you sure of what you saw?" Margo asked with concern. "You said you've never done drugs before."

Mia shook her head as Kris knelt by the drain. "I don't think it was a hallucination."

"Wait a minute," Kris said as she picked up something that was tangled in the grate. She held up a gold chain with a simple heart charm on it. "Carly was wearing this."

Margo's eyes widened as she reached out for the necklace. "Do you know what this means?" she said in a low voice.

"That Elenora is the crazy bitch I've always secretly thought she was," Kris replied grimly.

"If she killed them and took them—" Margo broke off.

"She could be the one making and killing vampires. But it's impossible. Elenora would be the last person to do that."

There was silence as the three women contemplated the implications of such a thing. Mia could feel in the air that they just didn't believe her.

"Shit," Kris said, rubbing her forehead. "I'm drunk, and I want to get more drunk. Can we just throw this on the back burner and tell Eli tomorrow? This is supposed to be Mia's night."

Margo grabbed Mia's hand. "I agree."

Mia was about to protest, but she stopped herself. She was new to this world. Who was she to tell them what to do? Besides, part of her wanted to forget about Elenora and keep having fun. That seemed messed up. Was this a vampire thing, too? She knew vampire time moved differently, but this felt important.

The women made their way back to the dance floor. "Ah, there you are!" Oscar shouted, grabbing them and hauling them over to a booth where Toby, Izzy, and Gianna were already sitting.

Toby held a giant bottle of Tito's up in the air. "Bottle service, bitches!"

CHAPTER THIRTEEN

The rest of the night was a whirlwind. From body shots to a buffet of secret biting, Mia felt the opposite of dead. The memories of what she'd seen in the basement faded into the back of her mind. Toby taught her how to take a shot of tequila, salt and all. She'd never had so much fun. All night Mia had been intensely aware of the strange connection building between her and Margo. Every time they danced, Mia wanted to reach out and touch the other woman, but she never managed to work up the courage. Mia just watched these people that she could consider choosing for her new Family, her forever Family. Tears flooded her eyes. Not once had she felt a connection with anyone like she did these people. In her entire human life, she had never really had a friend. Even though she'd only met the Bellamys a few hours ago, they completely accepted her. Mia felt anything but hollow; she had never felt so full.

//////

Three in the morning hit, the music died, the lights came on, and the voice over the loudspeaker told everyone to clear out. Oscar again said he was going to walk. Izzy chased after him, running at an embarrassingly slow pace for a vampire.

"Is Gianna okay?" Mia asked drunkenly as she fell into the back of the car with Kris and Margo. They hadn't seen her for the past two hours.

Kris let out a belly laugh. "She's in love."

"Gianna hasn't left Cedar Hollow in six years," Margo said, shaking her head. "She has a soul mate here."

Toby fell into the front passenger seat. "Nope, it's like Bella and Edward, but reversed."

Mia's eyes were huge. "He's *human*?" she shrieked as Margo pulled onto the street. "Is that even allowed?"

"Yep, and they have no idea that Gianna's a vamp," Toby coolly replied.

They were back at Noir House in no time, and everyone piled out of the cars. The silence of the house after having their ears blasted with loud music all night was deafening. They climbed the steps to the second floor and then split up, heading for their rooms. Mia stripped off her sweaty mesh dress and relaxed in a silky robe, enjoying the lasting effects of the night while Margo used the bathroom. When she was done, Mia took a brief shower to wash off the sweat, alcohol, and blood before falling into bed. The covers flew around her, and she pulled them over her head, taking in the smell of the champagne-scented body wash on her skin.

The down duvet felt like a cloud. Mia shut her eyes and pictured Margo's dancing body in her mind.

A small clicking noise came from the connecting door. Mia lifted her head to see Margo peeking around the door. "Are you up for a sleepover?"

Mia sat up fast and patted the blanket beside her perhaps a bit too eagerly, and Margo stepped into the room. She was only wearing boy shorts and a white tank top. Her hair flowed loosely down over her left shoulder. She sprang onto the bed and landed on her hands and knees in front of Mia, who leaned back, trying to assess Margo's intentions.

Margo tucked her hair behind her ear and then reached out, brushing her fingers against Mia's thigh. "Is this okay?" she asked softly, her words floating through the air to surround Mia. Margo didn't even try to make eye contact with her. It was the first moment Mia saw her fierce exterior falter.

"Yes," Mia answered, tilting her face up to the other woman's. She could feel her heart pounding hard and knew Margo could hear it, too. The next thing she knew, Margo's hand met her shoulder and she pushed her down. Margo's lips were on hers. They fell heavily into the pillows, Margo's tongue moving expertly in Mia's mouth. She tasted like the plum notes of her perfume. Mia felt hands exploring her body, so she slid her own hand along the curves of Margo's hips. Her skin was buttery soft; the indentation of her lower back felt like a secret place as Mia's fingers moved slowly across it. The covers started to get trapped in strange folds as they moved across the bed, their passion starting to feel like a race.

Mia's voice sounded like a hungry kitten as Margo pulled off her nightgown. She admired the way Mia's skin glowed under the moon. She started to lightly bite the soft places: Mia's inner thighs, her hips, the spots just beneath her breasts. She made sure not to break Mia's skin, but she knew how easily she could.

Mia's hands were in Margo's hair now, pulling it softly at the roots and directing her to Mia's mouth. She needed to taste her again. She needed to feel Margo's body pressing hard into hers. The urge she felt to tear her clothes off, to bite Margo, was so overwhelming. Yes, she wanted to fuck her, but she also wanted to consume her in every way possible. This new feeling was amazing, terrifying, but the best she had ever felt.

Mia had been in bed with a few people, but nothing had ever been like this. Maybe it was the drug-laced blood, or just the blood in general, but she felt like she was on fire. Every inch of her body was tingling, and she sighed between their kisses.

Margo pulled away. "Is something wrong?" she asked worriedly.

"Not at all," Mia replied dreamily. "I feel amazing." She pulled Margo back onto her, loving the woman's weight on top of her.

"I know Kris said I'm a flirt," Margo murmured into Mia's hair, "but not with you. I haven't felt like this in a long time." She kissed Mia's neck passionately. "I don't know what it is about you, but I feel like I know you. You remind me of someone."

Mia cupped Margo's face in her hand and saw a sad look cross over it. She lifted her head and kissed Margo, the sensation like fireworks. After a minute, she pulled away, panting. "Is this a vampire thing?"

"Do you like it?" Margo bit softly into Mia's shoulder, licking up the side of her neck as she pulled away.

"Yes."

"I think it's just an us thing."

Margo rolled off Mia and lay on the bed facing her, both women on their side looking into each other's eyes in the dim light of the room. She traced Mia's face with her fingertips.

Mia wondered why Margo had stopped kissing her. "Am I bad at this?" she asked anxiously.

Margo laughed. "No, not at all." She stroked Mia's hair. "I had this feeling once before, a long time ago. I want to tell you about it before we go any further."

Mia put a comforting hand on Margo's arm and waited for her to continue. "It was when I was alive," she said. "The last time I felt this way about someone was the reason I died." She paused a moment, searching for the right words. "As I said before, I was the daughter of a powerful man who betrothed me to a man I'd never met, the intention being to join our two families." Mia nodded, recalling the story. "My father wasn't just rich; he was a king. I was his only child. My mother passed away at my birth. My life was not my own. I was essentially my father's property, to be wed to whomever he desired. I had turned down more than a dozen offers of marriage, and he had grown tired of my 'maidenly shyness,' as he referred to it.

"I had no interest in the marriage for two reasons: not only was that man much older, but for the past several years, I had been in love with one of the castle hands, Emma. She was a peasant who worked in the kitchen, but I didn't care. I loved her. Most of the staff knew something was going on between us, and she had received threats to both her livelihood and her life for being with another woman." Margo let out a long breath before continuing. "She had begged me for a year to tell my father; she told me that if he loved me that he would understand and protect us. But she didn't know him like I did."

Mia heard Margo swallow, and she reached out a hand and touched her cheek. "You don't need to tell me if you don't want to."

Margo took Mia's hand in hers. "It feels easy now, but it might not later." Mia nodded. "I told her we could stay together in secret even after I was married. I promised her I would promote her to my lady's maid once I had charge of my own household, but she wouldn't have it. The day before the wedding, she went to my father in private and told him about us." A single tear fell from Margo's eye. She took a deep steady breath and swallowed hard. "He had her executed on the spot." Margo paused and the silence in the room was too loud. Mia grabbed Margo's other hand. "It wasn't until he called me out to see her body that I realized not only did I love her unconditionally, but that she was also my soul mate. And it was her love for me that ultimately killed her."

Mia pulled Margo into her body, feeling the wetness of tears pooling on her shoulder as Margo continued. "I didn't know Eli was a vampire then; my father had hired him to work with the horses. He knew of Emma and me and had been one of our allies. When I told him I couldn't live without her, he told me he could help, but only if I was sure. I said I was. I don't know why I didn't think he was insane when he showed up to my room after midnight and handed me a chalice, instructing me to drink it before I carried out my plan. But I trusted him, so I drank the mixture, and then I jumped. I honestly thought he understood I needed to die to be with her. That his potion would make my death painless."

Mia kissed Margo's forehead as the other woman sobbed. "The last time I felt like this was hundreds of years ago when I kissed Emma that morning. You have the same eyes. I have taken many lovers over the years, but it has never felt like this. I don't want to scare you; this is all moving so fast." Margo placed her hand on Mia's face and used her thumb to wipe away a tear.

"I have never really felt like this, either. If I'm being honest, when I see you, I don't know how to act." Mia laughed away the tears. "There is so much heartache in this Family," she whispered, her tone changing.

The night was long, and the two talked about their lives back and forth until the first light started to shine. Mia didn't even remember their final words, as somewhere between caresses and kisses, she fell fast asleep.

CHAPTER FOURTEEN

The light of the midmorning sun pouring into the room turned the insides of Mia's eyelids pink. She had expected to wake with a horrible hangover, but she felt perfectly refreshed. According to the clock, she had only slept for about five hours, but she felt like she'd had the best night's sleep in her life. She spread her hands over the high thread count sheets searching for Margo, but she felt only coolness. Sitting up, she looked to the bathroom door; it was open, and so was Margo's door beyond. Swinging her legs out of bed, Mia tiptoed into the bathroom, hoping the whole night hadn't been a dream. She peeked into Margo's room; it was almost a match to hers, but it sat empty.

Mia thought back to their night together and went over in her mind what she could have done wrong, but she could think of nothing. Perhaps Margo had just wanted to let her sleep. Looking at herself in the mirror of the bathroom, she observed her tousled black locks and the silky forest green nightgown that clung to her hips.

She brushed her teeth and sat at the vanity in her room, trying to replicate the brushstrokes Margo had used on her hair the night before. It didn't look quite right, but her hair bounced neatly enough. She opted for a lighter pink look when applying her makeup, and she delighted in how beautifully the highlighter shined on her cheekbones.

She giggled at herself in the mirror. She felt different; the cloudiness of the day before was gone. When she caught a glimpse of her family's photo, a stinging pain hit her chest, but she knew now that she no longer belonged to the Adairs. She was just Mia now. At least until she picked a new Family. She ran their names over in her head. *Mia Sutton. Mia Bellamy.* Both sounded equally strange.

The door to the closet revealed the mess Toby had made the night before. Mia stepped in and pushed through the clothing, searching for something casual that would impress Margo. The first item she chose was a black miniskirt, and for the top, a beige-and-pink blouse that looked to be vintage Versace. They matched the white platform sneakers she had spotted in the shoe cupboard yesterday.

Gazing at her reflection, Mia thought she looked like she fit in with the others.

She heard a few voices as she made her way down the stairs. Her steps echoed on the marble, and the voices quieted. Mia followed the sound of chopping and found herself in the kitchen, where Eli and Gianna were preparing food.

"Good morning, water lily. Did you get some beauty rest?" Gianna winked at her as she cut a loaf of bread.

"Yes, it was super comfy." Mia waved at Eli, then gestured to the food. "What's all this?"

"We are hosting an old-fashioned barbecue," he replied with a smile as he peeled a head of iceberg lettuce. "We don't do it very often, but we thought it would be fun."

"Oh, yes. Margo said we can still eat real food."

"Yes. What's the point of living forever if you can't enjoy a nice meal? It doesn't fill us up, so be sure to have a big breakfast." He pointed at the fridge, and Mia opened it before selecting a bag of B+ blood.

"Mugs are in the second cupboard to your right," Gianna said. "We don't always drink straight from the bag. We just did that last night because you were convinced we were lying, and we didn't think you'd believe it was blood otherwise."

Mia nodded and opened the cabinet. "You're right," she admitted, selecting a large white mug. She tore open the corner of the bag with her teeth like she'd seen Oscar do at breakfast the morning before.

"Margo told me you had a great night," Eli said as she poured the blood into the mug and placed it in the microwave.

"Thirty seconds," Gianna interjected as Mia felt her face grow hot.

"Um, yeah," she replied, punching in the numbers and hitting the start button.

"She said you danced all night at the Neon Viper?"

Mia exhaled in relief. Eli might have looked like he was no more than thirty years old, but he had the air of a wise dad. She wasn't sure she wanted him to know about her sex life.

"Yes, it was incredible," she replied.

"I am glad you had a good time." Eli dumped the lettuce into a green Tupperware bowl and started slicing the tomatoes. Mia's eyes were drawn to a quick glimpse of a sparkle on the counter. Immediately she recognized the small heart charm Kris had picked up off the ground at the club. Eli swiftly followed her eyeline and snapped the heart up. Mia was about to ask the obvious question, but Eli started talking as if to change the subject. "We each get you for only twenty-four hours, so we want to make sure you get a good idea of what life at Noir House would be like if you choose us. Speaking of which, you will be heading over to the Suttons' after lunch."

"So soon?" Mia said mournfully as she removed the blood from the microwave and tested it with a finger. She greedily licked her lips before sipping the mug's contents.

"I wish we had more time, but we do not want you to get too comfortable in one Family before you meet the other. We get just enough time to show you the bells and whistles."

Mia took another swig from the mug. "Do either of you know where Margo is?" she asked casually. Her desire for Margo was stronger than the desire to get answers about the drama of last night.

Gianna shut the fridge door and set some raw meat on the counter. "She just had to run into town with Kris on an errand. They'll be back soon."

Mia drained her mug and rinsed it in the sink, feeling satisfied with her meal but disappointed that Margo wasn't around. At least she knew for sure that Margo's absence had nothing to do with last night. Or so she hoped.

"Is there anything I can help with?"

Gianna pushed a stack of plates toward Mia before gesturing to double doors that led to the backyard. "Take these outside. Talli will show you where they go."

Scooping up the plates, Mia stepped outside feeling strange doing something so normal. Towering hedges and rosebushes surrounded the backyard, and the lawn was immaculately manicured. She spotted Talli sitting at an immense picnic table beneath a canopy, a book in her hands. Her hair was twisted up in a clip, and she seemed oblivious to her surroundings. Mia started toward her.

"Hello, Mia." Talli didn't even look up from her book. Mia didn't respond until she put the dishes down across from Talli.

"Good morning, Talli. Did you have a good night?"

"Yes. You did, too."

Mia gaped at her. "Can you—can you See that?"

Talli expressionlessly turned a page. "No. My room is across the hall from yours. The walls are paper thin." Mia couldn't help it; she felt fire pooling in her cheeks. A smile twitched at the corners of Talli's lips.

"You know that I can See." Talli finally looked up, closing her book and setting it on her lap. "What else do you know about me, Mia?"

Mia looked at her awkwardly. She figured that Talli already knew, but she said the words anyway. "Toby told me your story last night. I'm so sorry that happened to you."

Talli nodded her head and smiled at the ground. "Then you know that aside from my Gift of Sight, I just—*know* things." Mia nodded. "I am going to tell you something I would like you to keep to yourself." The world got quiet around them as Talli leaned in and motioned Mia to come closer. "You and Margo knew each other in another life," she said softly. "You see, Mia, most of the people we know in our life will be the same people we know in the next. Do you understand what I mean?"

"Reincarnation? But I thought vampires don't have souls."

Talli shook her head. "No, but humans do. I think some of that transfers to us when we become vampires, even if it's not a true soul. When you woke up and made eye contact with Margo, I saw the same spark pass between you that I see in humans. But I have to be honest; I don't think it would ever work. Call it the curse of the universe. You're meant for something bigger than love."

Mia started shaking her head, anger rising in her chest from the boldness of the woman's words.

She was interrupted when the back door flew open, and Toby bounded out. "Mimosas!" He placed a tray of champagne glasses on the picnic table. "What did I miss?"

Mia looked to Talli, but the woman had opened her book and was reading again. "Talli was just telling me where to put these plates." She took a glass from the tray and hugged Toby, but she couldn't stop thinking about what the woman had told her.

//////

Conversation flowed freely around the table as the Bellamys helped themselves to burgers, hot dogs, and salad. Mia saw that they used blood instead of ketchup and brought out a tray of Bloody Marys made with real blood after the mimosas ran dry.

Eli was wearing an apron with the words *Bite Me*. When he saw Mia raise an eyebrow, he grinned and shrugged. "It was a present from Kris," he explained.

Unfortunately, Margo and Kris weren't back from their errand yet, but the rest of the Family was enjoying the day. Eli was flipping another round of burgers when Alexander pushed a red wheelchair around the corner of the house. An old woman sat in the chair, her hair white and her skin shriveled like a prune. Eli put down his spatula, wiped his hands on his apron, and rushed to the chair's occupant.

"Thea, my love, how are you?" He bowed to the old woman and kissed her hand. Mia looked back at her plate and took a sip from her Bloody Mary, overwhelmed at the thought of meeting the matriarch whose light now resided in her body.

"Oh, you sit down, Eli." The woman held out an umbrella as if she was going to take a swipe at him, but she did it with a smile on her face. Alexander pushed his mother into the open space beside Mia before turning toward the house.

"Are you not joining us for lunch?" Gianna teased. Alexander looked across the group at Izzy and shook his head. Gianna rolled her eyes as the woman surreptitiously put down her plate and slipped into the house behind Alexander.

"Hello," Mia said to Thea as the woman adjusted the brakes on her chair.

"Hello, love," Thea replied. "You're just as I pictured you." Mia didn't know what she had expected, but the warmth from the woman seeped into her. "My Talli told me so much about you." Thea looked down the table at Talli, who was sitting silently watching. "Ah, I wish I could have met you when I was younger." Thea let out a loud laugh that ended in a harsh, raspy cough. The table fell silent for a moment before resuming its chatter. "I was a strong fifty-seven for nearly four centuries, you know." Mia turned her head and looked into the foggy eyes of the Family matriarch. "About twenty-five years ago, I started to age like any human."

The table quieted again. Thea waved her hand. "Oh, for Pete's sake. All of you stop. Taking care of your shenanigans for years has tired me out." Laughter drifted softly around the table as the Bellamys once again resumed their conversations and games. Thea fixed Mia with a serious look. "My dear, has your spirit-seeing Gift come back?"

Mia rubbed her hands together and wondered how much the woman could know. "No. I don't feel much different when it comes to that."

Thea pursed her lips. "Give me your hand, dear." Mia placed her right hand in Thea's open palm. Instead of looking at it, Thea held it and closed her eyes. A moment later, she flinched and opened her eyes. "That's the problem right there." She pointed to Mia's dad's wedding band on the opposite hand.

Mia inhaled sharply. "What?" She looked at the ring.

"Let me see that ring," Thea demanded. Mia reluctantly pulled the ring from her finger and gave it to the woman; pangs of fear rattled her body that the woman might take it from her. "Where did you get this?"

"It's my father's wedding band. My mom gave it to me after he passed away."

Thea ignored her and held the ring up to the sun, running her pointer finger around the inside of the band. "Do you know what this is?" She leaned toward Mia and held the band at an angle so that they could both see the ring's interior. Inside was the black line that ran the entire circumference of the band. "This here is a ring of obsidian crystal." Mia saw the familiar line, but she didn't know what Thea was implying. "Back in the fourteenth century, those with Gifts made these kinds of rings to dampen their powers when they were around common folk, so they didn't get accused of being witches. Where did your father get this ring?"

"My father's family owned it for generations."

Thea appraised her carefully. "No wonder. Your Gift has been passed down through your paternal line. I can feel it in you, Mia; you're going to be something special." Mia looked down at the ring in her hand.

"Why didn't my father ever tell me?"

"Gifts sometimes skip a few generations. Or he may have suppressed them as a child instead of embracing them like you did."

Mia stared at the ring in her palm for a few moments, then asked the matriarch the question that no one else had yet answered. "Is this why I was turned?"

Thea took Mia's other hand and glanced at the chattering group before whispering, "No, but we will discuss that soon." She patted Mia's hand. "Put that ring somewhere safe, and your Gift should return quickly." Mia sat for a moment, tracing the edge of the ring. Thea made a shooing motion. "What are you waiting for?"

Mia stood quickly and walked back into the house. The

inside was cold and silent. Her shoes made soft sounds as she made her way up the stairs to her room. She stood in front of the jewelry box and thoughtfully rolled the ring between her thumb and pointer finger. She wasn't sure if she was ready to see ghosts again, to hear the disembodied voices in the night, but she could always put the ring back on if she felt overwhelmed. Opening a small compartment, Mia kissed her father's ring and placed it inside. Closing the jewelry box, she became aware of Margo and Kris entering her room.

"Mia!" Margo exclaimed before planting a quick kiss on her lips. She smelled exotic. "I'm glad you're here."

"I was afraid you wouldn't be back before I left," Mia said happily, trying to let the last moment's feelings fall away.

Kris glanced from one to the other. "I'll meet you guys outside." She turned and headed back down the hall.

Margo gave her friend a wave and then spun to Mia. "I was hoping to be back earlier, but it took a little longer than I'd hoped." She looked a bit frazzled.

"What is it?" Mia bit back a smile. She was starting to enjoy how adorable Margo looked when she was overwhelmed.

"I wanted to get you something. It seemed like such a good idea when I was buying it, but now I think it might weird you out."

"I don't think anything could weird me out more than I already am." Mia laughed.

Margo let out a heavy breath. "Okay. Turn around and shut your eyes." Mia followed her direction, spinning and catching her reflection in the vanity mirror before closing her eyelids. She heard Margo rustling in a bag, and the next thing she was aware of was the shadows cast by Margo's arms as they lifted over her head, then the cool feeling of dainty metal touching her skin. "Open your eyes," Margo whispered into Mia's ear.

Mia opened her eyes and looked in the mirror, seeing the flash of the gold necklace. The word *Yours* was written in a simple cursive font. A grin spread across her face, and she turned to Margo. "What's this for?"

Margo had a tear in her eye. "I know you have to leave today, and I don't want you to forget about me." Margo pulled down the top of her blouse; a perfect replica of the same necklace sat on her chest. "I had to take Kris with me so she could put a Veil on the jeweler. I wanted to make sure they'd be finished before you left." Redness colored Margo's cheeks. "I know it's a bit much."

It all felt so surreal to Mia, and she flung her arms around Margo's neck. "No, it's perfect." Talli's words swirled in her mind as she kissed the other woman. She wasn't sure what they meant, but right now, she didn't care.

Margo broke the kiss. "I haven't felt so alive in centuries. I realized last night that I haven't been okay for a long time. But maybe—maybe now I will be. Even if we are just friends, I think I needed your energy around me."

Mia kissed her again. She had spent too much time not living, but now she was ready to jump into this with both feet. Even thinking that way scared her, but Margo was here, *right here*, connecting with her in a way that she never had before with anyone. "I don't want to leave," she murmured before leaning in for another kiss.

Margo laughed and slid her hand down Mia's arm. "Time will fly."

CHAPTER FIFTEEN

Mia went back outside as everyone was clearing the table.

"Oy, Mia! Over here." Alexander was wheeling Thea around the corner of the house. He beckoned to her. Mia swallowed.

"Alexander will take you to the Suttons'," Eli said, coming up next to her. Mia didn't feel ready to leave the house and all her beautiful new friends.

"Do you need anything?" Margo asked.

Mia held up her Gucci bag and nodded. She had packed her copy of *The Virgin Suicides* but had left the photo of the Adairs on the nightstand and her father's ring in the jewelry box for safekeeping. Margo had told her that she would have a fully furnished room and a new wardrobe at the Bruce Hotel.

"I will miss you, babe," Gianna called out. "Don't forget to choose us."

Toby let out a barking laugh.

Mia waved and then reluctantly followed the path around the side of the house. Alexander was folding up the red wheelchair and putting it into the trunk of a silver Cadillac. The back door was open, and Mia slid in next to Thea. The matriarch struggled to fasten her seat belt, so Mia reached out and clasped it for her. "Ah, you are so kind." Thea patted Mia's hand.

"Shit, I forgot my phone!" Alexander slammed the trunk and started back around the house. Thea made a hard line of eye contact with her son, and he paused as if they were sharing a wordless message before he moved on.

"I am glad I have you alone, Mia." Thea's words took her by surprise. "Has anyone told you about the dangers of your blood? And what has been happening around here?" Mia wasn't sure how to answer, so she just nodded quietly. Thea sighed. "I have always been so up and aware of things, so this whole situation has me extremely worried. We usually give a new vampire a week or more to choose a Family, but because people have been turned and then found dead, we needed to speed things up. You'll be safe soon."

Seeing Mia's confused look, Thea reached out and held her hands. "I began to lose my powers twenty-five years ago," she began, "and I knew that could only mean one thing: a new matriarch had been born. It's something that happens rarely, and it signals that the current matriarch has outlived her usefulness. It has happened with a couple Families in Europe."

Mia frowned. "What do you mean?"

"I lost a lot of my power on what we discovered was the day you came into this world," Thea explained. "The light that was my power was gone, and my abilities began to diminish. Talli used her Gift to See who could potentially become the next matriarch of the two Families. We were able to narrow it down to a few women, but when your mother published her book, it called out to Talli. As she learned more about you, she became convinced that you were the person we were looking for. When she visited the bookstore and saw you in person, she saw the light inside you, the same light that left me so many years earlier."

"I don't understand," Mia whispered, blinking her eyes.

"My dear," Thea said gently, "you are meant to be the next matriarch of the Sutton and Bellamy Families."

Mia took a sharp breath. "What does that mean for me?"

"You will take over my duties, my responsibilities. You will keep the Families safe. You will make sure they are following the rules, and you will dispose of any vampires who risk exposing us or any vampire; you will be the head of the Families." Thea patted her hand.

"I think you have the wrong person," Mia protested.

"I didn't decide this, Mia. The universe did."

"But I don't even *know* the rules yet! I don't know anything about this world. I do not feel powerful!" Mia exclaimed. "I've only been a vampire for two days; I barely know anything about them!"

"It doesn't matter how much you've learned so far," Thea replied. "We must complete the ceremony tomorrow."

"Tomorrow?" Mia felt panicked. This was too much.

"Don't you have to teach me how to do everything?" Mia felt aimlessly along the door's panel, subconsciously looking for a way out of the car.

"We need to do this as quickly as possible," Thea said firmly. "My powers are almost gone, and there is someone killing new vampires at a dramatic rate. We cannot risk losing you, and we cannot count on my abilities to last any longer. But we have arranged it so that you will receive all the instructions you need during the transfer of power."

Mia was stunned. How could this be? She was hardly qualified to lead an inventory check at the bookstore, let alone all vampires. She finally asked the question she'd been trying to answer for the last two days. "Did you make me crash?"

"No," Thea replied immediately and sharply. "We knew your life cycle was coming to a preordained end; Talli saw that. Or, at least, she had a general idea of when and where it would happen. The Families kept an eye on you for months. They knew that as my strength dwindled, the time was growing near."

"That's why you followed me. That's why Cordelia turned me," Mia said quietly.

"She may have plunged the needle into your heart, but Cordelia didn't turn you," Thea said quietly. "We all did. Blood from every member of the Families was in that vial."

Mia looked down as she tried to absorb what Thea was telling her.

"Mia," Thea said sternly. "You will have to be the one to put an end to the vampire who has been turning humans without permission. We do not take life for our own purposes; that is one of the strictest rules we have, and for good reason." Mia thought back to Talli's heart-wrenching story. "And I worry that it's someone in one of the Families."

Mia bit her lip as she pictured Elenora at the Neon Viper. She was already sure that the red-haired woman was responsible. "Could it be Elenora?" she asked quietly.

"God, no!" Thea jerked her head back as if Mia had slapped her. "A lot of people don't like her for what she did, but that was a long time ago." Mia looked at Thea, asking the question with her eyes. "This stays between you and me?" Thea's eyes burrowed into Mia's. She nodded. "Eli and Elenora parted ways in 1801 after she had an affair with another man. When Eli found out, he was devastated. He disappeared, and we had no idea where he was for more than a year. Elenora was also heartbroken. She had quickly realized her mistake, and she wanted Eli back.

"We finally tracked him down to a small village in Ireland after hearing reports of people waking up with puncture wounds on their bodies. He had seemingly fallen in love with a widowed pregnant woman. Not only that, but she was also a redhead." Mia squinted her eyes, trying to assess which direction the story might take. "Elenora had always wanted a child. She had become pregnant the last year of her human life, but she lost it in the womb because of the drought. Losing her child devastated her, and Eli says she was never the same after. Vampires cannot have children, so she and Eli never became parents.

"Elenora watched Eli and the woman from afar. She saw how he cared for her replacement, and she hated it. She felt she was a woman scorned. One day while Eli was out in the fields, Elenora did something unthinkable."

Mia was digging her nails deeply into the soft whites of her palms. "Elenora killed her, didn't she?"

"Not only did she kill the woman, she ripped her to pieces so that Eli would not be able to turn her."

Horrified, Mia's hands flew to her mouth. She pictured Eli coming home to find his love slaughtered, with no hope for her or the baby. Elenora was a monster.

"Eli buried the woman and packed up his things, but before he could, Elenora showed up pretending as if she had just found him. He knew immediately that she was the one responsible for the murders. He never really spoke to her again. She spent years trying to repent for what she did; she was a young vampire who had suffered horribly as a human, and her emotions were heightened. She still cries about it to this day. She learned lessons from what she did." Thea shook her head sadly. "Eli was broken, but after that, he started to build Bellamy Family, and she the Suttons."

"Found it!" Mia looked toward the window and saw Alexander holding an out-of-date flip phone in the air triumphantly. The car shook as he threw himself into the driver's seat. "I don't know how it even got into the refrigerator," he said, shaking his head in disbelief.

"That is strange," Thea replied, winking at Mia, who smiled. She was growing to like this old woman who seemed to have more tricks up her sleeve than just her vampire powers.

Alexander put the car into Drive and slowly maneuvered the Cadillac through the black gates. Becoming serious again, Mia voiced an observation. "So many of the Family members have such sad stories."

Thea patted Mia's thigh. "What is life if it isn't full of experiences worthy of being on a movie screen?"

///////

Most of the ride was silent, and Mia gazed out the window as they drove. The only sounds were the small coughs that Thea let out as Alexander's cigarette smoke filled the back seat.

She finally turned to Mia. "We will meet at a safe place tomorrow at dusk—just us, Elenora, and Eli." She paused as she unzipped the top of her lavender jacket and pulled something out. Around her neck hung a pendant, a simple purple stone wrapped in silver wire. "Last night, Elenora, Talli, and Cordelia helped me put the last of my energy into this. When you put it around your neck, all of that energy will transfer to you, and you will be the new matriarch of the Sutton and Bellamy Families. And then, I shall die."

Startled, Mia glanced at Alexander. He was looking back at her in the rearview mirror. "It's okay; I've had a long time to say goodbye to the old witch." She saw the smile pull at his cheeks, but that didn't take away the tear in his eye.

Mia shook her head. It all felt like such a huge responsibility. "I still don't understand what I'm supposed to do."

"All my wisdom and teachings will flow into you; all will feel like lessons you have already learned." The car started to slow, and Mia looked out the window, a heavy knot in her stomach. They were slowly climbing the long drive to the top of the hill where the Bruce Hotel was located.

It was the most massive building Mia had ever seen; the brown brick structure was castle-like. It was comprised of the main building and two rounded wings that rose up like turrets. A three-level balcony stretched along the entire front of the hotel. The roof was crisscrossed with numerous peaks, and dozens of chimneys soared into the sky.

Alexander drew the Cadillac into the crescent drive and stopped in front of wide stone steps. Cordelia and the boy called Luca were standing at the top of the stairs with thrilled faces. They ran eagerly down to the car as a bellboy opened Mia's door.

"Hello, Ms. Adair," he said, holding out his hand to help her from the car. "Welcome to the Bruce Hotel." Mia stepped out of the car, only to be immediately enveloped in Cordelia's embrace.

"Are you okay?" she asked worriedly. Her tone set Mia on edge, but when she pulled away, Cordelia's familiar face calmed her. Luca stood behind her, a hand on his neck.

"It's good to see you again," he said with a shy smile so white that it practically glowed. She stuck out a hand to shake his.

"It's nice to see you, too." Her small hand almost got lost in his. She turned back to Thea to say goodbye in time to see her pass Cordelia a briefcase. Cordelia gave the old woman's cheek a kiss, and Mia noticed that her eyes were watering.

Thea looked at Mia. "I will see you tomorrow," she said as the car pulled away.

Cordelia grabbed Mia's hand. "Come on! We'll show you around!"

CHAPTER SIXTEEN

Mia entered the Bruce Hotel through the thick, wide oak doors. The interior of the hotel was stunning, and she felt as if she had fallen back into a time when all things were classically beautiful. The floor was inlaid marble, the walls were a dark oak paneling, and the farthest wall had floor-to-ceiling windows that overlooked the grounds and the forest beyond. Lights hung from black metal chains. A baby grand piano sat in one corner, and a massive stone fireplace stood in the middle of the room. Though it was unlit, the scent of a fresh fire filled the air. An elevator with a cage gate sat empty waiting for guests, the floor numbers above it shining in gold.

Cordelia led them past the front desk, where a friendly brunette in a neat uniform stood assisting guests. "We rent the right wing of the hotel," she explained, ignoring the ornately carved main staircase and heading down a hallway. With her blue hair and distressed jeans, she didn't fit in with the hotel's old-world elegance. She stopped at another double-wide oak door and removed a heavy skeleton key from her pocket before sliding it into the metal lock. With a clink, the door unlocked.

"Welcome to the Sutton Family," Cordelia said as the door swung open into a great room.

Mia couldn't help but gasp. The spacious room was nearly identical to the main lobby, but the curved windows looked over a different garden and lawn. Another fireplace stood in the center, surrounded by armchairs, couches, and various tables. A bar stood on the left side, behind which was a swinging door that must lead to a kitchen. In front of the bar was a long table lined with enough captain's chairs to seat a small army.

On the other wall was a wooden staircase that resembled the main stairs but wasn't as wide. A balcony showed a line of doors that must lead to the living quarters. As Mia turned, she saw that the wall behind her was covered in bookshelves that held clothbound books and trinkets. Several floor lamps were placed throughout the room. The energy of the place was calming, and it almost felt like endorphins had been released in Mia's mind. Everything was gorgeous but looked delicate, and Mia had the feeling she wasn't supposed to touch anything.

"This is amazing," Mia breathed. "I love it."

Luca looked right at Mia, a goofy grin plastered on his face. She smiled back as she watched him exchange a glance with Cordelia. "What is it?"

Cordelia laughed. "We're just really excited that you're here. Honestly, we've been watching you for such a long time that this kind of feels like meeting a celebrity." The two looked so genuine that Mia felt her cheeks blush.

"Enough of this. Wait until you see your room," Cordelia squealed. She grabbed Mia's hand and bounded up the carpeted stairs, Luca close behind.

They led Mia down the upstairs hallway until they reached a room near the end. The whole way there, Mia watched Luca with interest. He seemed so introverted, but he could have been a model. His wavy hair bounced with every stride, almost as if it was permed to fall in such a perfect way. He was the kind of guy she would have been shy with in high school.

Cordelia paused at the door. "Ready?"

Curious, Mia nodded. As the door swung open, she gasped and staggered back a step, her hands to her mouth. Heat rushed to her face and tingled in her fingertips. This was impossible.

The bedroom was nearly an exact copy of her bedroom in the house she grew up in.

"Do you like it?" Luca asked anxiously.

Mia gingerly took a few steps into the room, tears gathering in her eyes. The wallpaper was the exact same as the wallpaper she had stared at every day of her life. The dresser, bed, and nightstand were almost identical to her own, and many replicas of her own possessions were placed carefully in their correct spots. She took another step and gathered the fabric of the comforter into her hand. The sage green material with pink embroidered flowers was just as she remembered. She walked over to the photo of her family, the same one the Bellamys had retrieved, and picked up the gold frame Sasha had given her for her twentieth birthday. The attention to detail was perfect. It felt kind of eerie but still beautiful.

A wave of emotion rose into her chest. "How?" was all she managed to croak.

"Luca and I visited your house a few times while you were all out," Cordelia explained. "Actually, this was all Luca's doing." Mia spun to meet the eyes of the man she had only met once, at the funeral home. "He even chose this room so the sun would rise in the same place as your old bedroom."

"You did all this?" She lifted a hand to her chest. "After I died, all I longed for was pieces of who I was." Mia didn't break her gaze. "I can't thank you enough." Her voice broke on the last syllable.

"He spent *so* many nights on eBay trying to find perfect replicas." Cordelia answered for Luca, who was blushing.

Mia shook her head and looked into Luca's eyes, trying to find the words to thank him. A warm feeling spread over her. At Noir House with the Bellamy Family, she'd had to make peace with leaving her old life behind. Everyone had made it seem like cutting ties with who she was, all the pieces that made her, would make everything easier. At this moment, it was maddening that they'd made her feel like stripping away everything from her former life was the only way she'd fit in with them. She had been in her most vulnerable moment, and they had used that to their advantage. They had shoved expensive clothing and jewelry at her; they had thrown her into her new life without even asking her how she was handling it. They just expected her to return their fake affection. She only realized this other side of her thoughts now.

Mia shook her head, suddenly confused. No, that wasn't right. She was overreacting. The Bellamys had kept her spirits high; they had given her space; they had welcomed her with open arms. And then there was Margo, who'd opened her heart to Mia. Suddenly, she realized Luca and Cordelia were staring at her as she tried to make sense of the overwhelming emotions.

"I'm sorry," she said. "I'm just so happy. Thank you so much, Luca. Never in my life have I ever been so surprised." She went forward, not knowing if he would accept a hug, but Luca's arms opened wide, and she practically fell into them. The kind embrace was the lever on the dam that held back her tears, and she started to sob. Mia felt so embarrassed. Then she felt Cordelia at her back, and a soothing feeling spread over her and seemed to pull the sadness right out.

She released Luca and wiped the tears from her cheeks. "Wow, way to bamboozle me first thing!"

Another familiar face popped into the room. "Yay! You're here!" Alyssa practically bounced into the room wearing a skimpy dress that barely covered her butt and yanked open a set of double doors. "Your wardrobe here is even better!"

Mia stepped over to examine the closet's contents: it was filled with designer clothing, handbags, and shoes, but they were more conservative than the wardrobe at Noir House. She thought back to Kris saying how strict the Suttons were and wondered how Alyssa got away with her own revealing outfits.

"Thank you, Alyssa."

The blonde woman scanned Mia's body appreciatively, assessing the outfit she had chosen that morning. "Look at you impressing me already." Mia felt accomplished somehow. "Come see everyone! We just got back, and we can't wait to see you!"

Alyssa floated out of the room, Mia following her as Luca and Cordelia shared a quiet sentence she couldn't make out.

///////

As Mia started down the staircase, she saw the other four remaining members of the Sutton Family distributed throughout the room. Miles, the soft-spoken man, was sitting on the couch. Annie was perched in an armchair across from him, flipping through a magazine, though she looked up and smiled as Mia approached. Alexander was slouched in an easy chair in front of the fireplace, and Isla was working on a jigsaw puzzle at one of the side tables.

Mia found a seat near Annie, and Luca leaned against the bar. Cordelia retrieved the briefcase Thea had given her and began handing out vials of something as Mia found a seat. "Thea said this is the last of it until Mia gets going." Cordelia pressed a vial into Mia's left hand.

"What is this?" Mia held up the glass tube for inspection. The liquid inside was gold and seemed to shimmer in the light.

"Think of it as vampire sunscreen," Cordelia replied.

Alexander laughed as he uncorked the top of his vial and threw back the liquid. "SPICY!" he yelled as he threw the empty glass into the fireplace, where it shattered.

"Oh, you piece of shit, the cleaners might cut themselves on that." Isla scowled at him. "Why can't you ever think about others?"

Alexander looked at the older woman with the pixie cut. "You are always such a refreshing ray of sunshine, Isla," he drawled sarcastically.

Mia watched as the others also consumed the contents of the vials. A few made grimacing faces. She finally uncorked her vial and hesitantly took a sip; it tasted like cinnamon and burned like vodka as it slid down her throat. "How does it work?"

Cordelia seemed eager to answer the question. "The sun doesn't kill us, but it can severely burn us and even temporarily blind us. Thea created this potion long ago to protect us. We used to only have to take this once a year, but as Thea got weaker, it became less potent. We started drinking it monthly, then weekly, and now it only lasts about four days. It's why she couldn't come to greet you when you first woke up. Doing this type of work wears her out quickly now."

"You don't really need to take yours, though, do you, Isla dear?" Alexander snorted. "You hide out inside all day waiting for the world to end."

In a flash, Isla was over Alexander, lashing out, but he was faster. As she leaned over to punch him, he stuck his foot up in the air and caught her in the abdomen. She struggled to reach him, but he just laughed. "Please just admit that you're crazy about me," he teased. Isla took one final swipe at him before muttering something in another language and stomping away. She climbed the stairs angrily, and a few moments later, Mia heard a door slam.

"Pay up, folks! That was less than fifteen minutes." No

one said a word. “You all suck. You know that, right?” Alexander stood and walked to the bar, where he grabbed a bottle of Jack Daniel’s. Mia noticed that he moved effortlessly, and his unkempt appearance would have been almost cool if he wasn’t such a prick. Yet, she had seen a more serious side of him in the Cadillac, and she wondered if his rough manner was an act. Alexander opened the outside door and left without looking back.

“Please excuse Alexander’s behavior,” Cordelia said nervously. “He’s got some issues.”

Mia nodded thoughtfully and glanced at the door Alexander had exited through.

During the next few hours, the remaining Suttons asked Mia questions about her life, and she surprisingly enjoyed the attention. The time flew quickly, and she found herself settling into this Family just as she had with the Bellamys.

Mia was in the middle of a conversation with Annie when a figure caught her eye, and she looked up. Elenora was standing at the balcony watching her. Instead of the risqué black dress she had been wearing the last time Mia saw her, she now wore a cream-colored pantsuit. A strange smile was on her face. “Welcome, Mia.” She glided down the stairs as elegantly as a dancer before taking a seat across from Mia. “Forgive my absence; I had some business to attend to. But tell us: How was your time with the Bellamy Family?”

Mia had no intention of telling this woman anything. “It was really nice,” she responded politely. Elenora nodded but did not ask her anything else.

Alyssa was filing her nails and took advantage of the lull in the conversation. “Mia, I’d like to pick your brain about being human, if that's okay? I've honestly forgotten what it's like, and that feels super strange to me."

Mia was about to reply when there was a crash and Miles fell to the floor. Annie rushed to him as Mia jumped up, afraid he was hurt. One of the windows was smashed, and the bottle of Jack Daniel's that Alexander had taken outside was spinning slowly in the gleaming shards. Mia wondered if the outburst was linked to the fact that this time tomorrow, Alexander's mother would be gone.

Annie held Miles in a tight embrace as he covered his ears and squeezed his eyes shut. She murmured to him, and his breath began to slow. Elenora was watching Mia. "Miles is what people call autistic nowadays. I saved him from some terrible people who were exploiting him." She paused. "It was the best thing I ever did. He is the smartest, kindest person I have ever met."

Miles had recovered and was back on the couch. He reached into his pocket and pulled out the oval stone Mia had seen him with at the funeral home, and as he ran his thumb over it continuously, she realized it was his comfort item. "Sorry about that," he said in a shaky voice. "I'm not a huge fan of loud noises. I also don't deal well with change, but that's difficult to avoid when you're a vampire and the world keeps changing around you." The softness that emanated from Miles was unmatched.

"I'm going to have a word with Alex," Annie said, getting up and smoothing out her skirt.

"I'll go with you." Miles stood and adjusted the glasses on his face. "I have a mind to tell him off."

"Wow, what a great introduction," Luca said as the two

went into the garden. The dark wood of the room made his blue eyes pop.

"Yeah, it really makes you want to choose us, huh?" Cordelia leaned against the back of the couch and stared at her shoes.

Mia shrugged. "Why is Alexander a Sutton, anyway? I'd have thought he would live with Thea."

"Thea prefers to keep her own company," Elenora remarked coolly. "Alexander is not technically a Sutton, but he stays with us as a favor to our matriarch. He can be a bit unpredictable and needs someone to keep an eye on him. When he lived with Izzy, places burned down." She smirked. "We are a bit more reliable than our counterparts at Noir House, Mia."

Mia started at the sound of her name.

"Would you mind accompanying me to dinner this evening? I would like to have a private word with you, discuss how we run things here in Sutton Family."

Mia looked at Cordelia, hoping she would save her from the date, but she was working on the puzzle that Isla had abandoned and didn't seem to be paying attention.

"Sure." Mia tried to keep her tone even.

Elenora flicked her sleeve back to read her watch. "It's four o'clock now. The hotel restaurant will be perfect. Chef Brandon creates the most exquisite plates."

Mia paused as Elenora took in her features like she was trying to read what was taking Mia so long to answer. The woman let out a loud laugh. "Oh, for heaven's sake! Don't look so worried. We will have some blood before we go." She motioned to Cordelia. "Bring out the good stuff."

Cordelia nodded and left for the main section of the

hotel. Luca moved over to sit next to Elenora. Mia tried not to fidget as they waited. A few minutes later, Cordelia entered, followed by the woman from the front desk.

"How can I help you, Ms. Sutton?" the woman asked cheerfully.

"Hello, Erin!" Elenora said brightly. "Please come here, dear. Luca, your assistance."

Luca glanced uneasily at Mia and stood as Erin walked briskly to him. He looked at her. "We will require some of your blood. Please stay as still as possible." Erin's face went blank as her smile dropped, and she held up her hand robotically. Cordelia handed Luca an alcohol swab, and he cleaned off her skin as Elenora pulled a cannula and a sterilized needle from her breast pocket. When he was done, she expertly slid the needle into the big vein in Erin's hand. Cordelia held out a crystal tumbler, and Elenora placed the other end of the cannula into it.

Blood flowed cleanly into the glass. When it had nearly reached the top, Luca put a gauze pad over the spot and applied pressure while Elenora removed the needle. Luca continued to press on the gauze for a few more moments before covering it with a bandage.

"Thank you, dear; you may go." Elenora waved her hand dismissively, and Erin's face broke into a smile.

"Please let me know if you need anything else!" She turned and left as if nothing had happened, closing the double doors behind her.

Cordelia handed Elenora a second tumbler and gathered up the used medical equipment, then headed toward the kitchen. Elenora poured the blood until it was even between the two glasses. "I will drink with you," she said, handing Mia a tumbler. She held up her own. "A toast!" she proclaimed. "To new beginnings."

"Mmm," Mia responded noncommittally before raising her glass, keeping her eyes on the woman.

Elenora drank first. "It tastes like Erin is back on the antipsychotics again. Seroquel makes everything so tangy." She watched intently as Mia drank.

Mia let a laugh escape her lips. What was she getting herself into?

CHAPTER SEVENTEEN

Elenora walked so delicately she practically floated down the hotel hall. They entered the lobby and passed the front desk, where Erin greeted guests, as if vampires had not just drained her blood. Mia stared uneasily at the woman, unsure of how she felt about the Suttons so casually feeding straight from humans. Even though she'd sampled Carly's blood last night, sticking a needle in the hotel staff seemed a blatant disregard of the rules; yet, it was clearly a common event. Perhaps Elenora considered herself too good for a blood bag.

In front of them was another set of magnificent double doors that marked the entrance to the restaurant. A man in a perfectly fitted black dress shirt and pants walked up briskly. "Hello, Ms. Sutton. We have your regular table ready for you."

Elenora paused, scanning the vast room, which was full of diners. "We will have a private room." It was not a request.

The maître d' nodded his head and spun on his heel. Elenora followed, with Mia trailing behind. As they passed through the main dining area, she saw that one wall was lined with windows, just like the lobby. Lacy curtains billowed in the afternoon breeze. A lonely-looking man sat at one of the tables next to the windows, staring mournfully out over the gardens. A waiter passed him without even checking to see if he needed anything. Something tugged at Mia, but before she could question the feeling, she found herself being ushered through a tapestry and into a secluded space that held a table and chairs; there was just enough room for two. Mia suddenly felt apprehensive about being alone with Elenora in this hidden room.

The maître d' handed the women two menus. Elenora did not even glance at hers, but she smiled at the man. "I will have the steak, please, rare, and with a glass of the house red."

Mia scanned the menu quickly and spotted a roasted chicken dish. She tried to match Elenora's cool manner and tone. "I'll have the chicken and the house white, please."

"Excellent choices."

The maitre d' made a slight bow before he gathered up the menus and left, and the two vampires sat in silence for a moment. Mia didn't want to be the first to speak, but she felt like there was no choice at this point. "Was there something you wanted to talk to me about?"

"Yes, Mia," Elenora replied. "I am sure you heard rumors about me from the other Family. I assure you they are only stories."

Mia frowned. "The Bellamys didn't mention you at all. Was there something in particular that you had in mind?"

"Not at all," the woman replied quickly. "There is just a bit of rivalry between the Suttons and the Bellamys. Of course, it is mostly one-sided. I have little interest in competition."

"Is this the reason you brought me to dinner?" Mia was irritated. Elenora couldn't possibly be interested in any rumors that Eli's Family would spread. It was so hard for Mia to sit and play pretend, when she knew what she'd seen. It was so hard for her to see Elenora the way the others seemed to think she was.

"Of course not," Elenora replied smoothly. "I would like you to keep an open mind during your time here. I am strict, but it is not without reason. My job is to protect my Family, not allow them to run around partying at all hours of the night."

Mia bristled. She opened her mouth to respond, but just then, the tapestry was pulled aside, and a waiter appeared with two wineglasses. He set them down and left just as silently as he'd arrived.

Once he was gone, Mia spoke. "What did you mean last night when you stopped Gary's car?" As Elenora took a sip of her wine, she tilted her head and screwed her face up as if she was trying to remember something.

"Who is Gary?" she asked nonchalantly as she set her wineglass down.

"Gary, the cabdriver who was taking me home. You showed up in the middle of the road and murdered him." Mia looked at her evenly.

Elenora shook her head slowly and looked at Mia, the corners of her lips curled up in amusement like she couldn't even picture the situation. "Mia, I have no idea what you are talking about." She took another sip from her wineglass.

Mia paused. She thought back to the moment Gary crashed through the windshield. Now she saw that memory from outside of the car, saw Elenora's arms as she threw him onto the vehicle, watched as his broken body fell to the ground before she descended upon him with a ravenous fervor. She blinked hard, and the image dissolved. Elenora was talking.

"The first night is always the hardest. You must have had a hallucination."

Mia held tightly on to her wineglass. "No. I know what I saw. I remember what happened. You murdered an innocent man and then forced me to drink his blood."

"It sounds like you had a good night and are trying to find someone to blame."

Now Mia was angry. She knew she saw Elenora that night, unless the woman had an identical twin sister who also happened to be a vampire. She shoved herself away from the table, trembling with rage.

Elenora rolled her eyes. "Don't be so dramatic; sit. I don't mean that in a bad way. All of us kill a few people in our first couple years." Elenora waved a limp hand at her as if it was no big deal. "And, Mia, there are a lot of redheads in the world. You are a new vampire; things get a bit scrambled in your mind for a while after the change. I am a friend, not a foe. Please give me a chance."

Mia found herself sinking back into her chair as her anger dissolved. She thought back to the story Thea told her in the car. That story matched the woman she'd seen the night Gary died and later that night at the club. Though Mia had planned to also confront the woman about Carly and her friend, she decided not to lay all her cards on the table.

If Elenora wanted to play with her, then fine. Game on.

"You're right," she said, trying to sound embarrassed. "I must have been seeing things." Elenora smiled and sipped her wine.

They had little else to say to each other until their dinners arrived. Elenora was delicately cutting into her steak when Mia looked at her innocently. "Why do you think someone is creating new vampires?" She lifted her eyes to Elenora and daintily placed a piece of roast chicken in her mouth.

Elenora shook her head slowly. "Did anyone tell you how powerful your blood is?"

Mia nodded. "Kris and the others told me."

"I am not a fan of that Kris." Elenora sniffed. "I wouldn't be surprised if she was behind this whole thing."

"Why do you think she would do such a thing?"

The other woman practically slammed her knife down. "Do you know what my Gift is, Mia?"

Mia tried to hide her sudden terror. She shook her head.

"I see people's true colors—literally. I read their auras, and Kris's varies between green and black. She is not someone to trust. Kris is a vampire because she had always wanted to be. She sought us out as a child, and she was born into this life with Gifts that most of us could only wish for. She could have been so powerful. But instead, she spends her days partying or off on secret ventures. She disappears for months at a time."

Mia nodded politely and cut another piece of her chicken.

"I need you to understand something, Mia. I'm sure that Eli and his Family painted me in a bad light, but every situation has two sides."

Mia had lived that truth before, and even after what she had seen Elenora do, she knew that every person had soft sides. Cordelia was the kindest person she had ever met. There was no way she would stay with Elenora if she were completely evil. Luca also seemed to have such good intentions.

"Luca is very taken with you." It was as if Elenora had heard Mia's thoughts.

"Excuse me?"

Elenora laughed as she took the last bite of her steak. "He has enjoyed following you around. Compared to the last half century, I have never seen him put so much work into anything as he did that room of yours." Something flickered across her face. "I know you had a great time with the Bellamys, but Sutton is the kind of place where someone like you can grow. We can have fun, but we also try to make the world a better place. We are connected here. If you stay, you will experience all the best that immortality has to offer."

Mia lifted her hand to her chest, where the *Yours* necklace rested hidden beneath her blouse. Sutton Family didn't have Margo.

"Do not forget, but you are about to go through a big

change. I know Thea told you about becoming the Family matriarch." Mia nodded. "A lot of power is going to flow through you tomorrow night, and I doubt Eli is going to be able to help you navigate those waters." Elenora's face relaxed, like a mother reassuring her child. Her voice was musical and lovely. Mia found herself wanting to trust her.

A warm feeling flowed through Mia. If she chose the Suttons, Elenora would take care of her and give her everything she wanted.

Don't fuck this up. The memory of Elenora's cold voice cut into her stupor, and Mia blinked. What had just happened? For a moment, she had been nearly convinced that Elenora was innocent. Had she been somehow enchanted? Could vampires cast a Veil on other vampires?

"I like power, Mia, and I think you will, too." Elenora purred as she pushed her dishes to the side of the table and leaned into the space, staring into Mia's eyes. "Do you understand me?"

Mirroring the older woman, Mia also leaned across the table. *Play her game.* "I do."

CHAPTER EIGHTEEN

Elenora didn't say a word to Mia as they walked quietly back down the hallway, but every time Mia snuck a glance at the red-haired woman, there was a confident smile plastered on her face. She seemed so sure of herself. Mia followed her silently through the door into the Suttons' wing, and when Elenora didn't seem to notice she was still there, she headed up the stairs to her room. Even though something strange was going on, she was excited to take in the space and further explore all the things that looked just like the ones that filled her old bedroom.

Turning into the doorway, she was surprised to see Cordelia sitting propped up on her bed.

"How did it go?" the blue-haired woman exclaimed, pulling herself to her knees. "Did you like Elenora?"

Mia nodded her head because after her dinner with the head of Sutton Family, she wasn't sure if anyone else was involved in the murders.

"The food was amazing," Mia said, squeezing the air with her hands as if it contained something juicy.

"We eat there a lot," Cordelia replied. "Blood is great and all, but there's nothing quite like a good tiramisu to keep things interesting." Mia nodded in agreement. "I thought we could go for a walk, and I could show you the grounds before you settle in."

Mia looked out at the garden from her bedroom window. She was eager to spend some time with Cordelia, the only person here that she had known from before this all happened. It was still so weird that it had only been two days since she had woken up in the casket. It already felt like a lifetime.

Cordelia bounced off the bed and grabbed Mia's hand as she passed her. They ran down the stairs and through the great room to the back door. A set of steps led down onto a private patio, where Alexander, Miles, and Annie sat around a firepit.

"Everything cool here?" Cordelia asked.

Miles shot a hand up in the air. "As cool as Mount Everest."

Alexander shook his head. "Speak for yourself, mate! The whisky has me warm as a Viking funeral." He held a fresh bottle up to the sky. "Want some?" His hand fell with the weight as he was obviously drunk.

"I think we're okay." Cordelia turned, but Mia hesitated. She looked at Alexander.

"You're not happy here, are you?"

"*Happy* here? Of course I'm not happy here. I'm not

happy *anywhere*. I'm almost four hundred years old, and I'm stuck with this lot; what do I have to be happy about? But we can't have any rogues running around *unsupervised* and *dangerous*."

He threw back his head and chugged from the bottle as if it contained water instead of whisky.

"Time to go." Cordelia took exaggerated steps away from the firepit, and Mia followed. She thought back on what she knew about Alexander. Could he have been Elenora's accomplice? He certainly didn't seem to have any inhibitions, and Elenora had alluded earlier that they had to put up with him. Why, if not because he knew her secret and could expose her?

Lost in thought, Mia barely noticed they were on a gravel path until the woods towered up in front of them. The dense canopy blocked out most of the light, leaving the women in the gloom.

Mia realized Cordelia had been talking. "—and this circles around, coming out near the fountain. So, what do you think of the Bruce? By the way, you can call me Cord. Everyone else does."

It was the most Mia had ever heard her talk, and she couldn't help but grin at the woman who had captivated her attention months ago. She tried to push her thoughts of Alexander and Elenora to the back of her mind.

"I do like Cord; it fits you better, I think," she said. "When I think of Cordelia, I think of *Anne of Green Gables*. Or *Buffy the Vampire Slayer*, and that particular Cordelia killed vampires." Cordelia made a face and laughed. "Cord sounds so much—" she searched for the word "—newer? More modern?"

Cordelia laughed and agreed. "Both Anne and Buffy were so big in the nineties. God, I miss the nineties! The original Disney Channel, Saturday morning cartoons. Oh! And Nick at Nite!" The longing in her voice was palpable. "I was turned in 1990, and I kept growing, so I kind of watched all the other teens be teens, but I didn't get to have the full experience. I had to live vicariously through television." The sadness in her voice took Mia by surprise.

"Isla was the one that turned you, right?"

Cordelia stayed silent for a second. "As I said, I'm a healer. As a human, I had performed some small miracles. Isla read about me in the *National Enquirer.*" Mia frowned. "It was a magazine back in the day that featured articles about aliens and human–dolphin hybrid babies and things like that. Every once in a while, they accidentally printed something real." Cordelia rolled her eyes. "Isla found me, and after she was convinced that I truly had a Gift, she asked me to heal her. She wanted to make her less—I don't know—fucking depressed all the time?" Cordelia shrugged. "It didn't work. Personally, I think it's because she creates her own misery. She's happier being sad, you know? But she thought that if I were a vampire, my Gifts would be heightened, and I could fix her. As you can see, even that didn't help."

Mia put a hand on Cordelia's shoulder. "I'm sorry."

"I probably wouldn't be so mad about it if it wasn't classic vampire behavior, doing things that have permanent consequences for others just because it's convenient for them. I've never met anyone as selfish and obsessed with themselves as these people. For all their talk of how we all have to follow the rules, they sure do break them a lot."

She sighed. "At least she didn't kill me right away and try to use my blood."

Mia stopped in her tracks and gave Cordelia a sharp look.

The woman paused. "Oh, relax. No one's going to kill you. That kind of thing doesn't happen very often . . . at least, it didn't used to."

"Is your family still alive, then? I mean, your human family?"

Cord didn't skip a beat. "My mom is sixty-four now, and my baby brother is thirty-six." She looked at Mia with an emotionless face. "It's super weird to be frozen in time."

Mia had never thought of it that way. She had never in her life imagined her mom or Sasha getting old and dying. She and Sasha would read the obituaries in the paper in the morning as a kind of macabre pastime, but now it crossed her mind that she would one day read her little sister's name in the death notices. How old would Sasha be when it happened? Would she live to be an old woman while Mia stayed twenty-five forever?

"Sometimes in the winter, I go back home and drive by. The last time my mom saw me, I was nine, so even if she thought I was still alive, she wouldn't expect to see me in my twenties. I stayed in my old town a few years ago and went to the grocery store for something mundane, like cleaning supplies. I ran into my mom there. I looked up, and she was standing there just staring at me." Mia felt goose bumps rise on her arms. "She looked at me for a hot second, like she was trying to place me. Then she smiled politely and walked past without saying a word. I walked out, leaving my cart in the middle of the aisle. I haven't been back since."

Mia shook her head. "That is so sad, Cord. Like, *really* fucking sad." Cord waved her forward.

"It's okay. It was a long time ago, and I'm over it. Anyway, I still get to help people. I'm the one who retrieves the blood from the donor clinic at the hospital, and I always stop by the children's ward and try to work some healing in."

Mia was blown away at Cordelia's kindness; if she hadn't known she was a vampire, she would have never guessed. She had never felt so much compassion exude from someone before. When she'd first seen the blue-haired woman at the bookstore, Cord had struck Mia as someone special, and it was true.

Cordelia tossed her hair. "We thought we'd take you to the beach tomorrow while Eli, Elenora, and Thea set up for the ceremony, but I have to stop by the hospital for snacks beforehand. Would you like to come?"

Mia wasn't much of a beach fan, but she wanted to watch Cordelia in action, so she nodded.

They were coming to the end of the path when Mia noticed a woman with long brown hair and blunt-cut bangs standing in the middle of the path, not ten yards from them. Mia started, then slowed her pace and nudged Cordelia.

"What?"

"It looks like we have company," Mia said in a low voice.

"Who?" Cordelia scanned their surroundings carefully, but she didn't seem to notice the woman, who stood unmoving in front of them. Mia saw now that she was staring at them and slowly shaking her head back and forth.

"You don't see her?" Mia was surprised. The woman

was wearing a red, knee-length dress and silver pumps. "She's literally right there." Mia pointed.

Cordelia frowned. "There's no one here but us."

Mia moved her thumb to her right ring finger, suddenly remembering that she had put the ring in her jewelry box at Noir House. Could it be that her Gift was coming back?

"You don't see the woman in the red dress who is standing right in front of us?"

"No," Cordelia said with concern. "Mia, are you feeling okay?"

Don't listen to him. The words were as clear as if they'd been whispered directly into Mia's ear. She flinched.

"Seriously, Mia. You're starting to scare me."

"You didn't hear that?"

"No."

Suddenly, Cordelia understood. "Do you think your Gift is coming back?" she murmured. Mia nodded, not taking her eyes off the spirit. "What does she look like?"

Don't listen to him. The woman faded from view.

"We can go now," Mia said with relief. As they exited the forest, she described what she had seen. Cordelia grabbed her arm and looked at her with serious eyes.

"There's something you need to see." She pulled out her phone and scrolled through for quite a while. Finally, she held the device out to Mia.

She took the phone and stared at the photo before her. Oscar and Gianna had their arms around a brunette. It was the same woman.

"That's her!" Mia exclaimed.

"Holy shit," Cordelia said, shaking her head. "That's Alison. She was a member of Bellamy Family. She'd been a vampire for about six months when she went out clubbing by herself. She never came home. They found her body in the forest a few days later, completely drained of blood."

"Do you think a rogue killed her? The one who turned and killed all those other new vampires?" Mia asked casually.

"Yes." Cordelia shivered. "But hey! I guess this means that your Gift really is coming back! From what it said in your mom's book, it sounded like you sometimes had a hard time controlling it when you were younger."

Mia nodded. Was there anyone in this Family who *hadn't* read that damned book? "I had spirits in my room almost every night asking me for help."

"That will change now," Cordelia said excitedly. "As a vampire, your Gift is not only amplified, but you'll have better control over it."

Darkness set in as Cordelia showed Mia back to her room. As Mia went to push the window open, she saw that it was actually a floor-to-ceiling door that led out onto a private balcony. Wrapping her arms around herself, she stepped out and felt the cool breeze.

The day had felt as long as a year, and Mia was eager for a hot shower. She could hardly believe she'd woken up at Noir House just that morning, and she wanted a moment to process the day before crawling into bed. She wanted to weigh her options and pretend that the hot water was Margo's touch. Mia suddenly longed to hear Margo's voice, and she ducked back into the room to look for a telephone. She abruptly laughed at her reflection in the mirror. Even if there was a phone in the room, she had never asked for Margo's number.

After seeing various bath salts and oils sitting on the tub, Mia opted for a bath instead. Both Families were full of people she knew she would come to love, but there was no question in her mind. She couldn't wait to get back to Margo. They had spent such little time alone together, yet they already felt so strongly for each other. What would a week, a month, or a year mean for their relationship? Yes, she probably could still be with Margo if she was part of the Sutton Family, but her one-on-one with Elenora tonight had convinced her that the woman was, at the very least, strange. She wanted no part in that. But then she pictured sweet Annie and Miles. If she was meant to be their protector, what was her next step?

//////

As the water drained, Mia pictured herself and Margo in various scenarios. On the road to Paris. Partying with Toby, Kris, and Gianna at Burning Man. Their lives were free, whereas the Suttons—with the exception of Alexander—gave off an air of structure and routine. It didn't make sense to her that the people of the Family couldn't freely move between houses as long as Eli and Elenora stayed apart.

Steam billowed from the bathroom as Mia exited in the thick white hotel robe. She immediately stopped in her tracks; a black, leather-bound book was lying on the bed, and she knew it hadn't been there before her bath. She gingerly walked to the doorway and peeked out into the hallway before shutting the door and picking up the book. Opening to the front page, she saw that someone had written in a heavy hand and black ink.

I heard you were running water and didn't want to bother you.
I have a surprise. Meet me on the lawn. Dress comfortably.

Luca

Mia smiled at the words. She walked to the closet and searched for pajamas; she found a set of expensive-looking silk bottoms with a matching top. They were black with white piping around the neck and down the front and, going by the label, were made somewhere in France. Looking through her shoe collection, she spotted a pair of matching slippers. She pulled on the soft fabric, which felt delicious against her skin. She then brushed her hair and ran a mascara wand across her lashes before silently making her way downstairs. The hotel was eerily quiet, and she crept outside.

She paused, her breath catching in her throat. Near the tree line was a giant blow-up movie screen lit up like the moon. Someone was sitting in front of the screen on a large, fluffy blanket. As she sprang across the dewy lawn, Luca turned and smiled at her with the biggest grin she had ever seen. "I'm so happy you made it," he said. Mia could feel her smile reaching her ears, matching his. "When I was taking reference photos in your room, I couldn't help but see the album on your dresser," he explained sheepishly. "I took a peek and noticed there were a lot of photos of you and your sister at drive-ins."

Mia took in a big breath of fresh air and sat down on the blanket next to Luca. She and Sasha hadn't been to a drive-in since her father died. Those times were some of her best childhood memories. She loved the mixture of the big screen, the starry sky, and the smell of popcorn.

As if reading her thoughts, Luca set a bowl in her lap. "I hope you love butter." Mia just stared at him. The moment couldn't be more perfect.

"What are we watching?" Mia felt Luca shift his weight so that he was slightly closer to her.

"From spending way too much time at your bookshelf and your DVD collection, I could see that you love romantic dramas. So . . ." He paused, a self-conscious expression on his face. "Is *The Notebook* okay?"

"You just want to watch me cry, don't you?"

Luca glanced at her anxiously. "No! I thought you'd enjoy it!"

Mia giggled. "I'm just messing with you. *The Notebook* is absolutely perfect." He relaxed, and she suddenly felt guilty. She couldn't believe she had just been thinking about Margo, and here she was flirting with someone else! There was something incredibly attractive about this boy who had spent so much time learning about her before he'd even met her. She remembered what Elenora had said at dinner, and her cheeks warmed. Luca had gone out of his way to make her feel welcomed and appreciated. She needed to give him a bit of a chance.

They watched the movie for the next two hours. After the credits rolled, they remained on the blanket, talking about their lives or the lack thereof. As the night grew chilled, their conversation deepened. Luca wanted to know all her most profound thoughts. She told him things about herself that she'd never told anyone for fear they would think her weird, but instead of spooking him and causing him to run away, it only seemed to strengthen his attraction to her.

"What happened today?" she asked at one point. "Did you Veil that woman?"

"Who?" Luca frowned. "Oh, Erin? No, I'm afraid I can't Veil anyone. Elenora has a few of the staff sort of hypnotized. When she says the right words, they fall into a trance so she can extract their blood."

"Doesn't that seem kind of, I don't know, *wrong*?"

"No. They have no idea what's happened, and we don't harm them. I'm sure Kris and Toby let you sample a few necks at the club the other night."

Mia was grateful for the darkness; her cheeks burned.

"I don't want to talk about Erin, though," Luca said softly. "I want to know more about you."

"I thought you already knew me from the time you spent in my bedroom," Mia teased.

"That just told me what kinds of curtains you had and what books you like. I want to know the real Mia." He brushed a strand of hair behind her ear and gazed at her.

This was totally different from her time with Margo. With her, Mia felt like she was being pulled along in her wake. Margo was outgoing and surrounded by people who adored her, and it was clear she called the shots. Luca seemed more laid-back, less sure of himself, but he looked at her with such happiness in his eyes.

Mia finally confided in him about the spirit she had seen in the woods. Something flickered in his face, but all he said was, "How do you feel about your Gift coming back?"

She shrugged. "It's been so long since I've seen spirits, so it was a bit startling. But if Cordelia uses her Gift to help people, maybe I should, too." He simply nodded, then changed the subject. Mia sensed something strange.

As the night wore on, the guilt continued to gnaw at her; even though she was attracted to Luca, she already had Margo. While she wasn't sure yet about how she felt, she didn't want to lead him on.

"There's something you should know," she began nervously. "I've got—feelings—for Margo." Luca's face fell, and something twisted inside Mia. "I mean, I like you, too!"

"That's not it." He looked up at her, a dejected look in his eyes. "You know the woman you saw in the woods? Alison?" Mia nodded. "She was Margo's girlfriend."

Mia couldn't hide the shock on her face. Margo hadn't said anything about one of the dead vampires having been her girlfriend.

"The night that Alison went missing, she and Margo had a fight. Next thing you know, she turns up dead." He glanced at Mia sideways. "What I mean is, be careful. Margo has always been a flirt, but she's also had a lot of girlfriends. She was obsessed with Alison; that's why she turned her. She's also turned quite a few vampires who ended up going rogue."

Mia felt as if she'd been slapped. She couldn't reconcile the Margo she knew with the woman Luca was describing. But she thought back to Kris's warning, telling her Margo was a flirt. This was a lot to take in; she would have to think about what she'd just been told.

The magic spell of the night was broken, and Luca walked her back to her room. When they reached her door, Luca took her hand. "I like you, Mia," he said quietly. "I like you a lot."

"I like you, too," she replied.

He leaned in for a kiss, but she took a step back. Luca looked wounded.

"I need time to think," she said soothingly. "I know that sounds like a cliché, but everything is so new that I'm not sure how I feel about anything."

Luca nodded. "Have a good night, then," he said, and turned to walk away. Mia caught his arm to stop him and gave him a hug.

"Thank you for the movie," she said, planting a kiss on his cheek. "It was absolutely wonderful, and I had a fabulous time."

Luca grinned and ducked his head before strolling away. She watched him for a moment, her insides in knots, and then entered her room.

Immediately, a soft tapping came from the window. Her first thought was that it was a moth knocking against the glass, but when she pulled back the curtain, Kris's worried face peered up at her. Mia searched for an opening, but it was a solid pane.

Kris made a motion of pinching her lips together with her fingers, then held up a piece of paper. Scribbled on it were the words, *Gary's body is gone, and the women from the club are officially listed as missing persons.* Mia slapped a hand over her mouth. She'd been right all along. Kris nodded grimly, then flipped the paper over. *LOCK YOUR DOOR.* Mia nodded and crept to the door before closing and locking it. She pushed the dresser in front of it for good measure.

She turned back to Kris, but the woman was already gone.

CHAPTER NINETEEN

Mia tossed and turned all night but still found herself shocked when she heard a knock on her door. "Who is it?" she called, slipping on the white robe.

"It's Cord!" Her voice sounded so cheery.

"Coming," Mia replied as she looked at the alarm clock. It was somehow already eleven, and she was supposed to go to the hospital to watch Cordelia on her rounds. She hurried over to the door and pulled the dresser back, then turned the lock. As she opened the door, the blue-haired woman frowned.

"Did you lock your door?"

Mia shrugged and thought fast. "Force of habit. I think I forgot this isn't a regular hotel room."

"And you usually shove furniture in front of your hotel room doors, too?" Cord frowned at the dresser.

"Of course," Mia replied coolly. She glanced at Cord's outfit. "What are you wearing?"

"Scrubs. These are for you. They'll help us fit in." Cord shoved a dressing bag at Mia. She peeked inside and saw a name badge, white lab coat, stethoscope, and scrubs.

"Wow. This is not what I imagined when you said we were going to the hospital," Mia said as she headed to the bathroom to change.

"It's easy to get around if you blend in," Cord replied.

Mia yanked off her pajamas and climbed into the scrubs. She quickly took care of her other morning grooming before exiting the bathroom.

"Perfect," Cord said with approval. "We'll hit the hospital and still have a couple of hours for the beach before the ceremony." Mia nodded as she ran a brush through her hair. She could feel the urgency in Cord's voice, and she applied the barest amount of makeup while the other woman packed her a bag.

"There you go," Cord said when she was done. "Swim stuff and a change of clothes." She handed Mia a thermos. "That's breakfast." Mia opened the top and took a quick swig, and found herself pleasantly surprised at how much she enjoyed the feel of blood sliding down her throat. She was getting used to being a vampire.

Cordelia swept out of the room without another word; Mia was quick to follow. They skipped down the staircase and into the hotel's main lobby. A bellboy saw them coming and hurried to open the door.

Mia happened to glance at the restaurant and started.

The same man from the night before was sitting at the same table, staring out into the garden with a sad expression. She stopped at the front desk, where Erin greeted her with a friendly smile.

"How can I help you?"

"Do you know who that man is?" she asked, pointing toward the restaurant.

Erin stepped out from behind the desk and looked at where Mia was pointing. "What man?" she asked, looking directly at the bank of windows.

"At the table by the window?"

"I don't see anyone." Erin frowned.

"Never mind," Mia replied hastily. "I thought I saw someone." She paused, noticing the bandage on Erin's hand. "Did you hurt yourself?"

The woman glanced at her bandage. "Oh, it's nothing," she said, laughing. "I'm a bit of a klutz, and I must have cut my hand on something. But thank you for asking." She resumed her place at the front desk, and Mia rushed back to Cordelia, who was waiting patiently.

"What was that?"

"A ghost, I think," Mia muttered as they exited onto the broad stone steps. A baby blue Mercedes convertible was parked on the gravel driveway, and she was surprised to see Cord dart around to the driver's door.

"This is our ride," she said as she climbed in, and Mia opened the passenger door. Seeing the look on Mia's face, Cord laughed. "What, did you think they'd let me have a Cadillac?"

"I just thought a car like this would draw too much attention."

They peeled out of the crescent drive and nearly took out a peony bush. They descended into Cedar Hollow a little too fast for Mia's taste, but the sound of the wind and the highway kept them from speaking. The ride was short, and in less than fifteen minutes, they were turning into the Cedar Hollow General employee parking deck. Cord flashed a badge at an automatic gate and the arm lifted.

"How did you manage to get ahold of hospital credentials?" Mia asked, impressed, as Cordelia drove up the ramp.

"It's amazing what connections we've been able to make over the course of a few decades," Cord said with a smile. She chose a parking spot and jumped out of the car.

"Does everyone here think you're a doctor?" Mia climbed out as well, though with less exuberance.

"It's a big hospital. You'd be shocked at how few people ask questions if you have a uniform and a badge." Cord grabbed a wheeled cooler out of the back seat and winked. Mia smiled. She loved this woman's fire and was proud that she was her friend. She found herself wishing she had grown up with her, which, of course, would have been impossible since Mia hadn't even been born when Cordelia was turned. She and Luca were quickly becoming reasons for her to stay with the Sutton Family, but after what Kris told her last night, she knew she couldn't. It was strange to look at the whole situation from different perspectives. If she looked at it from Elenora's mind, Kris did make sense as a suspect. She'd been with Carly at the club, and she was also the one to move Gary's car. But Mia was sure about what she'd seen. She didn't trust Elenora, and she was looking forward to getting back to Noir House as quickly as possible. She just had to get through the ceremony tonight.

Maybe once she was the matriarch, she could change things and somehow merge the two Families.

"Hello? Earth to Mia." Cord smiled. "It's time to go."

The women made their way through the garage to a set of glass doors. Mia held the door for Cordelia, who went through and swiped her badge to activate the elevator, then pushed the button for floor three. As the doors closed, Cord donned a surgical cap to hide her hair, put on a surgical mask, and handed a second to Mia. "Ready to operate, Doctor?"

"I'm always ready," Mia joked, slipping the elastic bands over her ears.

"Excellent. Except you have your mask on inside out. Please try to be professional, Doc." She giggled.

"What?" Mia looked at how Cord was wearing hers before laughing and switching the mask around. Now that it was on correctly, Mia pushed the metal band firmly over her nose.

"Perfect."

The doors slid open with a ding, and Cord set off down a hallway before taking a left at the first corner. She barely even glanced around before opening a door with her badge. Mia's heart caught in her throat. She took a good look before she ducked in after Cordelia. The woman was already at a refrigerator, stuffing blood bags into the cooler. There were so many bags that Cord's removal barely made a difference.

"You seem awfully confident that no one will catch us," Mia remarked.

"They're on lunch until one o'clock. No one's on this entire floor." She held up a bag. "Want one for the road?"

"Are you crazy?" Mia pushed the bag back at Cord.

"What? No one will wonder why you have a bag of blood. You look like a medical professional, remember?" She threw the blood back at Mia like they were playing a demented game of water balloons. Mia shoved it into the pocket of her coat as Cord grabbed a few more bags and then slammed the cooler lid shut before offering the handle to Mia. "Easy peasy," she said, heading back out of the room.

They went back to the garage level and stowed the full cooler in the trunk of the car. Cord looked at her watch. "If we hurry, we'll get to the children's ward before the nurses start their rounds." She took off with Mia at her heels. When they got back to the elevator, Cordelia punched the button for the sixth floor.

"Time to see if we can find a kid to help," she said. "I don't cure anyone these days; I just heal them enough so it looks like they've recovered on their own."

"Why?" Mia was surprised.

"It would look weird if the hospital started experiencing miracles every single week," the woman explained. "You know the number of religious folks that would start pouring into town? There goes our cover."

When the doors opened, Mia discovered that this floor had a lot more activity than the one they had just been on. Cord exited the elevator with her head held high and a self-important look on her face, so Mia mimicked her. She was surprised to find that Cord was correct: no one gave them a second look. They blended into the mix of doctors, nurses, and techs who hurried on their way to their destinations without glancing at them.

Whipping her badge up, Cordelia swiped for access to a door that read, Children's Wing. When the indicator light turned from red to green, she pushed the door open. Walking briskly down the corridor, Cord slid into an unoccupied office. A whiteboard was covered with photos of at least a dozen children. Beneath each picture was a name, a brief description of their illness, and a room number.

Squinting, Cordelia looked at each photo. "Perfect," she murmured, pointing to the photo of a small boy who appeared to be approximately three years old. He grinned broadly and wore a *Paw Patrol* T-shirt. The word *Terminal* was written in marker beneath his name. It looked harsh in the fluorescent lights. Cord ran her finger along the boy's information until it landed on the room number. Cord crooked her finger and then disappeared around the corner.

What they walked in on wasn't the same smiling boy in the photo. Mia felt her eyes begin to fill with tears. The diminutive child was on the bed hooked up to too many machines to count. His arms and legs were stick-thin; his eyes were half-closed, his breath ragged and labored despite the oxygen tubes in his nostrils. His mother was fast asleep in an uncomfortable chair in the corner. The entire room was full of beeping sounds. Another whiteboard was mounted on the wall with his most recent vital signs and a medication list; there were at least a dozen.

Cord put a finger to her lips and walked to the other side of the bed. There was a tiny patch on the boy's chest that was free of monitoring equipment. Mia watched as Cord pressed the palm of her hand onto the bare flesh. After a moment, Mia saw a redness similar to a rash bloom beneath her hand. The little boy's eyes fluttered open, and his breathing slowed to a more natural rhythm. He sighed.

Cord looked up at Mia. "You okay?" she whispered. Mia became aware that her entire face was awash with tears.

The boy's mother began to stir, and Cord hastened around the bed and pushed Mia toward the door. They walked down the hall with purpose, but just before they reached the security doors, a little girl of about seven stepped out of a room and ran toward the women. She stopped in front of the doors and stared.

"Can you help me, too?" she called. Before Mia could respond, Cord grabbed the door and swung it open. It passed right through the little girl. She still looked at the women tearfully.

"I'm sorry," Mia whispered. "I don't think we can make you better, but people are waiting for you on the other side. You should go to them." The girl slowly nodded; a moment later, she faded away.

Mia turned to find Cord watching her from in front of the elevator. She jogged over, and Cord pushed the button. "What was that about?" Cord asked briskly as a nurse passed by on her way to the ward.

"Nothing," Mia replied, swallowing a lump in her throat. Maybe she, too, had helped a child today.

///////

Cord and Mia pulled up to the beach soon after, but Mia had spent the entire drive in silence, absorbing everything she had seen at the hospital. Using the car as a shield, they took turns changing into their swimsuits as the other held up a towel for privacy. Mia loved Cord's sensible choice for her: black short bottoms and a swim tank. Cord was decked out in a floral one-piece. Once she was changed, she grabbed a few bags out of the cooler and slid them into a beach bag, then added some red Solo cups on top. Mia placed her unopened bag on top of the pile.

When they arrived at the beach entrance, they spotted Isla, Alexander, Alyssa, Miles, Annie, and Luca set up on the far left by the birch trees that littered the edge of the sand. Lugging the heavy bag, they made their way to the others.

"We were worried the eye candy wouldn't make it," Alexander called out as they approached.

Mia did a double take; Isla was sitting in his lap with a smug expression on her face. Was she happy? It threw Mia off.

"Don't mind us; we're all just drying up like prunes out here." Alexander pretended to reach up for a high five but instead grabbed the beach bag that Cord was setting down. He grabbed a blood bag and cup; ripping the bag, he filled the red cup with the cool liquid. Cord flopped down in the sand and gave him a dirty look.

"Could you be more obvious?" she said, rolling her eyes.

Isla filled a red Solo cup behind Alex's back with a bit more finesse as Mia spread her towel beside Luca and lowered herself onto it.

"How was your first hospital adventure?" Luca asked, trying to read her face. The picture of the little girl flashed in her mind.

"It was interesting," she replied. "Cord was amazing."

The next hour Mia felt like she was with old friends. They weren't as straitlaced as the Bellamys had made them out to be, but they were a bit more interested in pursuing hobbies and learning new things than partying. When she shared with them about the night at Neon Viper and how she'd tried the laced blood, she wasn't sure how they would react. To no surprise, Alex told her how he had once taken 127 Xanax and didn't wake up until six months later. While he was unconscious, Miles and Isla found an old-fashioned coffin and filled it with dirt before placing his body in it, so when he finally opened his eyes, he found he was arranged like Dracula. He laughed about it, once again showing that he wasn't the total asshole he acted like most of the time.

Everyone laughed and shared their own escapades, especially the ones in their early years, before setting off into the water. They all splashed, and Mia felt like she was in a sunscreen commercial. No matter where she turned, Luca was waiting, ready to toss her into a wave or steady her. Luca's eyes kept finding a way to connect with hers, his smile growing bigger and brighter. His hands were warm in the cool water and seemed to emanate desire. She wasn't dumb, she could feel the tension building between them with every wave that crashed against their bodies. He seemed too good to be true. His smile kept pushing Margo's face further out of her mind. She could barely even picture her anymore.

The day wore on. Miles and Annie had taken to creating the most beautiful sandcastles, and the others were lying in the sun. Luca gave her a sly grin and jerked his head toward the water. She followed him into the shallows, and when he swam away from her, she followed, laughing and calling out his name. He disappeared into a cavern on the side of the beach. Mia looked over her shoulder at the rest of the group. They hadn't noticed she'd left. The water just covered her hips as she walked into the cove.

"This is pretty," she said, looking around at the light bouncing off the ceiling of the cavern.

"Almost as pretty as you." The words almost caught Mia off guard, and she swung around to look at Luca, but he was too close, and their bodies connected. She looked up at Luca, and she was right. It had been some time since she let a man get close to her. His body pressed hard into her soft curves. His eyes were bearing down into hers; she could feel her awkwardness building inside her. In the past she would have pulled away, made some silly joke about the sky. But not now—vampire her was different. She wasn't old Mia anymore. Or was she? The push and pull between who she now was and who she used to be was so strong. So much had changed in such a short time. Mia closed her eyes for just a moment and Margo's face flashed on the back of her eyelids. Opening them, she looked back into Luca's face. Before she knew what was happening, Luca had bent down, and his lips connected with hers. His lips felt like the warmth of the sun. They moved so slowly and passionately against hers. It felt safe and familiar. Mia knew she should have pulled away from the kiss, but something made her return it. His head tilted as he slid his hand from the middle to the small of her back, her hand reaching and grasping his shoulder. She was getting lost, so lost. Pure vertigo slowly started to take her as everything from the past few days flooded into her mind. She took a step forward and stubbed her toe on a rock. Suddenly, she came to her senses and pulled away.

"Luca, I told you I needed time to figure out what I wanted." Mia heard the words come out of her mouth; it was almost as if she hadn't even been the one to formulate the thought. Her mind spun—was this old Mia or new

Mia who'd decided this? She blinked hard and looked out across the water, trying to steady herself. Trying to make sense of what had just happened.

"You came out here with me," he protested. "What did you think was going to happen?" She didn't like his tone; it didn't match the moment that had just passed.

"I don't know, but not that!" Mia was getting angry.

Luca licked his lips and reached for her, meeting her eyes with his. Another warm rush started to flow through Mia's body, and the memory of their movie night flashed into her mind: popcorn, giant screen, sharing stories about their lives. *Don't listen to him.* Alison's words echoed in her head and chased away the image. Now she knew what the woman had meant.

"You *are* Veiling me, aren't you?" she cried. It all made sense now, didn't it?

"I told you I can't do that," he replied calmly. "If you feel guilty, maybe it's because you want me more than you want Margo."

A hot rage reared up in Mia. "What I want is to go home." She started trudging through the waist-deep water as fast as she could. Luca called after her in the same calm tone as before.

"She's just going to disappoint you, Mia. I'm the one who truly cares for you."

"Why do you even like me so much?" Mia said louder than she wanted to. "Am I just a new shiny thing to you?" Mia instantly wished she could rewind and take the words back. She saw the hurt cross Luca's face. He didn't respond. A large pause lay suspended between them.

"I'll figure that out for myself," she said quietly as hot tears poured down her face. She couldn't understand why Luca would Veil her. To make her stay with the Suttons? But why? And now that she thought about it, it wasn't sweet that he had replicated her old room; it was actually kind of creepy. She wasn't that Mia anymore.

She stormed up the beach, then grabbed her towel and kept going, much to the shock of the others. She had just reached the parking lot when Cord caught up with her.

"Hey, what's wrong?" she asked with concern.

"I'm going home," Mia said through clenched teeth as she wrapped herself tightly in the towel. Without another word, Cord slung the beach bag into the car and climbed in. They were on the road in less than a minute. Mia fumed the whole way home, feeling betrayed and confused. If she couldn't trust Luca, how could she trust Cord? They seemed inseparable. They were pulling up behind the hotel, alongside a line of garages, when she finally spoke.

"Luca kissed me." She spat the words out.

"He did *what*? Jesus Christ." Cordelia slammed on the brakes so hard that Mia was afraid her neck would snap. The woman's surprise left Mia flabbergasted. "Luca just told me about you and Margo this morning. He told me he was going to step back and not get involved, give you time to think." She eased the convertible into one of the garages, and Mia hopped out.

"He's clearly changed his mind, then." She reached into the back seat and collected her belongings. She couldn't deny he had seemed willing to give her space last night. In fact, he'd been a real gentleman about it. "Can Luca—"

She broke off as another car pulled up next to the Mercedes, and Mia turned and hurried toward the back door with Cord close on her heels. Rushing through the back door, she ran up the stairs. When she reached her room, she was irritated to see Cord had followed her.

The woman closed the door behind her. "Can Luca what?" she asked.

Mia closed her eyes and tried to calm down. Cord was her friend. "Can he Veil people?"

Cord frowned. "I don't think so."

"What about Erin? The hotel clerk?"

"That's one of Elenora's workings. He just has to recite the words." She stared at Mia. "Why are you asking?"

"I think he's been Veiling me," Mia admitted in a low voice. "He keeps looking right in my eyes, and I get a warm feeling, and then I start thinking things I normally wouldn't. When he kissed me, it felt so right, but then I stubbed my toe, and it was like a fog cleared."

Cord had a worried look on her face. "That definitely sounds like a Veil," she replied, matching Mia's low tone. "Why would he keep such a Gift from us? And why would he be working a Veil on you?"

"I think he wants me to pick you guys, but I don't know why. He can't possibly be that into me."

"He has been a bit obsessed with you," Cord replied uneasily. "But it doesn't make sense that he'd be so intent on you choosing us."

A realization struck Mia. "Elenora was doing something similar at dinner last night. She kept suggesting that the Bellamys were bad news and that I would be better off here." She looked up at Cord and felt guilty; her friend seemed so distressed. After all, this was her Family they were talking about. Elenora had raised her.

There was a knock at the door, and the women exchanged glances. Cord opened the door and peeked around, then opened it wide. Alex stood there, and Mia clutched her towel tightly around her body. "I hate to interrupt your girl talk, but were you planning to let the rest of the blood rot in the trunk?"

"Oh, shoot." Cord flashed Mia an apologetic look. "We'll talk later." She hurried out of the room.

Alex didn't move from the doorway. He glanced down the hall, then turned back to Mia. "Are you okay?" The old, drunk vampire didn't sound like himself. There was sincere worry in his voice. Again, Mia wondered what he was playing at, but then she remembered that this was a big day for him, too. He'd be losing his mother.

"Yes," she replied. "I think I'm just nervous about tonight."

"About that," he said. "I know I'm not supposed to influence your decision—"

"Why not?" Mia whispered. "Everyone else has tried."

Alex nodded. "I know. But don't choose the Suttons." He darted his eyes down the hall again as voices drifted up the stairs, then lowered his voice to a whisper. Mia had to lean forward to catch what he was saying. "I'm not with the Suttons because I want to be. Elenora's got something up her sleeve, and I don't like it. I've been keeping my eye on her for a while, but every time I think I've figured out what she's doing, I find myself losing interest." He looked over his shoulder. "The last few years have been strange. Some other families have been starting rumors. I have known Elenora for years. Well, centuries. I have seen her, gotten to know her in ways you will only understand decades from now. Something's just not sitting right with me. I don't know if it's bad intentions exactly, but you are about to really change, and I don't want her to take advantage of you." Alex leaned out into the hallway to make sure the path was clear.

"So yeah," he said in a louder voice. "We'll be doing shots at the bar to celebrate. See you in a bit." He lifted an eyebrow and winked. He took a couple steps down the hall before turning for a few final words. "I hope you don't mind, I will be leaving now, taking a sabbatical of sorts. I have said my goodbyes to her, but I need to have a stiffer drink in town to celebrate my old mumsy." With a spin on his heel, he was gone before Mia could say another word.

Mia stood in the center of the room for another few moments, feeling dazed. "Holy shit," she said to herself as she moved to the door and locked it. Then she headed to the bathroom to take a shower and try to clear her head. She opened the door and stepped through. She hung up the towel to dry, turned back around, and nearly screamed.

CHAPTER TWENTY

Kris was standing behind her.

"What the *hell*?" Mia hissed as Kris leaned against the sink. "What are you doing here?"

"I was waiting in your room for two hours," Kris replied. "And then when you finally showed up, I had to run in here because you brought a friend." She grinned. "Frankly, after seeing you with Margo, I was afraid of what I might hear."

Mia glared, but Kris ignored her and held out a small leather pouch. "Just a token for tonight," she said as Mia opened the bag. She flipped it upside down, and a black square fell into her palm. She poked the item; it was made of cool metal and was inset with a raised circle.

"We have no idea where Thea will be taking you tonight, so a few of us put this together. Press it if the shit hits the fan, and we'll be there."

"Thank you, Kris," Mia whispered. "I've kept my eyes open like you told me to, and you're right; there's something strange going on in this house."

Kris looked concerned. "What is it?"

"I'm 99 percent sure that Elenora is the one killing new vampires, but what that has to do with me, I don't know. Alexander knows something strange is going on, too. I think this whole drinking thing is an act, and he's been staying here on purpose to figure it out."

Kris raised her eyebrows in surprise. "Alexander? And you trust him?"

"At this point, I don't really trust anyone," Mia said. Kris looked at Mia with heavy eyes that said, *Even me, eh?* Mia kept with the prior conversation. "But I think he's telling the truth."

"Well, isn't that interesting," Kris mused. She glanced at her watch. "Crap. I need to go, and you need to get ready. Keep that token on you, and if you get into trouble, we'll be there."

Mia leaned forward and loosely hugged Kris, who immediately stiffened. "Thanks," Mia said again. Kris nodded, then paused by the window-door a moment, listening. A second later, she slipped through and was gone.

As Mia stood under the hot water and washed the sand off her skin, she went over everything she knew about Elenora. If she was killing new vampires for their blood, what was she doing with it? She recalled her talking about the Darwrites. From what she knew of that family, they were billionaires who lived in a penthouse in New York City.

They derived their wealth from the hotel chain someone's father had started back in the fifties. Was Elenora selling blood to them? Were they just middlemen?

Regarding Elenora and Luca trying to convince Mia to pick the Suttons, Elenora by bad-mouthing the Bellamys and Luca by trying to make her fall in love with him, what was the point? She didn't know enough about vampires to figure out their ulterior motives.

She turned off the water and stepped out of the shower. She took her time toweling off, then blow-dried her hair. Mia used precision as she artfully applied her makeup, choosing dark colors so she'd look more badass. She knew if she looked the part, then she would feel it. She had a black leather jacket at home that she liked to wear when she needed to feel confident. She wished she had that jacket now.

Alyssa knocked on the door, and Mia let her in. "I love your makeup!" Alyssa exclaimed. "I hope you don't mind, but I think I figured out the perfect outfit for tonight."

Mia sat on the bed in her robe while Alyssa swept aside hangers in the closet until she found what she was looking for. Finally, she pulled out a pair of black leather leggings, an airy white blouse, and a sharp blazer.

Mia nodded appreciatively; it *was* perfect. Alyssa dove back into the closet and returned with a pair of spike-heeled booties with a snakeskin print. Mia held one out to admire it. "Thank you," she said, and Alyssa spun out of the room.

She dressed and then stood before the mirror in the bathroom. Gazing at her reflection, Mia felt a calmness wash over her. Not only did she feel in control, she looked powerful. Her eyes slid over her own body, and she decided she loved what she was becoming. She retrieved Kris's token and shoved it into the left pocket of her blazer.

Mia took a deep breath before she descended the staircase. Her heels were muffled by the deep red carpeting, but as she stepped onto the marble floor of the great room, they clacked loudly. The members of the Sutton Family were clustered around the bar, and they looked up as she approached. A few cheered. Mia looked around, but there was no sign of Elenora. Alexander poured a half dozen shots and held one out for her.

"You look unbelievable!" Cordelia crowed as she accepted the liquor. Mia blushed as Alexander held up his glass.

"To the next matriarch," he proclaimed. Everyone else held up their drink as they echoed his sentiment, then downed the shots at the same time. Alexander refilled most of the glasses, but Mia's glass was untouched. "What? You don't like tequila?"

"I just want to be on top of my game tonight."

"Your loss," Alex said, knocking back her shot.

"Shouldn't we be going soon?" she asked.

"Who do I look like, your chauffeur?" he answered in his regular flippant tone. "Thea will be sending a driver for you." As if on cue, the phone rang, and Cordelia answered. It was the front desk.

"Your car is here!" she squealed. Annie and Alyssa each gave her a big hug, and Miles flashed her a smile and a thumbs-up. Isla actually grinned, and Alex just gave her a solemn nod.

Luca had disappeared somewhere after his second drink, but Cordelia was there to see her off. She walked with Mia through the hotel lobby.

"Whatever happens tonight, whichever Family you choose, we will still be friends," Cordelia said.

"I certainly hope so," Mia replied, giving her a hug. "I'll see you soon." A bellboy opened the door for her, and she held her head high as she walked down the steps. A black Cadillac waited for her.

"Hello, Ms. Adair. I'm James. I'll be your driver tonight." The stoic man stood beside the car. Mia assessed him—definitely not a vampire. His eyes were almost a white blue. The smell of half-burnt cigarettes lingered in the air surrounding him. Mia held his eyes for a moment too long; she guessed he was Veiled. James held the door open, and she stepped into the back seat. The leather of the Lincoln was warm, the windows tinted so dark that the surroundings were warped. She watched James get in the front seat; he adjusted the rear-view mirror and gave Mia a wink before the transmission clunked into Drive. The car eased down the hill and into Cedar Hollow. Mia breathed deeply to quiet her nerves as they rolled smoothly along the road. She touched the black leather seats, remembering how she had awoken on a similar seat just two days ago. How quickly her life had changed! She was so lost in thought that she didn't take in any of her surroundings on the drive. Mia looked at the clock on the dash and realized they had been driving for nearly forty minutes. The town was only a five-minute drive from the Bruce. As if the man noticed what she was realizing, his voice interrupted the silence of the car's cabin.

"They told me to take you on a short drive before we reach your destination; they weren't quite ready yet, and hey, it'll help you clear your mind." Mia had a strange feeling come over her body.

"Where am I headed?" she asked James.

"The Closet," he replied.

The name seemed vaguely familiar. "What's that?"

"Well, it was originally a theater house when it was built in the late 1800s, then a music hall until that shut down in the 1980s. It bounced from owner to owner, then until about ten years ago, it was a massive thrift shop, though it's abandoned now."

The sun was nearly down when they turned onto the main strip, then slowed just down the street from the Neon Viper. James parked the car and jogged over to open her door.

"Where do I go?" Mia asked. He pointed to a building at the end of the street, and she turned to look. It was an old, dilapidated structure. She hadn't noticed it during her previous trips into Cedar Hollow.

"How inviting," she joked apprehensively before starting down the sidewalk. Outside the building, she looked up, and her eyes locked on a peeling sign.

The Closet.

She suddenly remembered why it sounded so familiar. Elenora's voice echoed in her mind. *"Take them to the closet,"* she'd said.

"Oh shit." Mia reached her hand into her left pocket and touched the cool metal of the token Kris had given her. She regretted getting into the car with James; how could she be sure that Thea had sent him? Perhaps if she went inside, Elenora would be waiting for her and her precious blood.

There was only one way to find out. Mia took the steps two at a time.

//////

Mia was surprised when the door easily swung open. Musty air rushed her face. The space beyond was utterly dark, a large expanse with the shadows of boxes and clothing racks. The light pooled in from the street and lit up the cobwebs that surrounded the doorway she entered. Mia could hear a murmur of voices coming from somewhere close. She thought she could make out Eli, and she felt marginally better. A light glowed from a doorway across the building, and Mia headed toward it. The floorboards creaked quietly as she passed over them, some felt soft with age. She tried to release her hands from the tight anxious fists they had made.

With one hand, she pushed the door open. The room it opened on was immense, and on the other side was a stage; its heavy red velvet curtains hung closed, the edges tattered from age. In front of the stage sat a folding card table upon which were perhaps a dozen candles as the room's only illumination. Thea sat behind it with Eli to the left of her and Elenora to the right. A vacant seat was placed in front of them.

"Hello, everyone," Mia said, looking at the three vampires. She was surprised that her voice held no weakness.

Thea beamed up at her. "Here is our wonder girl," she announced, motioning to the chair.

Mia sat down and folded her hands on the table. She knew it was time to put her game face on. Be the new strong version of herself. She wanted to crack a joke.

"To be honest, after seeing your houses, I expected something a bit fancier," she remarked, hoping to break the tension. "This seems a bit on the nose, doesn't it?" Eli smiled, but Elenora didn't react. Eli could take a joke, but apparently Elenora couldn't; Mia had half expected that.

Mia's eyes bounced between the two vampires. Eli looked calm, slouched in his chair with his kind face staring at her, waiting. But not Elenora. She sat rigid, as if she was made of granite. Mia just then felt the energy of the room—it was as if she'd interrupted something. She looked back to Eli, who was looking at Elenora, and something passed across his face.

"It's good to see you again, Mia," Eli said. Elenora laughed, and his expression changed. He looked like he wanted to punch his former wife.

"Be still," Thea ordered, looking from Eli to Elenora. "Tonight, we have our newest creation. Ms. Mia Adair." She addressed Mia with a powerful glance. Her chin was pulled in tight to her chest, and she looked up at Mia through thick brows. Her intention felt strong. "As matriarch, you will hold the power to keep all the vampires in your Family, and everywhere, safe. You will hold the responsibility to decide the fate of those who walk into your path. But first, you must claim a Family."

Thea held her hands out to her sides, pointing at both Eli and Elenora, the candlelight casting morbid shadows against her pale arms. The way her head was tilted, the shadows had found resting spots in the hollows under her eyes. Mia took a deep breath in; she passed her eyes over the two Family leads. Eli was staring at her, but Elenora was looking past him into the darkness. Mia followed her gaze but saw nothing. When she looked back, Elenora was staring at her, expressionless.

Eli then gave her an encouraging nod. Thea lifted her right hand and placed it in front of Eli. "Do you choose the name Bellamy?" She placed her left hand in front of Elenora. "Or the name Sutton?"

Shifting her gaze from Thea's face, Mia focused on the candle in the middle of the table and took a few measured breaths. She lifted her head and smiled broadly at Elenora, who smiled back at her. She seemed quite confident that Mia would choose her.

"This has been a hard choice, but I would prefer not to take the name of a murderer." Thea gasped, and Eli frowned, confused. "Thea," Mia said, "Elenora is the one creating new vampires and then killing them for their blood. She has been giving it to the Darwrite family." Mia's eyes kept passing between everyone. She could tell Elenora was trying to hold her composure. That she was trying to think of an excuse.

"What is this?" Thea cried out angrily as Eli's frown deepened. "I told you Elenora could not be behind these heinous crimes. How dare you accuse her of such savagery?"

"I saw her with my own eyes," Mia replied. She pushed her chair back and braced her arms on the table. "She has been attempting to Veil me ever since she murdered the cab-driver two nights ago. She forced me to drink his blood." Thea's face went white. "Last night she tried to convince me that I had killed him on my own, and I almost believed her, but her Veil faltered, and I regained my memories."

Thea gaped at Elenora, clutching her chest with one hand. Mia looked at the redhead with all the confidence she had. She expected to see the woman's face angry and ready to defend herself, but she hadn't moved; she sat composed, her hands folded on the table.

Mia continued. "What she doesn't know is that I followed her at Neon Viper and watched as she turned two young women." At this, Elenora's nostrils flared, but her expression otherwise remained motionless.

"Therefore, I choose Bellamy Family," Mia concluded. "And we might need to think about stopping her—" Mia took a deep breath as she looked at Elenora "—if you know what I mean." Elenora's cheeks turned bright red. She knew exactly what Mia meant.

Thea was fuming. "These baseless accusations against my daughter will not be tolerated," she hissed, slamming fists on the table.

A short laugh sounded, interrupting Thea's rage. "But she's right." Mia's jaw dropped as Elenora said the words. She had never expected her to confess. Eli shoved himself away from the table, disbelief in his eyes.

"Explain yourself right now!" Thea screamed the words so forcefully the wheelchair shook.

Elenora laughed again. "We all know that new vampire blood heals. It cannot turn humans into vampires, but it can slow the aging process. Everyone nowadays is so vain. Everyone wants beauty, to stay young forever. Kings claim to get heart transplants to live on—did you think that was true? I have been collecting blood for the past decade as I move across the continents. The world is so overpopulated with people, shitty people who care about nothing but themselves. So I chose to take care of me. I have turned thousands of people. Hell, I might have turned a hundred thousand people over the decades. The fresher the better. I bleed them and then I sell the blood to the highest bidder. The people of this century are so vapid, they'll pay any price to avoid getting older. I know you all value life, but why? What did life do for you?" Elenora's eyes darkened. "You know what works for me? Power. Power over humans, power over all of you."

Elenora looked at the three people around the table. Eli held his head in his hands, and Thea was shaking. Neither of them had seen this coming, and Mia thought she knew why. "And one other thing: I have been drinking the blood all this time." She stood up and pulled a bottle out of her purse. She drank it down in one gulp.

Mia looked to Eli. She had heard the whispers of others, and vampires drinking other vampires' blood was a rule they didn't break.

Mia stared in horror as first Elenora's eyes turned black, then her mouth and the areas around her eyes. She bared her teeth, and not only one pair of fangs protruded from her upper mouth, but three. Mia looked to Thea and Eli to see if this was normal. The looks on their faces told her they had never seen anything like this before.

"The consumption of the blood of young vampires has perfected me." Elenora's frame started to grow, her eyes sinking into the black expanse, her mouth cracking at the seams and pulling back from her teeth. "This is our true form, this is my power, you are nothing." Elenora's voice cracked and deepened into a demonic tone as the sound of rearranging bones filled the room.

"Elenora, STOP!" Eli yelled, desperation in his voice. Tears streamed down his face, and Mia knew that seeing his former love turn into the ultimate evil was destroying him. His eyes appeared to be glowing as the light from the candles bounced off them. She saw him reach for his chest as if he was grabbing at the memories of her. Even with all the hate he now carried for her, it wasn't enough for him to look away as she transformed into what could only be described as darkness.

Eli's breath quickened, and he couldn't break his gaze. "Elenora, why?" he said in a quiet voice. For some reason Mia couldn't understand, he reached out to her, like he wanted to help her. Eli was just that kind of man. Mia realized she was holding her breath, she was so caught up in his emotion.

The woman ripped the stopper out of another flask and swallowed a mouthful. Her frame began to grow and become more pointed at every joint.

"Why are you doing this?" Thea cried.

"Why not? I lost so much." Elenora's back made an uncomfortable cracking noise as she swung her body in Thea's direction. "I've built new life from the wreckage of the old." She took a step forward and bent, putting her face mere inches from Eli's. "I may have lost my Eli—" she tried to straighten her spine, but her new body was not shaped like a typical person's "—my chance to have children, my chance at a sweet normal life, but none of that matters now—why would I want to be normal when I could instead become the most powerful being in the world? I owe this world nothing; it has done nothing but ruin me. It has broken my heart in too many ways. This world owes me. It owes me." Mia watched as Elenora took two steps back from everyone. "My only mistake was thinking that

I needed to control Mia the same way I controlled you all these years." Elenora let a small hiss drift in Thea's direction. "I have become more powerful than she will ever be! I don't need Mia as a kill switch," Elenora growled as she towered over Mia. "I *am* the kill switch!"

"What do you mean, you controlled me?" Thea demanded.

"I've been killing humans for years, right under your nose," Elenora said, sneering. "Don't you think you would have figured it out by now? I had to make sure you didn't suspect a thing." She put on a mocking expression. "'*Dear Elenora. Sweet Elenora. She couldn't help herself when she destroyed that poor pregnant woman.*'" Eli choked back a sob, and she rolled her eyes. "Pathetic."

"You're insane," Thea whispered. "How many have you killed?"

Elenora paused and tilted her head as if listening for something. "Well, to start, there are currently forty-seven bodies upstairs dissolving in lye." She laughed. "I haven't been able to keep track of the others. You can come out, love!"

Mia spun, and all the air left her body as a man walked through a doorway next to the stage. It was Luca. He didn't even look at Mia as he walked up to Elenora. She held the flask up to him, and when he took a swig, his face pulled into the black mess. He set the flask on the table and kissed Elenora. Mia couldn't help but feel a pang in her heart: Luca had been the man with Elenora in the club. He was the one who brought the bodies to "the closet."

And this monster had kissed Mia.

She thought she was going to throw up.

"Elenora, you need to stop this right now. You are out

of control," Eli pleaded. Elenora matched his stance. She now stood inches above her ex-husband. "This is not you, Elenora. The things you did in the past were not your fault; you did them from a place of deep pain." Eli reached out and tried to hold the distorted hand of what Elenora had become.

"Please, remember." He let out a long breath; she stood silent. "Remember the flower fields—you're her, deep down you're her." The desperation in his voice was so heavy, it felt so sincere, but Mia wondered if he was grabbing at straws. You could tell from the energy in the room that they were not headed in a positive direction. Mia looked at the ground—she needed to look away from the sight of it all. She tried to imagine them in another life. She knew Eli hated Elenora so much, but right beside hate is love. Their lives had been intertwined for centuries. If anyone could stop this, it was him.

"SIT DOWN!" she screamed. Eli didn't budge. "Well, then," she said, switching to a seductive voice. "Luca dear, show the audience what they've won." They watched in horror as Luca walked to the side of the stage and pulled a dirty gold rope. The curtains parted, and Mia gasped. All the remaining members of the Sutton Family sat in a row of chairs, slumped over in sleep.

"That loser Alexander gave me the best idea today," Luca said, holding up a pill bottle. "I was surprised when you showed up here, Mia. I thought a party girl like you would have at least one shot of tequila to steady your nerves." He smiled. "If you think about it, what's about to happen is all your fault." Mia paled.

"What are you doing?" Thea yelled.

"Watch, Mummy. Let me show you how much I have changed." Elenora moved jaggedly toward the stage. "First, I am faster." In the blink of an eye, something white shot out of her hand, and a squishing noise came from the stage. A quartz stake protruded from Alyssa's chest. Mia screamed as her friend's body crumpled to the floor like a rag doll and deflated.

"Shut your mouth, or I will do it again," Elenora said calmly. Mia sat and covered her mouth, holding back a whimper. Eli was hyperventilating. The hideous creature turned toward Thea. "Give me the necklace."

Mia had nearly forgotten that she was there for the transfer of power. "I will never!" Thea shrieked.

Elenora lifted her arm, and Annie's body fell to the floor. Mia cried silent tears for the quiet, gentle woman. Luca let out a girlish giggle. Mia felt helpless. What could she do? How could she save her friends? She suddenly remembered Kris's visit and shoved her hand into her pocket. Grabbing the token, Mia pressed it over and over.

"GIVE ME THE NECKLACE!" Elenora screamed, causing the walls to shake.

"Over my dead body," Thea said, suddenly calm.

"That's easy enough," Elenora snapped. She advanced upon Thea.

Eli blocked Thea with his body. "Please, Elenora, don't do this!" But she shoved him aside as if he was a dead leaf. With one swipe of Elenora's hand, Thea's head rolled off her body, leaving the old woman's unmoving body slumped in her wheelchair. A grotesque statue in this house of horrors.

"Look how strong I have become," Elenora cooed to Eli

as he fell to the ground in grief. She snatched the necklace from Thea's gaping neck and strolled over to Eli.

"Oh, love, our story has been so long." Elenora knelt down next to the man, who struggled to sit up. "It's progressive for just the woman to get the happy ending now."

"No!" Mia ran at Elenora, but Luca reached out and caught her by the arm, folding her into a chokehold. Mia could only watch as Elenora pushed her hand deep into Eli's chest. Cracking sounds filled the room. His eyes went wide. "I want to feel your heart stop, my love."

Mia swung her head as she heard the door fly open, but she had no time to react. Footsteps pounded through the blackness of the hall. Luca flew off the stage and toward her. Before she had time to turn her head, he shoved her away, and she used her hands and feet to scutter back against the wall—at least from there she could take it all in, make a plan. She knew she needed to get off the floor to help, but she felt paralyzed.

Mia now saw the entire Bellamy Family as they stepped into the candlelight. They had all come into the room, faces blazing. Oscar started to run to Eli but stopped and crumpled to the floor before he could reach him. Mia knew they didn't stand a chance against Elenora, and she worried she was useless.

A figure appeared before her and shoved something into her hand. It was Kris. "Put this on," she shouted over the noise. Mia saw a flash of silver and immediately recognized her father's ring. She jammed it on her finger without a thought, by instinct. It almost felt magnetic, as if it had flown onto her finger.

The second the ring made contact with the base of her finger, the room immediately filled with white light, so bright that it was as if the building had been hit by lightning. Blinded, everyone stopped and tried to shield their eyes. Mia felt her body lift off the ground. Panic set in and she reached down for the floor, but saw it drifting away from her. It was painful and powerful and amazing all at once; she could hear the voices of millions as all of Thea's power rushed through her. Visions filled her mind's eye as she saw all the times through history. It was like a slideshow as fast as light. Somehow it all made sense to her as she absorbed the knowledge. Through all of it, she heard the cries of her friends and her new Family. She felt she needed to stay in this suspended state, but she wanted to get back to the ground. She recognized voices as they fell silent. She heard the cracking of bones, smelled the blood. Mia lifted higher and higher into the air, and the light grew more intense. A dense low humming filled her ears.

A sharp cracking sound came from somewhere up above, like the sound of thunder, and Mia landed feet-first on the floor. She felt as if she were on fire. Kris stood right in front of her. "DO IT, YOU BAD BITCH!"

Somehow Mia knew exactly what to do. She lifted one knee high in front of her, stomped her foot as hard as she could, and let out a battle cry, Mia then thrust her palm toward Elenora. The movement slowed everyone in time, except Elenora, looks of fear, anger, and frustration plastered on their faces. They didn't get to witness the silver light emitting from Mia's outstretched hand. They didn't see it reach into Elenora. They didn't get to witness the childlike fear in Elenora's deep black eyes as the light entered her body. The light absorbing the blackness, the memories. Only Mia felt the energy in every vein of Elenora. She was the only one that got to feel her heart stop. Mia watched as the light returned back into her own body, but with it came all of Elenora's memories, her plans, her pain. Then Mia watched Elenora's body fall to the ground, lifeless. She turned her head and surveyed the room, everyone moving as if they were underwater. So many of her friends had fallen while the transformation happened, but Margo and Toby were trying to hold Luca down on the ground.

Mia stomped again and sent the white light at Luca. Part of her felt a sick satisfaction as he deflated. She looked at the room and all of her people. A scream was building in the back of her throat. When she could hold it no longer, she opened her mouth and wailed. The scream left her lungs as fire, which set the dry wood of the theater alight almost immediately, and as the final flames left Mia's throat, time resumed its normal speed.

Those who remained were running for the exits. Someone grabbed her arm; it was Margo. "We have to go!" she yelled.

Two of the Panameras were out front. Mia watched as her Family piled into the cars. Margo and Kris placed Cordelia's limp body into one back seat while Toby jumped in the driver's seat. Gianna and Izzy were struggling to fit Alexander's unconscious form into a second car.

"Where's everyone else?" Mia asked dazedly—she knew there had to be more.

"They're all gone," Kris said through tears. "We're the only ones left."

Mia began to sway, and Margo grabbed on to her. She helped her into the car next to Cordelia as sirens began to wail. A crowd had formed in front of The Closet to watch the flames that were now licking at the night sky. Toby hit the gas, and the car flew forward down the street.

"They're all gone," Mia repeated. She couldn't feel any emotion. Her body felt like it held the weight of the world, but at the same time she felt more empty than anything.

"You did everything you could," Kris said, turning in the front seat to look at her.

"I feel hollow." The words echoed in Mia's ears, and tears began to pour down her cheeks. She'd thought after what she had just experienced, she would feel the opposite. Margo straddled Mia's lap and took up her entire line of vision.

"We are going to be okay," she said, cradling Mia's face. Mia could feel the shock leaving her body. She still had Margo. She thought back to what Luca had told her, and she knew it was all lies. Margo had fought so hard to stop them in the final hour, to save her.

She looked out the back window at the other Panamera. They were going to be okay.

EPILOGUE

The two cars carrying all that was left of the Sutton and Bellamy Families drove throughout the night. Mia supposed they were the Adair Family now. Margo was asleep, her head on Mia's shoulder, and Cordelia lay across their laps. Kris dozed in the front seat. Toby hadn't spoken since they'd left Cedar Hollow, his eyes focused hard on the road.

Mia twisted the silver band on her finger. She didn't understand why Thea's power had been unleashed after she put the ring on. Sliding it off her finger, she turned it in her hands.

Something was different. Mia flipped on the overhead light and stared at the ring. The black line was gone; in its place was a vein of the same amethyst that had hung around Thea's neck.

"She knew, Mia," Kris said sleepily. "I don't think she consciously believed it, but deep down, she knew. I don't think she was willing to take any chances." Mia remembered how Alexander had forgotten his phone while she and Thea sat in the car. He must have been retrieving the ring.

Mia nodded and put the band back on her finger, then switched the light off and stared out the window. They drove in silence, not knowing where they were going. They had plenty of cash, enough to start over, but Mia wasn't sure if she wanted to think about that now.

"Oh, fuck," Toby cursed, slowing the car to a stop. "Cops."

Mia sighed. This was the last thing they needed.

"Don't worry; I've got this." Kris flipped her sunglasses up wearily as an officer strolled up to the car.

But the man stopped at the back window, motioning to Mia to roll it down. She complied and then blinked. Her eyes must have been playing tricks on her.

"Mia." It was just one word, but she would have known that voice anywhere. She leaned forward.

"Dad?"

He looked identical to the very last moment she had laid eyes on him.

★ ★ ★ ★ ★